The Dovecote

Stephanie Dummler

Published 2009 by Onlywomen Press, Limited, London, UK

ISBN 978-0-906500-98-9

British Library Cataloguing-in-Publication Data
A catalogue record for this book is available from the British Library

Copyright © Stephanie Dummler 2008
Cover Design © Spark Design 2008

Typeset by FiSH Books, London
Printed and bound in the UK by CPI Mackays, Chatham, ME5 8TD

For Lyn

Prelude

Adagio e mesto

Often at night, when sleep is impossible, I sit and look out at the dovecote. Here, in the oldest part of the house, the walls are so thick that a seat has been fashioned beneath each window. Sitting sideways, tucked up within the fabric of the house, I can almost believe that I'm part of the building, that the dovecote and I have a history in common and that it, like me, is keeping a vigil. In daylight, of course, the very idea seems madness; yet nightly the thought comes upon me again as I gaze out alone in the darkness.

Outside, nothing changes. Only the varying light gives the appearance of change, and marks one night out from the next. Not even the blackest of nights can obliterate the dovecote; its massive domed top, always there, unavoidable, dominates the skyline. From here you don't see the doorway, only the unbroken rotundity of the whole, seeming to lack a single straight line. The masons who built her so many centuries ago must surely have thought of the dovecote as female: protective, embracing, she invites love as certainly as she denies it. Inside, in giddying, tiered rows hollowed out of the stone, are hundreds upon hundreds of boxes, each designed for a pair of occupants. I try to imagine the look of them, the sound of them, all of those birds roosting together, victims of their need for community, each pair so faithful, their billing and cooing synonymous with the behaviour of lovers, their tender mutual preening binding them ever closer. Did they dream of flight, but, finding elsewhere no rest for the soles of their feet, long to return to the warmth, the security, the seductive, enveloping

1

darkness, where they mated and laid, incubated and hatched, each a devoted parent, each sitting, each feeding their young? And did they hear the ladder turning, feel the probing hand grasp squabs and filch eggs, the intruder who stalked and stole and strangled? What quantities of love and loss are celebrated here, at the heart of the homestead where I now watch and wait.

Sometimes, to beguile the time, and to see the other side of the picture, I pick up again that now standard reference work *A Compendium of Doves and Dovecotes*, written and illustrated by T. Procter and J. Menzies. Beneath the frontispiece image of vigorous doves pulling Venus' chariot, I see anew my name in the dedication: 'To Bobbie, who was a great help to us both in the writing of this book.' I look again at Pouters and Tumblers, Runts, Barbs and Turbils; I re-read the story of St. Remigius who, having baptised Clovis, King of the Franks, was brought a timely phial of chrism by a thoughtful dove; of Teresa of Avila, John Chrysostum and Gregory, each inspired by oracular doves whose perch was a saintly ear, the better to be heard. And I remember the girl-saint Agnes who, on refusing marriage to her Roman suitor, received from heaven a dove-borne ring. So much for *columba livia*, domestic table-bird and messenger of the divine.

I leave the window and wander through the house. When love comes again, as one day it might, the voice of the turtle will echo once more. Until that occurs, the dovecote and I will watch and wait and remember.

1

Molto vivo e risoluto

'Robina!'

My mother's voice, shrill and peremptory, sliced through the afternoon air. It was pointless trying to hide. There were plenty of spots in our old garden where I'd hidden for hours, havens known only to me, where she'd never been able to find me. But the desolate plot round our spanking new house was devoid of such useful features.

'Robina! What are you doing?' The voice, closer now, was laced with disapproval.

'I'm making a wall,' I said, indicating my careful construction of bricks and half-bricks. 'The builders left them behind. I decided to dig them up.'

'Turn round – let me look at you,' she commanded, ignoring my splendid achievement. 'Yes, just as I thought. You've dirtied your lovely clean dress.'

'If you'd buy me some shorts, . . .' I began. A hopeless cause, and I knew it.

'I will *not* have you dressed like a tomboy! Imagine how Miss Nelson would feel if she saw you wearing shorts.' It was thanks to Miss Nelson's remorseless dressmaking that I was regularly stitched into frocks.. 'When *I* was nine,' she continued . . .

'I'm only nine for sixteen more days,' I interrupted, in case she'd forgotten my birthday. I'd longed to be ten for ages, but had to wait till mid-August, the youngest child in my class.

'When I was your age,' my mother corrected, 'I'd have loved to own dresses like yours. But the War had just started, and we all had to make do and mend.'

The War, I felt, had a great deal to answer for. It was now 1960, yet my mother's wartime restrictions still cast their blight on my life.

'That's quite enough mess for today.' She eyed my embryo wall disparagingly. 'I don't know what your father will say when he sees you've been using his axe.'

'It's not an axe,' I said. 'It's a hatchet.' My mother was clueless with tools; she once called a mallet a hammer. The tools were my father's province, useful for chopping up sticks for the fire, or lifting up manhole covers prior to unblocking a drain. These struck me as much more exciting tasks than the shopping, cooking, cleaning and occasional embroidery which occupied my mother and seemed to comprise a lady's lot in life. 'I used the hatchet to chip off pieces of brick,' I explained, ' to make them fit neatly together. It worked rather well.'

'Rather well?' Her eyebrows shot up. 'But it's hardly something we want in the garden, is it?' A statement, not a question. With the toe of her shoe she nudged at the central brick. The whole thing collapsed, my afternoon's labour destroyed in a second.

I stared at the ruins in silence.

'Put everything back where you found it, Robina, and clean yourself up. I want to talk to you. I'll be in the lounge.' Having issued her orders, she marched back into the house.

At my old school I'd won a gold star for my composition on 'Famous Historical People'. Most of the class chose the Romans, but I chose the Huns; I'd read about their exploits in the *Children's Encyclopaedia*, which described them as 'uncivilised devastators'. Conveying a convincingly Hunnish outlook on life had been simple: I mentally put my mother on a horse, dressed her in primitive armour, deprived her of any restrictions, and wrote about how she'd behave. My teacher said I showed great understanding of the ruthless frame of mind. I never let on how I'd done it.

My mother had cat-like hearing. The words, 'Shoes off, Robina!' rang through the house the moment I entered the kitchen. This shoeless regime, now eight days old, was due to the brand-new carpets; their arrival added considerably to the list of things banned in this house. I took off my shoes, scooted upstairs to wash my hands and change my dress, decided to put on clean socks for good measure, and joined my mother in the lounge. Was ever room less aptly named? Lounging had long been forbidden.

'Sit up straight, Robina – don't fidget.' My mother sat perfectly upright in her mis-named easy chair. The furniture at least was familiar in this otherwise alien house, though it struck me now as faded and sad in its clinical, pristine setting. 'I've got something important to tell you.'

I braced myself for the worst. What my mother considered important was often some ghastly appointment. Dentist, piano teacher, dressmaker: there was ample scope in the holidays for endless unwanted encounters. I sat still and tried to look eager.

'Your father and I think it might be...' – she hesitated slightly before finding the word – 'wise if you went away for a while. On your own.'

I could scarcely believe my good fortune. 'Away?' I repeated. 'On my own?'

'You must understand, Robina, that your father cannot afford to take us on holiday this year, what with all the expenses of moving. And as yet you don't know anyone here in Oreley Wood who could play with you.'

Oreley Wood – oh, much hated address! Not the bosky spot I'd imagined, but a horrid West Midlands estate, pretending to be a village. Why we'd moved here from Edgbaston was a total mystery, till I overheard my mother describing the house on the telephone. 'Of course it's detached,' she gushed smugly. 'One's quite unaware of the neighbours. As Mrs Braithwaite said to me after she moved, semi-detached is all right for a while, but really one longs for detachment.'

Now she said sharply, 'Robina – you are listening? Some gratitude might be in order. Not every girl is lucky enough to have an auntie she can stay with.'

Theresa! I was being sent to stay with Theresa! My happiness instantly doubled.

'Thank you,' I said politely, but still I craved confirmation. 'Has she really invited me?'

'I rang her earlier, and she said she'd be willing to have you.'

Not quite the same as an invitation, I thought disappointedly.

'I can't understand Theresa.' My mother embarked on a well-worn theme. 'She still hasn't found a husband.'

So great was my mother's conviction that every woman should find a man and get married that she viewed her sister's single and childless state as a huge dereliction of duty.

'But lots of women don't marry,' I'd objected on Theresa's behalf the last time this subject was aired. 'Miss Johns, for instance. She isn't married.'

'Oh, headmistresses!' My mother was dismissive. 'They're exceptions. They wouldn't have time.'

'And Miss Nelson,' I persisted.

'Exactly!' My mother sounded almost triumphant. 'Poor Miss Nelson, making dresses for a living. If she'd had the wit to get married, she simply wouldn't need to. Her husband would keep her, just as your father keeps us.'

'Perhaps she likes keeping herself,' I suggested.

'Now you're being silly, Robina. Every woman wants to be married and have a man to look after her. And to have children of course.' She made this latter duty sound much less appealing. 'It's what we are meant to do. When you're older, you'll understand better. You'll see how convenient marriage can be.'

I'd thought about this a great deal. Certainly my parents' marriage had its convenient side. I saw how my father dealt with bills, drains, all things mechanical, technical or dirty, and anything that required a tool or some physical strength; everything else was left to my mother. This apparently suited them both, and the neatness of the arrangement impressed me: any gap in the knowledge or capabilities of one was precisely matched by a corresponding strength in the other, so that my parents did indeed fit conveniently together, like two pieces of a jigsaw.

'And now that she's no longer teaching' – my mother, I realised, was still harping on Theresa's undutiful life – 'she probably misses the company of young people. That must be why she sounded so pleased at the thought of you coming to stay.' This evidently struck my mother as unfounded, but made my heart fairly burst with joy. 'She'll be here to collect you tomorrow. It seems that she now drives a car.'

A car was on my mother's list of desirable objects, only slightly lower than the lawn and rose beds she was constantly urging my father to supply for the garden.

I asked the question I hardly dared ask. 'How long will I be away?' There were five long weeks of holiday remaining, and not a single attraction in Oreley Wood.

'We'll leave that for your auntie to decide,' my mother said primly. 'But we'll pack all your dresses, in case.'

When my father came home from work, late as always since our move, my mother harangued him for ages. I'd been using his hatchet, she told him. She wouldn't mind betting I'd ruined it, and when would he see to the garden? It was best to sow grass seed in August, but he'd first have to dig it all over – when did he plan to do that? She'd seen some roses she fancied, knew exactly where she wanted them, but he'd have to enrich the soil – could he find some well-rotted manure? And so on and so on, till I thought she'd never stop. How did my father bear it, forced to endure these endless tirades?

When she finally paused, I butted in smartly. 'I'm going to stay with Theresa tomorrow. She's coming to collect me.'

'I know, my pet.' He didn't seem cross about the hatchet, and gave me a weary smile. He glanced at my mother and whispered, 'Lucky old you!' Later he slipped me half a crown. 'Think of me when you spend it,' he said, and I wondered then if he'd miss me. My mother most surely would not.

I'd only met Theresa, my mother's younger sister, on a couple of occasions, though she'd definitely been at my christening, promising all kinds of impossible things in my stead. She was the one adult I knew who was fun to be with. The last time she came for a visit, she invented a game called Possum, with ludicrous rules and a great deal of shouting. We'd only been playing a few minutes when my mother came out and stopped us, pretending it was tea time. That was the longest I'd had Theresa all to myself. The prospect of having her all to myself for the whole of the summer filled me with rapture. I pictured how it would be: we'd play lots of games, just the two of us, all of them noisy and wild; we'd go shopping together, and I'd help her wash up, and we'd talk and talk and talk. Best of all, my mother wouldn't be there to snuff out the fun.

It was late the next morning when Theresa turned up in her smart new Morris Traveller. After greeting my mother, who offered her cheek to be kissed, she grinned at me and winked quite roguishly.

'Well, Bobbie, how you've grown! I'm so glad you're coming to stay.'

My mother winced at hearing my name so abbreviated. 'Robina!' she Hunnishly ordered, giving all three syllables due emphasis. 'Run and get your suitcase. You'll need to be off straightaway '

How, I wondered, could two sisters be so different? My mother was stout and unbending, but Theresa was lithe and remarkably lean; her healthy, weather-beaten face was clearly used to smiling a lot, while my mother, from being so cross and disgruntled, had bad tempered lines on her forehead, and a pasty, constipated air. I could tell that their tastes were dissimilar, too: when my mother started swanking about our ghastly new house, Theresa said very little, which made me like her all the more.

My bag was stowed in the car, and off we set. How much distance lay ahead of us I had only the vaguest notion: I felt I was entering uncharted land, where all was unknown and mysterious, and the farther we drove from the tiny world I inhabited, the more I was smitten by shyness and could think of nothing to say. Theresa, too, was silent for long stretches of time, but whenever I glanced in her direction, she gave me a smile or a wink, and I felt she was on my side. A sign informed us that we were in Wales, and we drove through a landscape of small fields enclosed by hedges, where sheep, or sometimes a few cows, grazed. For a while we passed through villages of pretty black and white houses, and after that every place name I saw seemed foreign and unpronounceable, as though we were truly abroad. At one point Theresa took her eyes off the road to rub my arm affectionately and said, 'I think we'll get on very well, don't you?' I was instantly filled to the brim with delight, and wished that the journey could last for ever, the two of us in the car and no-one to trouble us.

Some time later she said, 'It's not far now. The house is called Hendre, which means 'old town' in Welsh, and shows it's a very old settlement.' Then, staring straight ahead, she continued, 'I don't think I mentioned to your mother that I don't live alone anymore – I haven't for a while, in fact. I live with a friend called Jo whom I'm sure you'll like and who's longing to meet you.'

My throat went tight, and the happiness of the journey drained entirely away. I'd imagined Theresa and me doing everything together, and now she was telling me that it wouldn't be like that, that I'd be the odd one out, that Jo would be there, who'd want Theresa to himself and wouldn't want me. I stared out of the passenger window in silent disappointment, my eyes stinging with tears.

And so it was that I first passed the dovecote without seeing it at all, huddled grumpily as I was on the passenger seat. But when the car stopped and I saw Jo standing there to meet us, I realised I was wrong. For Jo was a lady, and Theresa was right: I did like her.

Over the years, I've repeated that arrival many times, and every feature of the place has acquired its own meaning and memory. But what struck me most on that first occasion was the extreme difference between the ordered, circumscribed spaces of the house that I'd left and the expansive spread of this new domain. The car drew up outside a long, white-washed two-storey stone house with a porch at one end covered in wisteria. In front of the house was a large cobbled yard, on two sides of which lay a range of recognisable outbuildings – stables and pigsties, cowsheds and barns. Most impressive of all, standing on its own in the middle of the yard, was a large, circular, stone tower. It seemed to have no windows, and its domed top was at least as high as the house chimneys. Standing at its base, squinting into the sun and wearing trousers tucked in to Wellington boots, was a youngish woman who waved at the car.

'Bobbie – hallo! You're just in time to help look for the eggs.'

I glanced at Theresa, motionless in the driving seat. She nodded. 'Yes, that's Jo. You two collect the eggs first, and then we'll have tea.'

Never having found eggs anywhere but in boxes at the grocer's, I was by no means certain how to conduct this quest. But as Jo led me into each outbuilding in turn, she told me about the hens they kept, how many were laying regularly and which were their favourite nesting sites. The floors were covered with straw, and there were wooden boxes in various corners; in some of these I found an egg, and occasionally two. Meanwhile, the hens themselves kept up a kind of murmured grumble as they pecked and scratched about at our feet. Most wonderful of all, we came across a hen actually sitting; at our approach she ran off uttering a series of outraged squawks. The egg I found when I put my hand in the box was warm to the touch, and fitted snugly in my palm like an old fashioned hand-warmer. Between us we collected ten eggs that first day.

'That's a very good total,' said Jo approvingly. 'We aim for six dozen a week. We sell them, you see, every Friday.' And she led me to a room at the back of the house, where she cleaned the eggs and put them to stand in large trays. 'I hope you're feeling hungry,' she said when she'd finished.

'I am – a little,' I conceded. In fact I was ravenous.

'Good. So am I. Everything's ready. When you've had a wash, come on through to the kitchen. That's where we eat.' And she went through an inner door, into the heart of the house.

The kitchen was vast and old fashioned, and laid out on a long wooden table was the most substantial tea I'd ever seen: sandwiches filled with salad, scones and dishes of jam, fruit pies and three sorts of cake. Theresa poured me a glass of milk.

'Tuck in,' she said, an instruction unknown to my mother. 'There's plenty more. And all of it made by ourselves.'

'I didn't know you lived on a farm,' I said, helping myself to a sandwich.

'It's not quite a farm – more a smallholding,' she replied. 'The chickens you've already met. We've a couple of goats, for the milk and the cheese, though sadly they don't produce butter, and a Tamworth sow called Caroline, who's due to have piglets soon. With luck they'll arrive while you're here.'

'Caroline?' I giggled. 'That's a funny name for a pig.'

'The names are taken from pupils I specially remember,' Terry said with a twinkle at Jo. 'The goats are Trudy and Sandra – a recalcitrant pair of terrors, but likeable all the same.'

'And Caroline?' I prompted.

'A sprawling lump of a girl, who once fell asleep in my lesson!'

'There's a logic to all of this,' Jo explained. 'The pig, you see, has the whey left over from making the cheese. And odds and ends of vegetables.'

'And apples from the orchard,' added Terry.

'You grow apples as well?' I was amazed at their productivity.

'Yes, there's a sizeable orchard – old trees, heavy croppers, that were here when we came. But we dug the vegetable garden ourselves, didn't we, Jo?'

'I've still got the blisters to prove it! And we bake our own bread....'

'...and make our own wine – even the water is wholly our own, pumped from a well that never runs dry.'

I was struck by their self-containedness, a degree of detachment undreamt of at home. 'You've got everything you need all around you, like living in the Garden of Eden!' I marvelled, recalling a recent Scripture lesson on the delights of that place.

'Yes, we've got all we need here,' agreed Theresa, smiling at Jo across the table.

Equally marvellous to me was the house itself. It was, in parts, very old indeed. The living room, with a huge inglenook at one end, and the bedroom directly above it dated back to the seventeenth century. Here the walls were almost two feet thick, rough and lumpy on the inside, not at all like our smooth walls at home. Originally a ladder would have led up from the ground floor to a sleeping platform above, but now there was a separate staircase, steep and narrow, with a door at the top and the bottom.

'No good for getting a coffin down,' Jo said cheerfully, as she showed me the removable floor of the landing, through which coffin and occupant could be lowered on ropes. 'Don't worry,' she reassured me quickly. 'No-one's died in this house for years and years. It's not a feature we intend to use often.'

Newer rooms, some of them a mere century old, had been added higgledy-piggledy to this basic structure, and the result was a house full of unexpected and delightful surprises, a patchwork of intimate spaces. It was a lived-in, companionable house, and I adored it instantly. When later I telephoned my mother to say we'd arrived safely, I pictured her in our stark, unlovable hallway with a rush of something like pity.

'What is it?' she asked, when I started to speak. 'I hope you're not homesick already.' Her telephone voice was distinctly forbidding.

'Oh no,' I said. 'I like it here. There are chickens and goats.'

'Well, be a good girl, and make yourself useful. Are you and Theresa alone?'

Some instinct made me cautious. 'There's nobody else staying here,' I told her, with strict regard for the truth. 'Only me.'

And so the occasion for mentioning Jo slipped quietly out of my grasp.

My bedroom, black beamed, looked out on fields at the back of the house, and when I woke next morning and saw the view in sunshine, I couldn't wait to get outside. Jo and Theresa were already busy in the yard. Theresa was milking one of the goats which she had tethered to the outside of the old stables. Her head rested against the animal's flank as she ran her fingers down the long, full teat, forcing out the milk which squirted foaming into the pail. Jo was feeding the hens, throwing down corn which caused them to peck deliriously among the cobbles. She motioned me to join her.

'Milking's a tricky business, and goats are very self-willed,' she told me. 'If she feels like it, she'll kick over the bucket and then we'd lose all of the milk. We take it in turns to milk them, so that the pair of them get to know us both. The other job is feeding the chickens – perhaps you would like to do that?'

And she showed me the corn bin and the measuring scoop and the barn where the hens were kept at night, so that I could let them out and feed them each morning.

'By the way,' she added, 'Theresa likes to be called Terry, just as I like to be called Jo. My parents call me Jonquil,' and she pulled a face. 'What about you?'

'My parents call me Robina, but I'd *much* rather be Bobbie.'

'Right you are then. Aren't we the bee's knees? Terry and Jo and Bobbie!'

I didn't know what being a bee's knee might involve, but I liked it.

After breakfast that first morning, Terry looked me solemnly up and down. 'Are you terribly fond of that dress?' she asked. I was wearing one of Miss Nelson's more sober creations, with minimal flounces and frills. 'We rather hoped we could put you to work while you're with us, but you can't do much in that garb.'

'I've got heaps of them,' I said miserably, 'all of them worse than this one. My mother won't let me wear shorts.'

'But I'm sure she won't mind if you adapt to native costume – like togas in Rome or mantillas in Spain. It just so happens...' And she produced a pair of old trousers from behind her chair, holding them up for inspection. 'I'm hopeless at sewing in zips, but what if we chop them off here' – she indicated a point above knee height – 'and undid the side seams and made them much narrower – do you think that would work?'

'Oh yes!' I was almost ecstatic. 'That would work very well.'

'I've got one or two shirts I don't wear any more,' put in Jo. 'They could be made to fit.'

By the end of the morning my hated collection of dresses was rendered redundant, consigned to the depths of the wardrobe.

Our days had a regular shape. While Terry or Jo milked, I let out and fed the birds; after breakfast, we all visited Caroline, with a bucket of pig nuts and various tasty scraps. Then there was the garden to see to, and here, too, I was able to be useful, harvesting beans and carrots, picking raspberries and hunting for courgettes which hid beneath their prickly leaves, plotting to turn into marrows. Under Jo's guidance I learnt to distinguish weed from seedling vegetable, and hoed rows of lettuce; I learnt to plait strings of onions and discovered the delight of searching for cold, hard potatoes in the newly turned soil. Some of this yield would appear at lunch, transformed into quiche or made into soup or salad. Jo and Terry, both excellent cooks, took equal share in the kitchen, and mealtimes, which at home I'd regarded as boring necessities, now became celebrations of labour and love.

Afternoons were devoted to pleasure. Occasionally we went in Terry's car to some local place of interest, and each Friday we took the trays of eggs to be sold at the local shop, but mostly we stayed at home and did as we chose. Jo was an artist. From September to April she ran classes twice a week in a local community hall, teaching people to draw, but she also had occasional commissions, and was currently illustrating a book on fungi, which occupied much of her time. Terry had been an English teacher, and there were books everywhere – even in the bathroom, their pages spotted with water from having been read in the bath. I spent most afternoons with a book, lying in the grass when it was fine, or curled up in a window seat; later I talked with Terry about what I'd read. It was my first entry into that adult world which takes novels seriously and lets them become the reference points of one's real, inner life. For entertainment in the evenings there was only the wireless, permanently tuned to the Third Programme.

Throughout the day and especially over meals, there was constant talk and a great deal of laughter. Two particular conversations have stayed with me always. One concerned the dovecote, that strange, windowless tower standing in the middle of the yard. Though I'd explored it, I hadn't guessed its full function, because part of the original structure was missing. Jo explained that when it was used, a central rotating ladder, known as a potence, would have allowed access to the rows of nest boxes which lined the walls and lower part of the roof. I tried counting these several times, but always became disorientated after a while. Terry said there were almost two thousand.

'Why are there so many?' I asked, horrified at the thought of such a multitude of birds confined together.

'Doves and pigeons like to live in a crowd. Each female would have her own mate, and they'd roost together, side by side. Unlike many birds, they mate for life and are utterly faithful. Not all of the eggs would be taken for food; most would be allowed to hatch. They breed all the time – unlike hens who take rests – and might have eight or more broods a year. The male and the female take turns to sit on the eggs, and both of them feed the hatchlings.'

'Oh, there's lots to be said for Mr Dove,' said Jo. 'Faithful, hardworking and devoted to family life – truly a model husband and father.'

Terry continued, 'The young birds are called squabs, and they make the best eating. While they're still being fed – they

15

eat what was known as 'pigeon milk', but is really regurgitated food – and before they fly, they're beautifully plump and succulent. But of course they're only small, and it would take quite a number of them to make a decent meal for a large household.'

'But wouldn't it be – you know – very messy in there?' I asked.

Jo's eyes lit up. 'Dove dung! There's nothing like it for the garden – it's the best manure you can find. Yes, you'd need to clean out a dovecote very regularly, every day, probably. If you didn't, they'd soon move elsewhere. They're fussy birds, and wouldn't stay long in a dirty dovecote.'

'"Fair dovecotes have most doves",' quoted Terry. 'You know, I've often thought what fun it would be to write a book about doves and dove keeping – and pigeons, too, of course. I was reading Mrs. Beeton the other day; she's full of the most extraordinary information. According to her, white is a dove's favourite colour. And a proper pigeon pie should have three of the birds' feet poking out through the top of the pastry, to let people know what kind of pie it is. Imagine if one had to do that with a pork pie!'

'Doves are always coming up in Scripture,' I said, remembering Noah's exploits.

'And in Art,' added Jo.

And so the idea of the *Compendium* began to take shape.

Another conversation that made a vivid impression – this time because of the extent to which it overturned my existing view of the world – occurred one day when the washing machine stopped working. When this had happened at home, my mother called out the repair man, who fixed it two days later. Proud of knowing the procedure, I was quick to suggest this course of action to Terry.

'Call out a repair man?' Her voice was incredulous. 'I don't suppose there's any need for that. It's probably just the fuse. Let's see.'

I watched, amazed, as she opened up the plug, removed the fuse and inspected the wiring inside.

'No, it's not the fuse this time. One of the leads has come loose – see.' She showed me where a bundle of wires was no longer held in place by the tiny screw. In no time at all she'd repaired it, and the machine whirred back into life.

'I don't think my mother can know about that,' I said. 'Know that a lady could mend it, I mean.'

Terry laughed. 'Ladies, my poppet, can do anything at all – if they want to.'

'Absolutely anything?' I thought of all the jobs my mother left to my father or to various repair men, and couldn't believe that none of it was necessary.

'Of course, silly! Men aren't *born* knowing how to mend a tap or unblock a drain. They have to learn, and the best way to learn is simply by doing it. Often there's very little skill or strength needed – it's more a matter of understanding how things work and thinking logically about what might have gone wrong. And women can do that just as well as men. Sometimes better.'

'Then why *don't* women do it?' I asked, puzzled.

'Because traditionally there are jobs that men do and jobs that women do. If you're a man and a woman together, I suppose it's simplest to divide out the tasks on traditional lines. Men tend to be stronger than women, which is why they get stuck with the heavier chores. But for two women like Jo and me, there aren't any rules at all. It's up to us to decide who does what, and it makes sense if we can both do everything. We keep things going here without any man to help us, which shows that it can be done.'

So far, her tone had been light, but now she looked me right in the eyes, and I knew what she said was important.

'Don't *ever* think that being a woman means you can't do something, Bobbie. There may well be things you can't do in life, but you probably wouldn't be able do them if you were a man either. You will only be happy if you're truly yourself, and that means finding out what *you* can do, and then doing it – every single bit of it. Live your particular life – make that your goal, and don't simply settle for what others think is best.'

It was the first time anyone had told me this, and so contrary was it to the ideas I'd previously formed that it felt as if a dam had burst and flooded all the known points in my world, destroying familiar landmarks. A whole new series of possibilities seemed to open up that made me feel strong and powerful, capable of doing anything. At the same time I saw Jo and Terry's life together in a new light. It was another kind of partnership, the complete reverse of my parents' jigsaw pattern, one that relied on similarity and sharing instead of on difference and complementarity. It must be grand, I thought, to live with someone who knows the same things you know, and not have to rely on someone who only knows the things you never learnt.

With so much new to occupy me, it was hardly surprising that my birthday crept up on me unawares. So to be woken one morning by the strains of 'Happy Birthday' and to find Terry and Jo, each holding a parcel, at the foot of my bed was a double delight. At home, presents always had a utilitarian edge – a pencil case, new socks or winter gloves – and I dreaded having to pretend gratitude for similar gifts now. I need not have worried. Terry's parcel contained a huge cake with *Bobbie* and *10* and lots of kisses in three different colours of icing.

'It's all for you,' she said, beaming at me. 'Every single crumb of it. And if it tastes awful, remember we both made it.'

I tried it; it tasted divine.

'And we both made this, too,' said Jo, handing over a small, flat package.

It was a book of funny drawings of me. In them I struggled to uproot mammoth vegetables, heroically weeded fields full of cabbage plants, searched for raspberries with a huge magnifying glass, and hunted for eggs in the unlikeliest of places. In each scene Jo and Terry were depicted as idlers and wastrels, playing cards or lounging about, while I slaved away under a remorseless sun. Accompanying each drawing was a verse describing my labours in mock-heroic couplets.

She grasps a giant Carrot as her prize –

'Tis half her weight, and more than half her size.
Was ever root of such gigantic girth,
Of such dimensions, harvested on earth?
Was ever such a monster glimps'd before?
She pulls, she tugs, she strains – and strains some more.
With might and main and unremitting toil,
She extricates the Carrot from the soil.

It was the best present I'd ever received, of no practical use whatsoever, and I have it still, all these years later. During the morning the postman brought a parcel from my mother. It contained a pen and pencil set and a hideous tartan beret, which I knew I'd be condemned to wear throughout the autumn.

'It'll keep you nice and warm,' said Terry bravely, but we all knew she was only trying to be kind.

The last few days of the holiday were coloured by one event: Caroline's imminent farrowing. I was desperately keen to observe it, birth being such an improbable process, even in farmyard pigs. Though I did what I could to speed things up, scratching the fat sow's back and passing on comforting details about the world outside the pigsty, she was frustratingly slow to respond. Then, on my second last day at Hendre, she began rootling about in the straw, pushing it into clumsy heaps. I guessed this meant that the piglets were on their way, but despite my urgent entreaties, none had appeared by bedtime.

That night I woke with a start, certain that Caroline needed me. I pulled a sweater over my pyjamas, slipped on my shoes and crept downstairs. It was a clear night with an almost full moon: looming above me was the dovecote, silvered by the moonlight. Never before had I been outside in the middle of the night, and the sheer quantity of stars, stretching from horizon to horizon in a curve which echoed the dome of the dovecote, was a revelation. Despite the bright moon, the pigsty was only partially illuminated, and even after my eyes had grown used to the darkness, I could make out nothing within. But as I stood there peering, I was aware of tiny snuffling noises and what sounded like a long sigh of contentment. Certain now that the piglets must have been born, I ran back indoors, bursting to tell Terry and Jo. I tapped on their bedroom door, and when this failed to wake them, turned the handle and stood in the doorway.

'Terry, Jo, I think the piglets have arrived. Do come and see! We need a torch and I haven't got one. Oh *please* come quickly.' I was fairly bouncing up and down with excitement.

Terry put on the bedside light. 'We'll be down in a minute, Bobbie. Wait till we come. We mustn't startle Caroline at all.'

'There's a torch in one of the kitchen drawers,' added Jo. 'See if you can find it.'

And away I rushed.

Good as their word, they appeared almost immediately, as hastily dressed as I. Together we crossed to the pigsty, and Jo shone in the torch. There Caroline lay on her side, a teeny pink piglet suckling contentedly at each of her enormous teats while others tried frantically to elbow them out of the way so that they too could feed. We thought we counted twelve, but the squirming mass of bodies made accuracy difficult.

'We'll count them again in the morning,' whispered Terry. 'Clever old Caroline! She'll be perfectly fine. Let's leave her now. What she needs is a good long rest.' And the three of us went indoors, gladdened by this miracle.

I adored the piglets. I spent most of the following day at the pigsty, gazing in rapture at Caroline and her litter, watching the tiny eager creatures feed and sleep. When I made a final visit just before dusk, Terry came with me.

'What will you do with the piglets?' I asked. They were motionless now, in a jumbled, satisfied heap.

'We'll keep them – for a while.' There was caution in her voice. 'But thirteen full grown pigs would eat us out of house and home.'

'I know,' I said sadly. 'And there wouldn't be room in the pigsty.'

'But we'll keep them until they're weaned – that's at least for a couple of months. If you come again at half-term, you'll see them then' She looked at me sideways in the gloom. 'If you'd like to, that is.'

'Oh yes, I would like to – more than anything else.' And I hugged her with all of my strength.

And so that joyous summer finally came to an end, and the day I was dreading arrived, when I had to abandon my shorts and put on a dress and pack the rest of my hideous clothes for the journey home in Terry's car. I felt quite different from the person who'd set out more than a month ago, and I looked different too, for the sun had tanned my face, my arms and even my knees, and had bleached my hair, so that I hardly recognised myself. This time there was no constraint between us on the drive, and we talked and played games the entire time; but we both grew silent as we approached Oreley Wood.

'Write to us, won't you – and come again soon,' said Terry, squeezing my hand as our new house came into view.

'I promise,' I said, and squeezed back even harder.

Then we said no more, for there was my mother waiting for us with my old life around her, ready to swallow me up.

But something momentous had changed in my absence: my father had left us. It was a couple of days before my mother got round to telling me this. At first she said he was away on business, which was only part of the truth.

'Your father's gone to live in Scotland, near Aberdeen,' she finally admitted with no trace of emotion. 'His firm offered him a position there, and he decided to take it.'

'Why don't we go and live there too?' I asked. Whatever it was like, it could hardly be worse than Oreley Wood.

'Because I want to stay on in this new house. Your father never really settled here. He'll come and see us from time to time, I expect – it's not as though we're divorced or anything.' She gave a nervous laugh. 'And there's no need to mention it to anyone. He's just working away from home for a while. To see how he likes it.'

The news completely stunned me. Everyone I knew had two parents who lived together, and just as I couldn't imagine how my mother would survive without my father, nor could I conceive of my father living alone. As far as I knew, he couldn't cook or wash clothes or go shopping. I pictured him wasting away in Aberdeen, ill fed and dirty, wishing my mother and I were there to look after him. It was several months before it dawned on me that my trip to Wales had been arranged to coincide with his extraordinary departure.

On one thing my mother could rely absolutely: I would tell no-one about our odd domestic arrangements, because there was no-one I could tell. The class which I joined in September consisted entirely of existing pairs of friends. Even when these friendships broke up, as frequently happened, it was merely a question of changing partners, as in some complicated dance, and I remained the odd one out. Admittedly this wasn't much of a trial. I continued to read a very great deal, and read during breaks and at lunchtimes, which made me seem odd in the eyes of my peers. As it was our Eleven Plus year, I was wrongly assumed to be a desperate swot, a type so universally despised that they left me entirely alone. In fact the Eleven Plus was of no particular concern to me, for I was determined to go to boarding school, and had begun persuading my mother that it would be a feather in her cap if I did so. All of the best stories, from *Jane Eyre* to *Mallory Towers* involved a boarding school, and I was convinced that only by attending one did I stand a chance of meeting a new set of girls who would know nothing of my outcast state and might actually like me. My mother, at first dismissive, warmed to the notion when I reminded her that Mrs Braithwaite had sent her daughter, Celia, away to boarding school. I guessed that where Mrs Braithwaite led, Mrs Sinclair was sure to follow.

As September wore on, I noticed a change in my mother. She seemed less Hunnish than usual, lacked some of her briskness, and hardly bossed me at all. I decided her symptoms were those of sadness caused by the flight of my father, and thought it would cheer her to hear about Caroline.

'I don't think I told you that Terry has a pig,' I began one evening after supper. 'She's a Tamworth sow called Caroline. And she had piglets. It's called farrowing,' I told her, in case she didn't know.

'So your Auntie's a swineherd now, is she?' she said with the tightest of smiles. 'Chickens, goats, pigs – whatever next? But aren't they very dirty creatures?'

I could bear no criticism of my beloved Caroline. 'Pigs are extremely clean,' I said hotly. 'It's nonsense to say that they're not. They're cleaner than some human beings. And when she had piglets, I saw them first. In the middle of the night.' Once embarked on my tale, I prattled happily on. 'I went out to the pigsty and was sure I could hear something, so I went up to the bedroom to wake up Terry and Jo and then we all saw them. Twelve little piglets.'

'Theresa *and* Jo?' said my mother, picking up on quite the wrong bit of the story. 'So your Auntie's got herself a boyfriend at last, has she?'

'No, of course not. Jo's a lady. And I watched them all the next day, the piglets I mean, and they...'

But my mother was no longer listening.

'Theresa and Jo were in the bedroom, did you say? The *same* bedroom?'

Something was terribly wrong. My mother was supposed to be interested in the piglets, not in Terry and Jo.

'Yes, in their bedroom.'

'But not in the same bed?'

I was growing more and more wretched. 'Yes, in their bed.'

'Do you mean to tell me, Robina, that your Auntie Theresa is sleeping with a *woman?*'

'Yes,' I muttered. 'With Jo, her friend Jo.' I sensed I was betraying them, and had to make a stand. 'She's my friend too. They both are. They're my very best friends and always will be.'

'We'll see about that, young lady. Now you just listen to me. As long as I live, you are *never* to go there again. Do you understand me? I forbid it. To think you've been exposed to such... such *filth!*' She spat out the word. 'It's a good job your father doesn't know about this. That a sister of mine should be so... so depraved, so utterly lacking in shame! And with a young girl in the house as well, her very own niece – her goddaughter! Well, I'll soon put a stop to all that. Never again, do you hear? And there'll be no more letters either. Heaven knows what harm they've done, putting notions into your head. Get yourself upstairs to bed at once, and I'll ring Theresa. There's nothing more to be said on the subject. To bed, young lady.'

I was powerless against my mother's outburst, the devastating force of which I could feel, but of which I could understand nothing. Terry and Jo's sleeping arrangements made such perfect sense, and were of so little significance, that I'd never given them a moment's thought, and was at a loss to know why they so inflamed my mother. But her words had a terrible impact. Never to see them, never to hear from them again! My sense of loss was immense, as was my wrath at my mother, but most of all I cast myself in the role of traitor, a Judas who'd betrayed all that was precious through a bungled attempt at sympathy. It also had the unwanted effect of restoring my mother to full Hunnishness. Not for an instant did she waver from the course she adopted, and Terry's name, much less Jo's, never again crossed her lips in my hearing.

Having stoically refused to eavesdrop on her telephone conversation, I had no idea what she actually said to Terry, and agonised over how to make her and Jo understand what had happened, for I simply could not bear it if they thought ill of me. That evening I tried writing a letter of explanation, but it was a sorry, confused effort, too full of whining self-justification, and I tore it up. Only as I made my miserable way home from school the following day did the solution occur to me: I, too, could telephone Terry – not from home, naturally, but from the kiosk outside the Post Office. If I spoke to her, all would be well. That night while my mother was cooking, I secretly consulted the telephone directory and learnt about reverse charge calling. If Terry didn't wish to speak to me, she could refuse to accept the call.

The next day I carried out my plan. My heart began thumping wildly as I entered the telephone kiosk. I gave the operator the number and heard it ringing. Then there was absolute silence. Had I perhaps been cut off? Suddenly a voice said, 'Go ahead, caller', and I heard Terry saying, 'Bobbie, Bobbie, is that you?'

'Yes. I'm sorry, Terry. She made me tell her things. I didn't want to.'

'Bobbie, it's all right. You did nothing wrong. I should have told your mother about Jo a long time ago. It's entirely my fault. You mustn't blame yourself.'

'But I can't ever see you again. She won't let me.' Relief had immediately reduced me to tears.

'Not for a while, no. You must do as your mother says. But perhaps you'll be at boarding school soon, and then it won't be so bad. We can come and see you there at least. Jo sends her love, and says you're not to be sad. There's really nothing to be sad about. Just be patient, that's all. Can you do that? Can you do that for us?'

'Yes,' I said. 'I can do that.'

When I look back at my ten year-old self, I'm amazed how steadfast I was to my purpose throughout that winter and spring. My one aim was to win, not simply a place, but a scholarship, at Lansdowne Abbey, an Anglican boarding school in Worcestershire, an establishment selected not only on the basis of its relative proximity to Terry and Jo in Wales, but also because Celia Braithwaite had happened to go there. A scholarship would overcome any objection my mother might raise about over-expensive fees, though I guessed that my father would pay. He was still working in Aberdeen, and sent me occasional postcards showing the Bridge of Dee, the Hill of Barra and other warlike sites.

In my single-minded pursuit of Lansdowne Abbey, I had more than Celia Braithwaite's support: a new and unexpected ally entered our life that autumn in the form of Mr Walters. With considerable astuteness, my mother joined an afternoon Country Dancing class in October, and it wasn't long before Mr Walters became her regular dancing partner. Recently retired, he had time on his hands, and his health and physical fitness were amply attested by his participation in so lively and energetic a hobby. It soon became clear that, while stripping the willow and gathering peascods, my mother was pouring into his ear the sorry tale of our garden, of the window that wouldn't quite shut in the bathroom, of the leaking kitchen tap. Over the winter he did so many little jobs around the house that it seemed natural he should appear the following spring with rolls of turf, spade and trowel and take on the role of gardener as well.

I heartily disliked the man, partly for his unfailing cheerfulness and partly for his habit of whistling constantly through his teeth like a manic kettle, but made a point of hanging irritatingly round him whenever he appeared, in the hope of filling him with the strongest desire to have me out of his way. It is quite easy to be irritating if you set your mind to it, and I worked at it with a vengeance. I asked endless questions about whatever it was he was doing, and when I ran out of new questions, asked the old ones all over again. I regularly moved his tools from where he happened to put them, and sometimes absentmindedly wandered off with them, obliging him to waste several whistling minutes searching for them. In short, I was thoroughly obnoxious. All the while, I rhapsodized endlessly about Lansdowne Abbey and the manifold benefits I'd receive there.

This double-pronged campaign worked wonders. Mr Walters – he must have possessed a Christian name, but I never learnt it – was soon a keen supporter of the proposal to send me to Lansdowne, and my mother, owing him so much, was as putty in his hands. I took the entrance exam early in February, was called for interview three weeks later and offered a Governors' Scholarship by the following post.

At last, I thought, my particular life could begin.

2

Hampstead 1960

Allegro con brio

Thursdays are the best days, the busiest days, the only days Alex looks forward to, if she's honest. Which of course she isn't. How can she be? Who at twenty-five is going to admit that she only enjoys one seventh of her life? Not Alex. Not yet.

And if she can't admit it to herself, it's certain that Matt, her husband, has no idea. For reasons she finds increasingly hard to justify (though unplanned pregnancy has a lot to do with it), Alex has been married for five years to Matthew Allardyce, the up-and-coming young composer, whose *Spectral Dances* for horn, strings and percussion has recently had its first performance at the Wigmore Hall. To mediocre reviews, it must be said. *The Times* was suitably scathing. 'Spectres take heed!' it warned. 'If Mr Allardyce should invite you to one of his dances, plead illness, bereavement, a previous engagement – plead anything at all, but do not attend. It will be dull, protracted and pointless, with nothing to recommend it.' It's a view with which Alex agrees, though she'd never dream of saying so. Matt blames lack of rehearsal time and an over-literal approach by the critics, and is now working on *Spectral Dances 11,* which strikes Alex as perverse if not downright bloody-minded, all things considered.

Not that she'd actually been at the first performance. No such luck. Maggie, their usually healthy four-year old, chose that very day to develop an alarmingly high temperature, and was so feverish and fretful when it was time to leave that Alex met the babysitter at the door and told her she wasn't needed, she'd changed her mind about going out. Of course she had to pay her, and the girl looked so thoroughly put out at the change of plan that Alex immediately assumed she'd arranged an evening of sexual debauch in their flat. That, or systematic robbery.

She'd got details of the rejected babysitter (who turned out to be called Tatiana Labinovitch, though one could hardly hold that against her; this is Hampstead, after all) from a card in a newsagent's window. She knew no-one else they could ask. They'd left all their useful babysitting friends in Manchester when they moved to London three years ago. Alex's mother had just died, and with the money Alex inherited she bought the flat in Hampstead. That's still a sore point with Matt, though they'd only moved for the sake of his budding career. And how does one go about making friends in Hampstead? Since Maggie started at Nursery, Alex has done her best to strike up friendships with the other adults there. But most turn out to be either foreign *au pairs* with very little English, or mothers with busy schedules who are off-hand and daunting. 'Do hurry up, Cressida darling,' these mothers trill in prefect-like tones to their offspring. 'You know we've got ballet at two.' Alex has once or twice had the urge to yell in similar fashion, 'Do come along, Maggie. We've got the tiger shoot at two and tea at the Palace at four.' But so far her courage has failed her.

Thank heavens for Maggie, she thinks. At least she is someone to love. Alex loves bathing her and inventing games with her and reading her bedtime stories. But most of all she loves the way Maggie loves her: absolutely, unconditionally, with total trust and without question. Alex longs to be loved in exactly this way by an adult, but so far all the adults she's known – her parents, her teachers, even Brown Owl, and now Matt – always seem to want something from her in return. She tries to give them what it is they want, but it's never enough. Or perhaps what she gives them is not what they're expecting. It seems to Alex that Maggie alone isn't disappointed by her. Not Maggie. Not yet.

'I do envy you,' Alex's school friend Cassie had written, when she learnt of their move to Hampstead. 'Mixing with all those arty people. And it must be heaven to be married to a composer' – Cassie was married to a statistician called Higginbottom and lived in Market Harborough – 'and be part of the creative process.'

Alex has never replied. She doesn't know what to say. So far she hasn't met any arty people. From time to time someone might call at the flat to play something through with Matt. But she's clearly not welcome in the large, bay-windowed front room in which Matt installed the Bechstein and which he grandly describes as 'my studio'. Once when she ventured in to offer coffee to the visitor, Matt glowered and snapped, 'Not now, for heaven's sake. Can't you see that we're busy?' She's never done it again. He hates any disturbance while he's working, and Alex has to stop herself from whispering to Maggie when they're together in the kitchen, next door to the studio.

And there's certainly nothing heavenly about being married to Matt. He will never admit that he's wrong. Alex is used to hearing him blame others – at length and vehemently – for mistakes which she guesses are properly his. She felt keenly sorry for the original horn player in *Spectral Dances* – a man she's never met and has only heard referred to as 'that bugger Colefax' – who made what seemed to her a perfectly reasonable suggestion about tempo markings, and so became the target of Matt's anger.

'Bloody jumped-up bandsman – what does he know about tempi? If he can't get it right at my speed, he's not bloody well up to the job. He'd better watch out or I'll find someone else for the horn.'

And that's what he'd done in the end. That poor bugger Colefax was doomed from the moment he tangled with Matt.

For Matt enjoys arguments, especially winning them. These days they're becoming more frequent. There's usually one first thing in the bedroom, often about socks or some other item of clothing.

'What have you done with my socks? I can't find them anywhere.'

'They're in the third drawer down, where they always are.'

'No they're not. I've looked.'

'They must be there. Look again.'

'What do you mean 'Look again'? I've already looked, and they're not bloody there.'

He cuts a ridiculous figure, storming about in his underpants. Alex is tempted to laugh, but knows that would anger him further. Instead she says, 'You'd better let me have a look.' I'm a slave to the sock drawer, she thinks, as she investigates for herself. 'Let's see – what have we here? Socks, socks, socks. Black socks, grey socks, green socks, those horrid stripy socks you wear on holiday...'

'But no brown socks,' Matt says triumphantly. 'It's the brown socks I want.'

'Oh, the *brown* socks.' She might have known. The brown socks are the only ones that need darning. 'They have a hole in them.'

'I thought you were going to mend them.'

'And so I am. I just haven't got round to it yet.'

'Well perhaps you could do it now. Or would that be too much to ask?'

And Alex obediently gets out her sewing basket and finds the brown wool and the darning needle and sits on the edge of the bed in her nightie mending the heel of a brown sock which Matt could perfectly well manage without, if he cared to. Lately, she spends Wednesday evenings frantically checking his clothes – tightening shirt buttons, removing spots from jackets with miracle chemicals, even ironing his ties – to avoid the possibility of delay in the morning. Because on Thursdays she cannot afford to be late.

Hopeless, of course, to expect Matt to do anything at all domestic. Better not to try. At first, Alex supposed it was simply innate clumsiness. Why else would he drop so much of the washing up? He broke handles off cups, chipped milk jugs and plates, cracked glasses. Before long, the only way she could guarantee they'd have any china and glassware left was to do it all herself. Which of course was his aim all along. And as for asking him to help with the cooking, she's given that up since some chops he was grilling caught alight and set fire to the tea towel he'd left on the cooker. He'd only popped out for a moment, he said, to jot down an idea he was working on. But she'd still had to repaint the kitchen ceiling.

Her mother, of course, had known what would happen, had seen it all coming.

'Head in the clouds most of the time,' Alex once overheard her describing Matt to a friend. 'Doesn't know what day of the week it is, I shouldn't wonder. The *creative* type, according to Alex. Selfish, I call it. Get everyone running round you while you swan about, waiting to be struck by the Muse. Muse, indeed! I know what I'd like to strike him.'

But who listens to her mother? Not Alex. And by then it was too late anyway. Maggie was already conceived. On a spare bed in a friend's house after a party, when Alex got her weeks muddled up. And by the time she was certain, Matt was already talking about marriage. It just had to be sooner than planned. And they'd had to pass Maggie off as premature, of course. 'I don't know how you could let him touch you. Not before you were married,' her mother said. Which suggested to Alex that her father must have been considerably less insistent in that department than Matt. Touching was the least of it.

And Matt's still insistent. No change at all there. The more they argue in the morning, the more insistent he becomes at night, as though the one can make up for the other. Especially if his work is going well. Alex doesn't know which is worse, his bad temper when things don't go as he wants, or his sexual appetite after a successful day. Not that there've been many of those lately. *Spectral Dances 11*, even more glum and lugubrious than its predecessor, is progressing badly from what she can gather. And he's recently been passed over as composer-in-residence at one of the London colleges (much swanning about, plus a small amount of teaching) in favour of 'that bugger Enright', an older man whose jaunty compositions smack of Edwardian complacency, according to Matt. Alex rather likes them, though she'd never dream of saying so.

He was counting, it seems, on the college job to help tide them over. With nothing in the musical pipeline but the gloomy *Spectral Dances*, the future is bleak on all fronts. Which is why, even if there's no argument in the bedroom, there's almost bound to be one over breakfast, when the post arrives. Bills and bank statements. The bank statements are the worst – the sums involved are so much larger. Enormous, in fact. Post of this nature is addressed to them both, but Matt naturally commandeers it all, reinforcing Alex's sense that she's somehow an afterthought, being only 'and Mrs' on the envelope. Even after five years, she's still not used to being Mrs. Allardyce. And anyway, the person she thinks of as Mrs. Allardyce – the *real* Mrs. Allardyce – is a corsetière in a Manchester department store, flattening Mancunians' stomachs and smoothing their spreading hips. And 'Alexandra Allardyce' sounds too much like the pen name of someone who answers readers' questions on the problem page of women's magazines. Alexandra Allardyce Advises.

Matt digests their financial state while Alex digests her breakfast. Over the years she's learnt to interpret his limited range of reactions to post. Putting the offending piece of paper carefully and silently back in its envelope means that he's cross, but not dangerously so. Studying it at length to an accompaniment of tut-tutting sounds means an argument's in the offing. Flapping it about in front of her face is definitely a prelude to outright rancour and strife. If she flinches as he thrusts the bank statement perilously close to her eyes while flicking it up and down, he merely sees it as guilt.

'That's right,' he says savagely. 'Shy away! You run up debts and then don't want to know about them.'

'What do you mean? I don't run up debts!'

'How do you explain this, then?' An explosion of even more furious flapping and flicking.

Alex stays perfectly calm. 'Explain what?'

'Don't play the innocent, pretending you don't understand.'

'If you'd just let me read it, I might understand better.'

'Read it? You don't need to *read* it. It's the bank statement. Just look at the colour of the figures. A child of six could understand it.'

'I assume that the figures are red.'

'Damn right the figures are red. And we've exceeded the agreed overdraft again. You've got to stop spending so much.'

The injustice of this stings Alex. 'I spend almost nothing as it is.'

'What rubbish! You're always coming home with something new.'

'For Maggie. She's growing, Matt – children do. They grow out of things and need new ones.' He's never grasped this simple fact of life. 'Of course, if we're talking about buying new clothes, what about your new suit – the one you wore to the Wigmore Hall?'

Matt instantly bridles. 'I suppose you'd have liked me to go there looking scruffy?'

'Of course not. But did you have to buy such a wildly expensive suit? And *five* new shirts, one in each colour? You could surely have managed with one.'

'They'll last me for years,' he says doggedly.

'They'd better,' she mutters.

'Don't try to change the subject. I'm saying you've got to spend less, and you're trying to change the subject.'

'No I am not.' Alex speaks slowly and carefully, to make sure he understands. 'I am saying I cannot spend less. I've bought nothing for myself in over a year. Just look at me, Matt. My mother gave me this cardigan four Christmases ago. I wore this blouse at college, but you probably won't remember – you were always too keen to get it off me. This skirt was my mother's, for God's sake. I don't remember exactly when I bought these shoes, but it was in Dolcis in Manchester, so it must be more than three years ago. I buy things for Maggie, yes, but only things that she needs. And just now she really needs a new pair of shoes...'

'That's it then,' he snaps. 'Things bloody well can't go on like this, one expense after another. You'll have to find a job.'

'A job?'

'Yes, a job. Why should I be the only one working? You can get yourself a job and see how you like spending *your* hard-earned cash.'

And so the next phase of Alex's life begins.

At first the prospect of a job terrifies her. But the more she thinks it over, the more it seems a real possibility. She could teach music in a school, give piano lessons. She pictures eager little hands on the keyboard, rooms full of children singing merrily while she plays. That evening, after she's put Maggie to bed and read every single word of her current story books ('No, Mummy, don't miss any words out. It's not the same story if you miss words out.'), Alex rummages in the cupboard which houses her files from college. There are her undergraduate essays on Beethoven's string quartets and Mahler's use of the orchestra and yes, the notes she made for her LRAM Pianoforte (Teacher) exam. She even finds her certificates, unframed and rather battered – so different from Matt's, ostentatiously framed in his studio. She writes to each of the nine Prep schools in the area. There are, she realises, some advantages to living in Hampstead after all. Seven reply. Six regret they have no suitable position at present. The seventh, Frognal Preparatory School, rings her up, and invites her to meet the Head at 10.30am the following Monday.

The school is clearly desperate for a music specialist. The Head all but begs her to join the staff. She is, he says, the answer to his prayers. Yes, and to the prayers of all those Hampstead mothers who complain that music isn't on the curriculum, thinks Alex. And the result? One full day's teaching a week. Each Thursday, she'll play the piano in the Hall for School Assembly, have Forms 1, Lower 2, Upper 2 and Lower 3 in turn for a class music lesson, rehearse the school band for half an hour at lunchtime, and have three little girls in turn for piano lessons in the afternoon. And if she leaves the school promptly at a quarter past three, she can be home in time for tea as usual with Maggie.

If Matt's pleased, he doesn't say so. 'Only one day a week? I suppose it's better than nothing. What are they paying you?'

Alex names a sum which seems princely to her, but cuts no ice with Matt.

'Is that all? You should have held out for more, as the wife of a gifted composer. It was probably mentioning my name that got you the job.'

Like hell it was. She used her maiden name on all the letters. As far as the school is concerned, she's Miss Alex Taylor. If only.

Of course it takes some organisation. Mainly of Matt. He now has to collect Maggie from Nursery on Thursdays at half past twelve, and keep her safe for three hours. Hardly too much to expect. She doesn't dare ask him to take the child in the morning as well. She knows his limits. And if she runs, or at least trots, between the Nursery and Frognal Prep – down Fitzjohn Avenue, into Netherhall Gardens and then a hop, skip and a jump along Frognal – she can do it in fifteen minutes. Just in time for Assembly and only a little out of breath.

Once started, the day speeds by. The children do all that she asks. They stand, breathe in, sing a phrase, tap a rhythm, learn sol-fa. Even the poor plodding pianists in the afternoon do their best. She feels better than she has done for years – for five years, at any rate. She's doing something at last, something she enjoys and is good at. Something that doesn't disappoint anybody. Though trust Matt to insist on making love every Thursday night, just when she feels most exhausted. Not that he notices. She sometimes thinks she could be sound asleep and he still wouldn't notice. She has, in fact, dropped off once or twice, just for a moment. It's not as if she's missing anything. What is there to miss?

Then one Thursday, just as Alex is bringing band practice to an end, collecting in the triangles and packing away the drums, the school secretary appears in the Hall. The Nursery has been on the phone. Maggie has not been collected. She's perfectly safe, Alex isn't to worry, but if someone could just pop over and pick her up, the Nursery staff really can't hang about any longer. Damn the man, thinks Alex as she looks for her handbag. Damn and blast him to hell. But the secretary's still hovering. Is it far? She knows Alex has a piano lesson in five minutes. Can she give her a lift? The little girl can spend the afternoon in her office.

Alex feels like kissing her. But she can't remember her name. Something to do with the kitchen. Saucepan? Teapot? Kettle – that's it.

'That would be wonderful, Miss Kettle. If you're sure it's no trouble.'

'Absolutely sure. Come along now, you don't need a coat. And please call me Gladys. Everyone does.'

A note for the piano pupil telling her to practise scales for five minutes. Into the car with Gladys, who instantly turns into a demon driver and gets them to the Nursery in three minutes flat. Thanks all round to Nursery staff. Apologies. Can't think what happened. Something must have come up. Won't occur again. Maggie cheerful but curious. 'Where's Daddy?' A wink from Gladys. 'He asked me to look after you today. He wants you to count my paperclips.' Curiosity satisfied. Grateful look from Alex. Piano pupil practising diligently when she returns. Bloody man. Bloody, bloody man. What the hell was he thinking of?

The answer of course is himself. No surprise there. There'd been a phone call. Someone from the Third Programme, interested in a discussion about sponsorship of the Arts. Could they possibly meet for lunch? Of course, says Matt, and grabs his coat.

'But she's your daughter, Matt. You forgot her, for heaven's sake.'

'But no harm done, eh? She told me she enjoyed herself.'

'Counting Miss Kettle's paperclips, yes. Not waiting for a parent who didn't turn up. She hardly had a whale of a time then.'

'Look, Alex, I've said I'm sorry.' He hadn't, of course. 'Now can we forget it? Actually, it was a bit of good luck meeting up with old Tomlinson. I was telling him how that bugger Enright waltzed off with the composer-in-residence job, and he happened to mention...Alex – are you listening?'

'I'm listening. I just can't believe what I'm hearing.'

'And he said there was another coming up.'

'Another what?'

'Another residency. For a composer. At a university.'

'In London?'

'No – Perth.'

'In Scotland?'

'No – Western Australia.'

And so the next phase of Alex's life begins.

For a while she says nothing at Frognal Prep while Matt waits to hear from Australia. She doubts that he'll get it. He's sent them a tape of some recent work – himself playing his piano pieces *Fugitive Fires* and *Concatenations*, as well as a re-dubbed recording of *Spectral Dances* – which is surely enough to scupper his application. But no. Australian ears are made of sterner stuff. They offer him the post. A two-year residency, starting in October. Return flight paid and accommodation provided. Accommodation for one.

'Only two years, Al. Twenty-six menstrual cycles. Then I'll be back.'

'And in the meantime? What am I supposed to do?'

'Ask at that school of yours. Can't they give you extra work? Or there's always more piano lessons.'

Alex is damned if she'll become a piano teacher. She doesn't want pupils to the flat, the odd lesson here, another lesson there, always being tied, and Maggie's life disrupted. She discusses it with Gladys. Gladys, it so happens, has a cousin who's a record reviewer for a glossy monthly publication called, unsurprisingly, *Record Review Monthly*. Gladys lets her cousin know that Mrs. Matthew Allardyce would be interested in joining the reviewing team. Could he have a word with the editor? As luck would have it, the editor has just fired one of the regular reviewers, a volatile Spaniard, over his blatantly chauvinistic attitude to recordings of some rather minor works by de Falla. He agrees to give Alex a trial and sends her a parcel of records. If her reviews are satisfactory, he'll employ her. They are, and he does.

If Matt's pleased, he doesn't say so. 'Reviewing? I won't have my wife known as a reviewer. A bunch of hacks and mountebanks, that's what reviewers are. What on earth made you join that vile breed?'

'Necessity, Matt. And no-one will know I'm your wife. I won't even use my maiden name. I'll call myself Alexandra Schneider. We Taylors were Schneiders before the First World War. Will that suit you? Though why should you care? You're buggering off to the other side of the world. You'll be swanning about in Perth, where no review of mine can touch you.'

'Yes – but I'll be back. It's just for a couple of years. I promise, Al.'

And he doesn't doubt himself for a moment. Not Matt. Not yet.

3

Allegretto e grazioso

One morning in my fourth year at Lansdowne, a very strange thing happened: I opened my desk to find a bar of chocolate inside. Attached to it was a message which read 'Sweets for the sweet', and was unsigned. When I showed it to my friend Holly Carstairs at break, we agreed that the only thing to do with chocolate was to eat it, and did so. Two days later, a red rose was similarly concealed, along with the message 'O my Luve's like a red, red rose'.

'Obviously from a Scot,' was Holly's comment. 'No-one else could bear to read Robbie Burns, much less quote him.'

From then on I received a gift and an accompanying anonymous note almost every other day, and grew to dread opening my desk for fear of what it might contain. There was a small rectangular mirror ('Who is the fairest of them all?'), a picture of a Great Dane ('Love me, love my dog') and, most unimaginative of all, four sugar cubes sitting on a cut-out paper heart ('Sugar is sweet and so are you').

'You know what this means,' said Holly when I showed her these astonishing trophies. 'You've got an admirer. Someone in this school is in love with you.'

'But who can it be?' I wondered. The whole idea seemed unlikely.

'Well, we know quite a bit about whoever it is,' Holly pointed out. 'Scottish, owns a Great Dane, can get into our form-room before or after school with no trouble, knows which desk is yours...'

'Couldn't it be a mistake?' I suggested hopefully. 'Perhaps they've put them in the wrong desk.'

'Nonsense. Your name is on each of your exercise books. Someone who can make sense of Burns would be sure to notice a thing like that.' She looked at me. 'Do you *want* to find out who it is, Bobs?'

We thought about it for a while.

'It might be the gardener – he's a little bit odd.'

'Or a cleaner. They come round after we've all gone.'

'Or Wacky Jacky.' Miss Jackson was our Form Mistress that year.

'Or the Head.'

We collapsed into giggles, but in fact each suggestion only served to increase my alarm. To be the unwitting object of any of these people's affection was a seriously disturbing notion.

'No, I don't want to know who it is,' I said finally. 'But I do want it to stop.'

At the end of school that afternoon, we penned our own message for the mystery admirer. Carefully detaching the centre page from my Geography notebook, I wrote at Holly's dictation: 'Alas, your gifts are in vain. I'm unable to give you my heart.' We considered the 'alas' to be especially effective. The next day the note was no longer there, nor were there any more gifts. But I often pondered in secret over the identity of my hapless lover, and sometimes wished I'd been brave enough to leave a message of an altogether different kind.

Holly was my closest friend at Lansdowne, a fellow boarder in my House. Only to her did I ever confide the secret of my father's prolonged absence, and she in return told me something of her own life at home, which sounded greatly more taxing than mine. Her parents, though living together, never spoke to each other directly but instead communicated through a third party.

'It's ghastly, Bobbie,' she told me. 'They behave as though they can't see or hear each other, even when they're both in the same room. At mealtimes, it's always 'Would you ask your father if he'd like more potatoes?', when the wretched man's sitting right there. They're each as bad as the other. I don't know how they manage when I'm not around to act as messenger, and I really don't care. They're childish and senseless and tiring to be with, and a dreadful example to the young.'

'Were they always like that,' I asked, 'or has it come on lately?'

'It's been going on for as long as I can remember. I think the only reason they had me was to act as their go-between, I honestly do.'

For both of us, school was the happier environment.

Lansdowne, like all well-run institutions, allowed for oddness and even catered for it: my fondnesses for Latin, literature and quadratic equations were accepted as a squint might be, or a club-foot. I began to enjoy my piano lessons, learnt to play the cello and was soon recruited into the school orchestra. No one laughed at me for my enthusiasms, or, even worse, tittered about them behind my back. They were part of me, and with increasing thankfulness I learnt that what Terry had once told me was indeed the case: that only by being truly myself could I fully embrace life and happiness. Being truly myself also involved a loathing of Games and all kinds of sport, and I told a multitude of lies to escape them. I was also very untidy, and year after year my Housemistress felt it necessary to write on my report 'Robina continues to use the floor instead of the wardrobe'.

In spite of this damning indictment, I was happy as a boarder at Lansdowne to a degree I hadn't thought possible, and though I'd gone there half hoping for deprivation and humiliation as in *Jane Eyre*, or excitement and escapades as in *Mallory Towers*, I soon learnt just how unreliably Literature can represent Life. For seven years I knew exactly what was expected of me, and on the whole was able to supply it. My prizes for classics and algebra satisfied even my mother, who turned up each year for Prize Giving wearing a new hat. Afterwards she would take me out for tea and fill me in on her latest activities.

'Mr Walters and I are now members of the Country Dancing Demonstration Team,' she told me proudly one autumn, over our plate of iced fancies.

'Is that very demanding?' I asked. Try as I might, I could not imagine my stout and unbending mother as a gifted dancer.

'Not at all – I enjoy it. We give demonstrations to groups who are interested in starting their own Country Dancing club – Women's Institutes, Townswomen's Guilds, that sort of thing. We travel all over the place, usually on Fridays.' Then, timing her announcement to coincide with the waitress's appearance with a pot of hot water, she added, 'Mr Walters and I have just been awarded the annual Top Couple Performance Cup. That's a *very* great honour.'

'It must be,' I said. 'Congratulations.' I guessed my achievements in Latin and Maths seemed decidedly pale by comparison.

'Not only that,' she continued, 'but the roses have had such a good flush of flowers this autumn.'

I was stumped for a moment to see the connection, until I realised that the roses, too, were the work of the whistling Mr Walters. 'I'm sorry I missed them,' I said.

'So you should be,' she answered crisply. 'But now you're at home so rarely, there's a very great deal that you miss.'

In fact the terms were punctuated by free weekends and exeats of which, I'm ashamed to say, my mother knew nothing. On some of these red-letter days I would find Terry and Jo waiting in the House Sitting Room, ready to take me out. As they were hard at work on the *Compendium*, our first excursions were to the dovecotes of the area. Worcestershire and Herefordshire proved splendidly rich in such buildings, and while Terry photographed them from every possible angle, Jo carefully sketched the interior. I was generally called upon to estimate numbers of nest boxes, and was always relieved when the total was less than Hendre's, for I longed to be connected with the biggest, most sumptuous, dovecote in Britain. I was useful in other ways too. In Lansdowne's library lurked some ancient volumes, including a copy of Varro's *De*

Re Rustica. Armed with a Latin dictionary, I painstakingly translated his account of how pigeons were kept and used in Roman times. My findings were treated with caution.

'But *why* would a Roman lady take a pigeon to the theatre, Bobbie?' Terry asked when I produced this particular gem. 'Are you sure you translated it properly?'

'They tucked them into their bosoms,' I said, keen to supply all the details, 'then released them and let them fly home.'

'But *why?*' Terry persisted. 'What on earth was the point? Unless they were proving how well they were trained.'

'They could have been using them to send messages,' I hazarded. 'Like Hannibal did when he crossed the Alps.'

'Now *that's* an idea.' Terry nodded approvingly. 'But what sort of message might they have sent?'

I was used by now to Terry's habit of turning everything into a game.

'Lions mauled by Christians,' I suggested.

'Milk all the asses – I feel like a bath,' was Terry's offering.

But Jo was the outright winner, and made us all laugh with 'Need a clean tunic – the bird's made a right mess of this one.'

It wasn't all dovecotes and doves. Sometimes we went for picnics, and in the winter months would visit museums and art galleries. Once, when I was thirteen, we went as far as Stratford, which was busily celebrating the four hundredth anniversary of Shakespeare's birth, for a concert of music played on period instruments. But we never went to Hendre, in view of my mother's embargo.

On one of these lazy Saturdays together, Terry, Jo and I were discussing *Tess of the D'Urbervilles*, which I'd just finished reading at school. I'd greatly enjoyed the novel, but felt Hardy simplified things by letting Tess meet so few men.

'It's always like that in books,' I complained. 'It's obvious Jane Eyre is going to fall for Mr Rochester, as there's simply no other man in her world at the time. And Tess gets involved with Angel and Alec, but it's not as though she has any real choice; again, there's virtually no-one else for her. It's as though women are bound to fall for any man they meet, and some of them are wrong and some right. But we don't see them choosing the right person out of a whole range of possibilities, if you see what I mean.'

'I do see what you mean,' said Terry, 'but I don't see it as a problem. Isn't that what it's like in life? When you think how vast the world is, we can only ever meet a very small number of people from which to make our choice. Your ideal partner may be sitting in Australia or Canada right now, or even in Lincoln or Hull, but unless you meet, he or she may just as well not exist.'

'Isn't that a depressing thought?' I asked. 'All those missed opportunities.'

'We can only work from the opportunities that happen to come our way,' Terry said briskly. 'Which is why it's so very important to make the most of them, to ensure that we meet as many people as possible who are like us, and whom we might like.'

I thought about this for a moment. 'How did you and Jo first meet?' I eventually asked. This was something I'd been curious about for a while.

'Oh, I taught her,' said Terry with a laugh. 'I'd been teaching for five or six years when she suddenly appeared in my Lower Sixth literature class. Jonquil Menzies. I can still see her name on the register.'

'Chaucer, Milton and Pope,' said Jo. 'Not, on the face of it, a promising mix.'

'You had a real understanding of language,' Terry said fondly. 'A feel for the weight of a word. It's the sort of thing you can't really teach. It's either there or it isn't, I've come to believe, like freckles or perfect pitch. Some of your essays were packed with insight ...'

'But that wasn't why ...'

'Oh no, that wasn't why – though it may well have helped. Then, after two years, you left and went off to Art College.'

'But before I left, you said to me ...'

'... "Do keep in touch". One says it a lot, but they rarely do, thank goodness.'

'But I did.'

'Yes, you did. You wrote me such letters – so funny and warm, with lots of amusing drawings.'

'But never a hint of love in them.'

'No, never a hint of that.'

It was like listening in stereo. I had the distinct impression that this was a story they'd delighted in telling each other many times before.

'We did meet up once,' Terry continued, turning to me. 'I invited her to tea.'

Jo smiled at the memory. 'And *I* thought you probably invited lots of former pupils to tea. I thought it was what you did. I had no idea that I was the only one.'

'Oh yes, you were always the only one. It wasn't a great deal to go on, though, was it? One polite tea-time conversation and twelve letters in four whole years.'

'But you kept all my letters . . . '

'And you kept all mine. Though we didn't know that at the time of course. Then the following year, when you were doing your teacher training, you wrote and said you were thinking of getting married. Imagine it, Bobbie! I was struck all of a heap.'

'What did you do?' I asked.

'At first, I didn't think there was anything I *could* do. But I felt so . . . so desolate. I think now it was genuine grief. And I couldn't get her out of my head. I found myself thinking about her all the time, from the moment I woke in the morning. It was like being gripped by obsession.'

'Were you really going to get married?' I asked Jo.

'I'm ashamed to say that I wasn't,' she answered. 'Wasn't it awful, to lie like that? It was a sort of test, I suppose. I didn't say a word about marriage to anyone else, only to Terry. But I had to know how she felt, you see – because I'd been think-ing about her all the time too. Every single minute. Then one day she turned up at my digs, completely out of the blue.'

'I'd armed myself with all the proper arguments,' Terry said with gusto. 'She was still very young. Did she know what she was doing? Was she utterly sure he was the right one for her? All that sort of thing. But what I desperately wanted to say was that I knew I couldn't possibly live without her.'

Jo smiled and reached for her hand. 'Which you did eventually get round to saying. And which was exactly what I wanted to hear, though I'd never admitted it, even to myself. It had been a secret, hidden life that only went on in my head. I didn't know if it could ever be real.'

'Of course, it wasn't straightforward,' Terry continued. 'These things, I'm afraid, rarely are. We had to be careful and not expect everyone to understand. That's really the reason we settled at Hendre, to give minimum offence – though Jo's mother, poor dear, still doesn't approve.'

'Like mine,' I said feelingly. 'Though I don't think she's got the faintest idea how good you are together.'

'Bless you, Bobbie.' Terry smiled at me warmly. 'You do say the loveliest things.' She looked over at Jo, who gazed steadily back, her face suffused with tenderness. 'So, when all's said and done, no regrets?'

'None at all,' Jo said quietly. 'Living with you has been all that I hoped for, and more.'

Terry seemed moved by this declaration. 'And will be for a long time yet, please God. But you'd better watch out, Bobbie!' she added, with a return of her former spirit. 'English teachers are by far the most dangerous. It's all that naked emotion – we don't always know how to cope!'

'You needn't worry,' I laughed. 'I've got jolly Mrs. Gallagher, and she's well and truly married. There's absolutely *no* danger there.'

But it was in Mrs. Gallagher's class at the beginning of Upper Sixth that I first found myself speaking about love between women. We were studying *The Rainbow*, a book I was enjoying very much until I hit Chapter 12. This chapter, to which Lawrence gives the prejudicial title 'Shame', describes the brief but passionate relationship between the seventeen year old Ursula and her teacher, Winifred Inger. Lawrence's description of Winifred's taut, striking physical and intellectual beauty put me in mind of Terry, and as I was reading I felt the powerful sexual attraction between the two women, only to have it dismissed as negative and perverted a few pages later. For the first time I felt I was reading something false in a novel, and was sufficiently affronted to object. I timidly raised my hand.

'Why is Lawrence so harsh about Winifred Inger?' I asked. 'He seems to switch half way through the chapter from admiring her to despising her.'

'Well, it wouldn't really do, Robina, would it?' Mrs. Gallagher answered. 'And the girl is so young – just your age, in fact.'

'But age isn't an issue here,' I persisted. 'Lawrence never suggests she's too young – he even minimises the age difference by referring to them both as girls. And in any case, Ursula has already been cavorting with Skrebensky with the author's full permission. No, it must be because she's with a woman not a man. But I don't see why it's so wrong. Why Lawrence thinks it's so sterile and abnormal, I mean.'

'Lawrence wants his characters' lives to be fulfilled in every conceivable way,' Mrs. Gallagher said smoothly, 'and that can only happen in a relationship between a man and a woman. I'm sure you can understand that. It's what's most natural, after all.'

'But he may be wrong,' I continued. 'It may be possible for two women to have a completely fulfilling relationship, don't you think?'

'Let's just concern ourselves with Lawrence's point of view, shall we, Robina? You are perfectly right: he does condemn this relationship, although he also makes us see where the initial attraction lies. And now if we can move on to Chapter Thirteen . . .'

And thus I lost my taste for Lawrence and his particular set of sexual prejudices, and dismissed Mrs. Gallagher as a hopeless cause.

The following Friday afternoon I was in Lower School Hall supervising Junior Prep when the Head came in, looking unusually agitated. Watched by fifty pairs of eyes, she made her way to my desk and spoke in a low whisper.

'Robina, could you go to your House at once. There's someone there to speak to you. I'll take over here.'

This was most unusual, but obediently I went. My Housemistress was waiting for me at the door. She, too, was agitated, but in a fussier way than the Head.

'In the Sitting Room, dear,' she said, taking me by the arm. That most uncharacteristic 'dear' told me something was badly amiss. 'There are two men to see you.'

When she opened the Sitting Room door, I saw two uniformed policemen perched awkwardly on the sofa. They looked very young, hardly much older than me, and their faces were red, as though they'd been running. They both stood up when I entered the room.

'Miss Robina Sinclair?' one of them asked.

'Yes.'

'And Mrs Eileen Sinclair is your mother?'

'Yes, she is. Is there something wrong? Has something happened to her?'

'Perhaps you'd better sit down, Robina. I'm afraid we've some rather bad news.'

I sat down. My legs, I noticed, had started trembling and I put my hands together on my lap to try and control them.

'Your mother's been in an accident, Robina. She was in a coach with some friends ....'

'Yes,' I said. 'That would be the Country Dancing team. They often go out on a Friday. Today I think they were going to somewhere in Cumberland.'

'Cockermouth.'

It was the only word the other policeman had spoken, and I had a dreadful desire to giggle.

'Yes, they were going to Cockermouth,' the first policeman continued. 'But there was an accident on the way. It looks as if the coach went out of control on a bend and turned over.'

'And my mother?' I asked, suddenly realising why they were here.

'I'm very sorry. Your mother was killed, Robina, along with three of the others. I'm very sorry.'

He looked so genuinely sorry and upset that I had to curb an instinct to tell him it was all right, it wasn't his fault. Instead, I sat and looked down at my hands.

'And Mr Walters?' I asked.

'Mr Walters too.'

'They always danced together,' I said. 'My mother and Mr Walters.'

'But they weren't married?'

'No, they were just good friends. My mother's still married to my father. Oh, my poor father! He won't know anything about it.'

'If you could tell us how to get in touch with him, someone will inform him.'

I gave them my father's address in Aberdeen.

'One of our colleagues in Scotland will give him the news as soon as possible,' they told me, and stood up to go, patently relieved that a difficult duty was over.

'I'm very sorry,' each of them said to me as they left the room.

When they had gone, I stayed where I was. The Sitting Room window was open, and I could hear the Chapel Choir singing 'The day thou gavest, Lord, is ended' as part of Evening Prayers. It struck me as sadly appropriate. After a while, my Housemistress came to sit beside me.

'Is there anyone you need to telephone, Robina?'

'Yes,' I said. 'My mother's sister.'

And for the second time in seven years I rang Terry's number.

My mother's death effectively brought to a close everything associated with my parents. She left no Will, and my father inherited her estate. Since this consisted of a house which he'd paid for, and a small amount of cash saved from the allowance he'd been sending regularly from Aberdeen, there was a certain justice in this financial adjustment. My mother had never earned a penny in her life, having married at the end of her time at secretarial college; whatever shorthand and typing skills she acquired there were acquired entirely in vain. My father, now settled happily in Scotland, told me he intended to sell the detached house he loved so little in Oreley Wood and look for a bigger flat in Aberdeen.

'You must come and stay with me there, Robina,' he said kindly. 'I'd like us to keep in touch.'

Unduly influenced, perhaps, by his postcards of battlefields which formed my only view of that country, I could not shake off the impression that Scotland was a wild and lawless place where I wouldn't be happy. He did not press me, but explained he'd continue to provide me with a quite generous sum of money each year on my birthday until I was twenty-one. After that age he hoped I wouldn't need it.

During the four surreal, timeless days between the accident and the funeral, when my father and I lived once again under the same roof, we grew no closer, although I did come to understand him a little better. Scrupulous in not once criticising my mother, he nevertheless let me see how difficult their life together must often have been for him.

'We really had little in common,' he admitted ruefully. 'Your mother depended on me for so many practical matters which I didn't feel up to shouldering.'

'Like the garden?' I suggested.

'Not only the garden, but all sorts of Do-It-Yourself and home decoration – she was always full of such plans. I probably let her down badly by not being more technically-minded. But I've now found the answer. In Aberdeen I live in a rented flat. If anything goes wrong, I just ring up the landlord and he gets it fixed. It suits me down to the ground.'

My jigsaw parents, it seemed, had never fitted together quite so conveniently as once I had blithely imagined.

Terry, looking most unlike herself in a black coat and skirt and a hat, came up on the day of the funeral and was beside me in the church and at the graveside. Among the mourners I recognised some of my mother's friends and neighbours from Selly Oak, who came over and said kind things to my father and me. There was also an unfamiliar group who introduced themselves collectively as fellow members of the

Country Dancing class. They seemed a likeable bunch, and I found myself hoping that my mother had been genuinely fond of Mr Walters, and he of her. The committal over, my father, Terry and I returned to the house, where the fruits of Mr Walters' labours were still strikingly evident in the rose beds, pergola and well-maintained lawn. Little remained in the house that was mine apart from clothes and books, and these were easily packed away in Terry's car. It had been agreed that I would go immediately to Hendre to stay with Terry and Jo, with whom from now on I would make my home. Later they would take me back to Lansdowne; the Head had insisted I need not return until after half-term, still almost two weeks away. My father would stay in Oreley Wood for a few more days, to make arrangements for the sale.

Thus, for the second and final time, Terry drove me from Oreley Wood to Hendre. As we left the West Midlands behind, I couldn't help thinking that my mother's death had finally brought about what I most desired, and that my previous visit had merely been a dress rehearsal for this final, inevitable journey. We passed through the border country, puddly and bleak-looking now under an autumn sky. There was mud on the road left by tractors, and alongside the hedges lay sluggish pools of rainwater which spattered the windscreen whenever we drove too close.

'It's strange how your mother always disliked the countryside,' Terry told me. 'Of course we grew up in a town, and she never lived anywhere else, whereas I managed to live in the country all the time I was teaching, first in Shropshire and then in Herefordshire, where I met Jo. I couldn't get over how silent it is in the country: it was like being given back something I hadn't known I'd lost, and I still love it. But I think the quiet and the total blackness of it all at night rather frightened your mother. She came to visit me once, before you were born, and couldn't wait to get back to pavements and streetlights and the sound of traffic. It was where she felt safe. She did so like to have tidiness around her.'

'But things can't always be tidy, can they?' I said. 'Life's rather messy when you come to think about it, especially the loving part. Think of Anna Karenina.'

'And Maggie Tulliver.'

'And Bathsheba Everdene.'

'And Dorothea Brooke.'

We continued in this vein for some minutes, until my literary knowledge was exhausted.

'I don't think my mother was cut out to be a great literary heroine,' I concluded.

'To be in charge of one's feelings is not always a bad thing, though, Bobbie. Unless we *are* great literary heroines, we probably look very foolish indeed when we chase our dreams of happiness instead of getting on with what others call Life. Look at me, giving up a good career to hide away in the middle of nowhere with Jo. But I'm afraid I'm unrepentant. I've always been a chaser of dreams, and always shall be. How about you?'

'I don't know,' I said. 'I haven't had to choose.'

'Oh, it's not a question of choice,' said Terry firmly. 'You'll see.'

That night I couldn't sleep. I was restless and could not relax, as though the business of the day wasn't over and there was something I still had to do. My bedroom felt close and oppressive, and at two o'clock, despairing of ever falling asleep, I pulled on some clothes and crept downstairs. Outside all was still, but as I crossed the yard I must have disturbed the hens, who, fearful of the fox, set up a cautious muttering. Finding myself at the door of the dovecote, I went inside and sat down on one of the projecting stones near the base. I sat there quite still for a considerable time, and in the vast, dark, womb-like space I was gradually overtaken by a sense of calm, as though the generations of doves had left behind a tangible legacy of peace. I felt no grief for my mother, but now I began to cry, and realised that this was what I so far had not done. The tears weren't for her, nor were they for my loss. They came from the terrible knowledge that I'd never truly loved my mother, and now I never could.

Back at school things were subtly different. Though many boarders had separated parents, or parents with spectacularly tangled and complicated love lives, no-one but I had a dead parent. This gave me an automatic uniqueness and, I guiltily realised, a cloak of tragedy which I hardly knew how to wear. In my House, all references to mothers, however oblique, were stifled in my hearing, and even the staff behaved with unfamiliar deference, as though my loss had somehow imbued me with new and adult wisdom. Only once did I consciously exploit this. On my UCCA form I listed six campus universities, feeling that after the genteel seclusion of Lansdowne, urban life might well be overwhelming. This was virtually heresy in the eyes of the Head, who prided herself on the school's links with Oxbridge and the major city universities, but all opposition ceased when I uttered the magic formula, 'I think it's what my mother would have wanted.' In fact my mother had never seen the remotest need for higher education, assuming that a year at Secretarial College would serve me as a stepping stone to marriage, as it had done for her.

The marathon of A-Levels over, the final term at Lansdowne ended with the traditional Leavers' Party. It was a strangely formal occasion. The Upper Sixth gathered in the School Hall and stood around awkwardly, eating sandwiches and vol-au-vents and drinking something euphemistically called 'Champagne Cup', a weak, rather fruity beverage of unknown but not unpleasant composition. The Head and our Sixth Form teachers put in a brief appearance, and after the food, there was dancing. As the evening wore on, I grew more and more dejected. Made maudlin by drink and sentiment, I was watching the bizarre spectacle of pairs of girls dancing together and trying to retain a sense of detachment when Janet Forbes, a science student and a member of another House, came and sat beside me.

'You're looking sad, Bobbie,' she said. 'Would you not like to be dancing?'

In seven years at Lansdowne, I'd had nothing to do with Janet Forbes, and could only recall that she'd once thrown a rounders ball a spectacular distance on Sports Day, trouncing my feebler effort. I wondered what similarly abstruse pieces of information she'd managed to glean about me.

We stumbled on to the dance floor, Janet Forbes, it seemed, as much a victim of Champagne Cup as I. At first we danced separately, but when the record changed to a slower number, she put her arms round my shoulders and drew me closer. Thus entwined, we rocked backwards and forwards, barely moving our feet. I started to say something, but she hushed me.

'No, don't say anything. It's perfect like this.'

My arms gradually held her tighter, and I sensed Janet Forbes was trembling. My body began to feel strangely alive, as though something had finally slipped into place and was letting me know it was there. The record seemed to last a very long time. When it ended, Janet Forbes brushed my cheek lightly with her lips and whispered, 'Thank you.' Then she was gone.

Some years later, through the Old Girls' Guild Newsletter, I learnt she'd become a vet and had joined a practice in Ayr, near her parents' home. She had always wanted to work with animals and was quite well known as a breeder of dogs: Great Danes.

4

Hampstead 1969

Con speranza

'Maggie!'

No answer.

'Maggie! Dinner's ready.'

Still no answer.

'Maggie! Your dinner's on the table.'

A door slams. Maggie appears in the kitchen: Alex resists the urge to tell her not to slouch. Perhaps all teenagers slouch? Maybe it's the physical equivalent of saying 'I don't give a damn'? Either that, or the unaccustomed weight of newly developed breasts. Alex doesn't remember slouching at fourteen, and her mother would certainly have told her if she had. Mind you, she doesn't remember developing breasts either. Certainly not the kind that alters one's centre of gravity.

Maggie slumps onto her chair and starts eating her meal in silence.

'So – how was your day?' Alex refuses to give up, although she's perfectly sure what the answer will be.

'OK.'

'That's good. So was mine. I finally got an interview with the pianist I was telling you about. The girl from Provence. Her English is a bit sketchy – I talked to her mostly in French – but I think we understood each other. She's playing tomorrow evening at the South Bank. Did I tell you?'

'Uh-huh.'

'And you know I'll have to be there?'

'Uh-huh.'

'That OK with you?'

'Uh-huh.'

'It's just I don't like leaving you.'

Maggie rolls her eyes heavenward in silent supplication. 'It's OK, Mum. I'm fourteen. I *like* being on my own.'

'That's OK then.'

'Yeah – that's OK.'

End of round one. Alex searches for another topic. She insists on conversation at dinner time, just as she insists on eating at a table and having proper knives and forks and table napkins in napkin rings. She believes they are civilising.

'You'll never guess who I bumped into on the High Street this morning. Gladys Kettle. Do you remember Miss Kettle? From Frognal Prep?'

'That old dyke.'

'Maggie! What an awful thing to say!'

'It's true.'

'It may well be true, but there's no need to put it so crudely.'

'She makes it so obvious, Mum. Those horrid tweeds she wears – yuk! Of *course* I remember her. She was always hanging round here after Dad went, like she fancied you or something.'

There was no 'or something' about it. It had just taken a long time for the penny to drop with Alex. Gladys had been such a help, virtually getting her the job at *Record Review Monthly*. And that first winter Matt was away, she'd felt so very lonely. She'd just had Gladys round for the odd drink occasionally. But the silly old thing got hold of the wrong end of the stick. Even now, the memory of that fumbled embrace at the front door, her lips just managing to avoid the other, more eager, lips, makes Alex cringe. Time for a quick change of subject.

'Any plans for the weekend?'

'Yeah – sort of.'

'That's good.' Maggie's always more cheerful when there are plans. 'Will you be at home?'

'Bev's having a party on Saturday. She asked if I could stay the night.'

Alex knows better than to say yes or no straightaway. She's learnt to take the scenic route. 'Who else is going?'

'Well, Trev, of course. And Nick. Rick'll probably be there. And Beth and Jo. And Seth and Mo, most likely. I said I'd have to ask.'

Alex is delighted by the paired symmetry of the names. It's like hearing about the Seven Dwarfs, though she'd never dream of saying so. She's quite forgotten whether Nick and Jo are boys or girls, and doesn't like to ask. She has a feeling she's asked before. Instead she says, 'What are they like, these parties you go to?'

'They're just parties, Mum – you know. We eat and we talk and we dance.'

And drink, most probably, Alex thinks. And smoke the odd joint. Still, she knows Bev's parents – Piers and Drusilla Hope-Patterson. They'll keep an eye on things. She'll give them a ring in the morning. 'Sounds fine to me,' she says breezily. 'I'll be going to the Prom on Saturday of course. Actually, it should be a good one – I'm looking forward to it. Colin Davies conducting *The Dream of Gerontius.*'

'Not my scene, I'm afraid.'

'I know.' She's given up with Maggie and classical music. Ever since that time they went to Stratford for one of the four hundredth anniversary concerts. Music for Shakespeare's plays. On period instruments. Maggie must have been about eight. Perhaps it was too much to ask. She'd whined so much they'd had to leave in the interval. Alex had just started writing the odd concert review, and was surprised how easy it was to make up something about the half of the programme she hadn't actually heard. Not that she does it often. There's always a chance the pianist will collapse, or the hall burn down in her absence. Much too risky.

'Actually, Mum, it's a real pain sometimes, being your daughter.'

Oh God – what's coming now? Alex runs through the list of her possible crimes – the erratic shopping, indifferent ironing, whimsical cleaning. She does her best, for heaven's sake, keeps the bathroom spotless. At the dentist's once she read an article about the terrifying numbers of germs that lurk in bathrooms, and has never forgotten it. But she can't always be defrosting fridges or scrubbing at grill pans – there just isn't time. And surely she's trained Maggie to overlook the odd bit of dust now and then?

But it's not a complaint about housekeeping. 'They all take it for granted I'm keen on your sort of music.' It's clear from her tone that nothing could be more unlikely.

'All? Which 'all' are we talking about?'

'The people at school. Teachers mainly. Mrs Pugh was on about it again at the end of term. 'We're expecting great things of you, Maggie. Such a talented musical family'.' She imitates the music teacher's North Walian accent to perfection. 'It's like Dad's J.S.Bach or something and you're...'

But there's no easy parallel. Not for what Alex has done. To be a woman, and a *young* woman – thirty-five's not exactly geriatric, whatever Maggie might think – *and* a well-known music critic is hardly run-of-the-mill. Some days her success still surprises Alex. Other days she adores it.

'Take no notice, sweetheart. That's all in Mrs Pugh's head. It's certainly not in mine or your father's. You do exactly what you want. Find out what makes *you* happy, and never mind anyone else. It's still early days. There's no need to rush – take your time. And Maggie,' she adds, ' I'm sorry. About not being just an ordinary mother like everyone else's. Like Bev's and Beth's and Jo's.'

'Jo's mother's a dipso.'

'See!' Alex smiles at her daughter. 'It could be a whole lot worse.'

And together they stack the dishes by the sink. As dinner time conversations go these days, that counts as one of the better ones.

Often at concerts Alex lets her mind wander. It's one way of getting through them all. During the piano recital, she thinks about the men in her life. Not a topic which usually detains her for long. But when the French girl starts playing a Rondo, it occurs to Alex that her life has taken the form of a rondo, the same old pattern returning only slightly disguised, pretending to be something different but really just the same. Or maybe a Theme and Variations, each episode starting out bravely, but shaped and controlled by the past.

It started, of course, with her father. Isn't that often the case? She'd so wanted to please him – why did that matter, she wonders? – and managed to do so, on the whole. But oh, how she'd worked at it! Her mother's constant carping never bothered her for a moment, but the slightest criticism from her father – a schoolmaster with a toothbrush moustache and a pipe – made her unhappy for days. Yet he wasn't a cruel man. Just a man with high standards. Perhaps it was lucky he'd died when she was eighteen – a heart attack on the golf course. Not knowing about Matt. Or Maggie.

And Matt, again, had been hard to please. Impossible, in fact, towards the end – though at first it had been so simple. Are all composers highly sexed? An overspill of creative urge, a continuous need for expression? It was sex that kept them together, of course. Once she'd given herself to Matt – and she'd held out as long as she could, she really had – that was most definitely It. A commitment. For life. In those days that's how things were. She rather admires the young of today, with their defiant sleeping around. (Should she talk to Maggie about the Pill? Surely not Maggie, not yet. She's only fourteen, after all.) Playing the field. That's what she's never done. And now? Surely it isn't too late? Please God, let it not be too late. Since Matt's departure – still in Australia, quite a Big Shot over there, those ghastly *Spectral Dances* rivalling *Waltzing Matilda* in popularity, by all accounts – there've been two men in her life. Douglas, who's no longer in it, and Richard, who is.

Douglas was a mistake from the start. Married, of course. Wife in Dorking keeping the roses tidy and insisting on separate beds. For Douglas and her, not for the roses. Early menopause. Hot sweats for wifey, cold shoulder for Doug. She met him in Oxford at a gathering of music publishers. What's the collective noun for music publishers? A score, perhaps. Or a stave. At any rate, he was the liveliest of them there. Definitely *con brio*. And a few dinners and late night drinks later, *appassionato*. But never *con amore*. Sex was more like gymnastics to Douglas. Bags and bags of energy but lacking the slightest finesse. She'd known from the start it was just a fling – they'd agreed, in deference to wifey – but she hadn't expected he'd take it quite so literally. He constantly flung himself at her, in lifts, on stairs, in taxis, throwing himself about, clutching and pawing at any accessible body part. In hotel rooms – he often invented reasons for having to stay in London, as though Dorking were on the other side of the world – the tousled state of the bedclothes after one of Doug's energetic frolics always astonished her. Surely such violent exertion can't be obligatory? As for herself, her body often failed to respond, though she jerked about now and again, just to show willing. In the end, she suspected Douglas just got tired of her. Tired of her lukewarm response. Third disappointed man in her life.

As the pianist launches into her final piece, – Schumann's *Kinderscenen* – Alex thinks there are probably things about sex that she's missing. Important things, like how to enjoy it. She assumes that enjoyment is chiefly the point. Matt must have enjoyed it, or wouldn't have been so insistent, and Douglas too, in his vigorous, flesh-grabbing way. Neither enquired if she had. Or is it, she wonders, a monstrous conspiracy? Is there really no more to the business of sex than bouncing and grunting and free-for-all fondling and a heap of rumpled bedclothes afterwards, and there's some sort of widespread agreement not to let on? Instead, people go round pretending it's the be-all and end-all, the very elixir of life, something to sing about and die for, when if they were honest they'd say to each other, 'Don't bother – it's frankly not worth it.'

Suddenly the music breaks into her thoughts. The French girl's arrived at *Träumerei*, and there's such longing in her playing, such soft and expectant tenderness, that Alex is wholly transfixed. It melts her completely. She's crying, she realises, as the phrase reaches its climax before returning to the simplicity of the opening. Yes, she thinks, there's still tentative hope. Her fling with Douglas was four years ago, and here she is, on the verge of doing it all again with Richard. Next Saturday night. She'll see him at the Albert Hall – he's a critic for a daily which prides itself on its coverage of the arts. And with Maggie away at her party, she can bring it about. If that's what she wants. She knows it's what Richard wants.

Applause brings her back to the present. She dries her eyes, gathers her things together and prepares to leave the Purcell Room.

Saturday night. The Royal Albert Hall. Alex is in her usual place in the Circle, an empty seat beside her. She's always given two complimentaries, but likes to go alone. The other seat's useful for handbag and programme, coat, umbrella, shopping, whatever she's got. No coat tonight, though. It's excessively hot, almost a full house, and there seems to be no air in the building. The programme comes in handy as a fan. Usual sense of vertigo looking down on the promenaders in the Arena. Usual sense of envy. For some, their first time here perhaps. For others, their first live performance of *The Dream*. For all, a sense of excitement, of something about to happen. They chatter and laugh and call out good humouredly to the stage hands adjusting chairs and music desks. Then, in turn, the choir, orchestra, soloists and conductor make their way on to the platform. And once the baton is raised, utter absorption, rapt attention. You could hear a pin drop.

A stirring work, stirringly performed. At moments Alex was close to tears. She only has good things to say about it. She'll write them up tomorrow and they'll appear in print on Monday. Meanwhile she's spotted Richard, who's making his way towards her. He's thirty-five – a year older than she is – but looks decidedly younger. That's what comes of being a bachelor. He's got a service flat in Pimlico. Alex didn't know such things still existed.

The two of them sit side by side in the centre of the Circle. Around them, the hall empties. Alex's heart and soul are still in the performance. She desperately hopes he won't say anything clever or smart or even vaguely intelligent. She'd rather like him to weep on her shoulder. Or to weep on his. For a long time he says nothing at all. She likes him for that.

'Some journey,' he says at last. 'It felt like I was making it, not Gerontius.'

'I know what you mean. Emotional exhaustion.'

Minutes pass in silence until he speaks again. 'As one limp rag to another, would you care for a reviving drink? I know a quiet place off Sloane Square.'

And she allows him to take her to a taxi. They are whisked through the phantasmagoria – she can think of no other word – which is London at night. Sometimes she hates it, all those other people, all strangers, all indifferent. Tonight in the taxi with Richard they are simply a passing sideshow put on for her enjoyment. The impact of the performance begins to wear off.

The quiet place off Sloane Square calls itself a bistro, and does not serve meals as such. They order a bottle of wine with a dish of olives and two crêpes, and settle down at a corner table. It's subdued rather than quiet – plenty of people but not much noise. A soothing, mellow place. The first glass of wine disappears quickly. So does the second. The crêpes are delicious.

'If you like, we can have coffee at my place,' Richard says. 'It's no distance.'

And it really isn't. The air is still warm as they cross Pimlico Road and head towards the river. In no time at all they're at Richard's flat. It's all very calm and well ordered. He's a calm and well ordered lover. Only after the coffee has been drunk does he suggest they move to the bedroom, where he gently removes Alex's clothes and kisses her shoulders and breasts. She's content to let it happen. Perhaps it's the music, perhaps it's the wine, but tonight everything seems easy and smooth. She's beginning to enjoy herself, to respond to Richard's caresses, when he suddenly forgets her, becomes someone quite separate, quite other, remote and distant. Wherever he's gone, he's left her behind. She's no longer real for him. After it's over, she resents his weight, the dead, heavy stillness of his alien body which in no way resembles her own. But when he stirs, she smoothes the hair from his forehead and lightly kisses his eyelids, because she suspects the failure is hers. And if it isn't, she'd never dream of saying so. She dresses, while Richard, in a cashmere robe, makes more coffee. He promises to be in touch, he'll ring her soon. Alex leaves the calm and well ordered flat and walks up towards Buckingham Palace Road, where a taxi takes her to Hampstead. Back in her flat, she showers to remove all trace of Richard, and goes to sleep thinking of Elgar.

It's more than a week till he phones – she's almost given him up. But then he suggests something so safe and bizarre that she says yes straightaway. A visit to a dovecote in Wales. Remarkably old, remarkably large. Some friends of his – members of some Preservation Society or other – are taking him to see it on Tuesday. Would she like to join them? There and back in a day. Pub lunch *en route*. Should be interesting. A day away from London, a breath of fresh air. Friends' car. Plenty of space. Yes, she says, how lovely, what a good idea, she'd love to go with them. She squares it with Maggie ('No sweat, Mum. I'll be at Nick's anyway.') and looks forward to a day as a blameless sightseer.

They come for her at eight o'clock. Richard introduces his friends, Sheila and Mike, both small and round – they remind her of squirrels or mice – and both hearty talkers. Mike drives, she sits in the back with Richard. Just before they hit the A40, she asks Sheila about the Preservation Society they belong to. Sheila's reply keeps them going as far as the Oxford turnoff. By the time they stop for lunch at a pub somewhere beyond Gloucester, Alex has quite forgotten where they are going, or why, and rather wishes she hadn't come. Not the faintest whiff of fresh air so far – she'd have had more on Hampstead Heath. But after lunch the scenery gradually changes. They switch to minor roads, and just when she thinks she's never been anywhere so quietly beautiful, Mike pulls off the lane in to a large cobbled farmyard. 'There it is,' cries Sheila turning round and pointing, as though she might miss it. And there indeed it is. A huge, circular domed structure. The object of their journey. The dovecote.

Alex gets out of the car, thankful to stretch her legs. The place appears wholly deserted. There's only an old Morris Traveller parked up by some pigsties. What an extraordinary spot, perfectly tranquil and still on this August afternoon. What can it be like to live somewhere so remote, so peaceful and undemanding? She wanders round, looking vaguely in the outbuildings while the others hover round the dovecote. She expects some old Welsh farmer to appear at any moment. But when she turns round to walk back to the others, she sees a young woman coming out of the house. She's carrying a book in her hand. Slim, short dark hair, neat features and a gamine androgynous look about her which makes Alex think of Audrey Hepburn in some old film. Mike says something to her – she can't hear what – and the girl replies 'Yes, of course. My aunt's expecting you. I'll just let her know you're here.' She crosses the yard in front of Alex, who can't take her eyes off her. There's such self possession in her walk, yet a great sense of fun in her smile, her eyes sparkling as though at some huge joke. She breaks into a run and disappears through a white farm gate between the outbuildings. Not a girl, but not quite a woman. Not yet. Alex continues to stare, but she doesn't reappear. Instead, two women come hurrying through the gate. The elder of them goes up to the group by the dovecote, hand held out in greeting. Alex decides she'd better join them. Mike tells their hostess she must be Miss Procter. The woman smilingly agrees. They all introduce themselves. So sorry not to be here to meet you. Small crisis. New pair of geese not settling in well. Panicky things, geese. It'll be alright now. Bobbie will see to them. Bobbie.

They look at the dovecote inside and out, marvel at its size, its antiquity. Discussion of dovecotes in general. Alex wanders off, hoping to catch sight of Bobbie again, but is summoned indoors for tea. Huge kitchen table. Sandwiches, cakes, scones. More introductions. My friend, Miss Menzies. Sheila talks incessantly. Doves, dovecotes, geese, it seems she's an expert on all of them. Alex wants to ask about Bobbie, the niece Bobbie, but there's no opportunity. Sheila and Alex use the bathroom in turn. An old house. A lovely, gracious, loved old house. And then it's time to leave. As the car swings out of the farmyard, Alex turns to wave goodbye and there she is, smiling and waving at the front porch, her arm on Miss Procter's shoulder. Bobbie.

Alex is quiet on the return journey. Not so Sheila. A remarkable building. Such a survival. And what charming people. Lesbians, of course, but none the worse for that. A simply delightful house – aren't some people lucky! And such a delicious tea! When she finally comes to a halt, Richard embarks on a long story about a windmill he once visited in Essex. Alex looks out of the window, haunted by Bobbie's smile.

They finally reach London and drop her off at Euston. Lovely day. So kind of them to take her. Must do it again sometime. Richard promises to be in touch. Home on the Northern Line. A strangely disturbed feeling, as at some new discovery, some new possibility. Maggie's already in bed, light on, reading. Alex tells her not to wake her too early. It's been a long day. She's exhausted. She could sleep for a week.

But in the middle of the night, Alex wakes from a deeply erotic encounter. She's with Bobbie, can sense the girl's body against hers in a warm and totally fulfilling embrace. She's seriously aroused. She caresses herself to get rid of the burning desire but is left with a much bigger ache, a yearning she's never known and cannot satisfy. It's a long time before she goes to sleep again.

Richard does eventually get in touch. He sends Alex a letter. Never having seen his writing before, she doesn't at first realise who it's from. He's writing to tell her he's getting married, to a girl he grew up with in Norfolk. Long standing friend of the family. They'll be living in Cambridge, but who knows, his path and Alex's may one day cross again. He'll always remember her with affection, those hot August evenings at the Proms, etc, etc. She assumes that he means the time they made love.

So that's that then. She sends him a card wishing him every happiness, and in her address book puts a line through his London address and phone number. Exit Richard, pursued by the past. Now she's alone on the stage.

5

Con deliberazione

'........or a chamomile tea, if you have it.' Dr Irene Treadgold, the moral tutor attached to the Hall of Residence, hovered vaguely in my doorway. 'But don't let me interrupt...'

'You're not,' I said as I plugged in the kettle. 'I've done all I can for today, and you'll give me the perfect excuse not to practise the cello.'

'Ah yes – the cello. Such a mellifluous instrument! But perhaps at this time of the evening...?'

I had to admire Dr Treadgold. She truly believed that my fellow students went to bed early and would be disturbed by my playing. Some, of course, might well be in bed, but not for the purpose of sleeping.

She perched herself, birdlike, on one of my chairs. 'And how are you settling in?'

I was used to this question: she asked it whenever we met. 'I've joined the Choral Society,' I told her. 'The standard for female voices isn't as high as it is for men.'

'Ah yes – all those vigorous basses! They're always quite desperate for women.' Anyone else would have loaded this statement with innuendo, but not Dr Treadgold. 'It's because of the Engineering Department,' she confided. 'So dispropor-tionately large.'

This was certainly true. The gender imbalance across the whole university was of Biblical proportions. There were men wherever one looked, in all of the senior and middle-ranking teaching posts and all the way up the administrative ladder; the meagre scattering of women among the junior lecturers was far too slight to leaven the masculine atmosphere. As with the staff, so with the students. I suspect it was the guaranteed surfeit of Engineers, all of them famously randy, that encouraged girls to apply here. Dr Treadgold's task, as our moral tutor, was to ensure that the sexes were chastely apart between the hours of eleven at night and eight in the morning – hence her nervous evening prowls. Inviting her in for a drink was a way of protecting her innocence.

'I don't think the Choral Society attracts many Engineers,' I said, 'though there are quite a few Divinity students among the tenors.'

She seemed pleased to hear this. 'It's good to know they're being properly trained. Singing is such an important part of the priestly function, I always feel. I know them, of course, the Divinity students. I have them twice a week. For Greek,' she added after a pause, in case there was doubt. 'And what is the choir rehearsing at the moment?'

'*The Christmas Oratorio,* which is comforting and straightforward, though far from easy. But we're also attempting a piece by Janáček that's alarming in every respect. I always get horribly lost. The best I can do is pretend to be singing and look enthusiastic.'

'Ah yes – very wise. But what a peculiar choice! If you as a Music student aren't able to cope, what hope is there for the rest?'

'Don't be misled by the cello,' I said. 'I'm only half Music; the other half is Psychology.'

'Ah yes – of course – Joint Honours. I suppose it gives one breadth……..'

I could tell she looked down on such shilly-shallying, and felt obliged to point out that a broad course of study has an ancient and honourable pedigree. 'To a medieval student, even my two subjects would seem paltry. Wasn't it the case that at Paris and Padua and Bologna they undertook to teach everything there was to know in the world?'

As an educational aim this was hugely appealing, and I often regretted being alive at a time when knowledge was so vastly expanded that no-one could grasp it entirely.

'And what, I wonder, would Socrates say about that?' Dr Treadgold, believing, perhaps, she was holding a seminar, happily contemplated her question in silence for several minutes. I hoped if I waited long enough, she'd forget that she'd asked it. Eventually she spoke. 'You always do raise such absorbing conundrums, Robina.'

'It must be the chamomile tea,' I said. 'Would you care for a second cup?'

'Thank you, but no – I really ought to be . . . ' She stood up in what, for her, was quite a determined manner. 'You've had my note about the sherry party on Saturday? A modest affair, just Freshers and one or two others. I thought it might be a way of helping everyone settle in.'

She clearly took the business of settling in very seriously.

'I'm looking forward to it,' I said, and watched her drift away, along the corridor and back to her flat, with no further thought for the moral welfare of those whose rooms she was passing. I felt I'd performed a useful public service.

The party was perfectly dire. As we each arrived – all of us female, all from the same Hall of Residence – Dr Treadgold dithered about with a bottle of sherry and asked, as she poured out a thimbleful, how we were settling in. Only a brave and unfeeling woman would dream of admitting she hadn't settled in adequately, and as none of us fell in that category, conversation instantly flagged. Our hostess was too preoccupied to make any introductions, but we undertook that office ourselves, and learnt where we came from, what subjects we studied and our views on refectory food. That being the extent of our interest in one another, a dismal silence descended, broken only by Dr Treadgold asking a late arrival, 'And how are you settling in?' When the silence was almost unbearable, she flitted about with a second dose of sherry and suggested we all sit down. As there weren't enough chairs, a few of us sank to the floor.

'Some of you,' Dr Treadgold began, 'are possibly living away from home for the very first time, and may be finding things a little...' – she searched for just the right word – 'unsettling. I want you to know that I'm always available if anyone needs to talk. Not just about problems with work, though I'll willingly deal with those, but also concerns of a more personal nature. New freedoms, new expectations, new responsibilities – they can all be so very...'

'Unsettling?' someone suggested.

'Exactly – yes – I'm so glad we agree. And if any of you should feel...'

'Unsettled?' This time there were undisguised titters.

'Exactly – yes – unsettled in *any* way, please drop in for a chat. I can't promise there'll always be sherry, but I can generally stretch to...'

We never did hear what beverage might be on offer, for there was at that moment a sudden incursion of gangly men, most of them wearing duffle-coats, all of them noisily cheerful.

'The door was ajar, good Doctor,' one of them explained, 'and we rudely let ourselves in. I do hope we're not too early, but we've brought more sherry as penance.'

What a change was wrought by their coming! Such patting of hair and adjustment of skirts, such modifications of posture the better to show off assets, such flutterings in the dovecote. Even Dr Treadgold perked up mightily and announced in an almost jovial tone, 'Ah yes – my Divinity students!' I detected a slight disappointment – they were not, after all, Engineers – but this was bravely borne. With the men a buzz had entered the room, a frisson of sexual challenge.

I recognised some of these wholesome youths from the Choral Society: they were earnest and sober and favoured strong shoes. I could picture them in a few years time working in challenging parishes, inspiring the Mothers' Union and teaching the Scouts to knot. Now they were honing their pastoral charm on us and Dr Treadgold.

'I'm Roger Trevelyan,' one of them said to me. He was tall

but without the gawkiness so often found in earnest young men. 'Third Year Divinity. And you, I believe, are an alto.'

'Robina,' I said, 'but everyone calls me Bobbie. Music and Psychology and clearly a Fresher – that's why I'm here. And yes, I'm an alto. An alto who struggles with Janáček.'

'I've given up struggling,' Roger confessed, with a grin that made him look boyish. 'I just open my mouth from time to time and hope it looks like singing.'

I was about to admit that I did the same when Dr Treadgold materialised with a welcome top-up of sherry.

'I trust you're sharing with Roger your views on education, Robina,' she said, dispensing the liquid frugally into our glasses. 'We had such an interesting exchange of views the other day – specialisation versus breadth, the eternal dilemma. You might both enjoy discussing that now, while I just...' And away she floated to paralyse further victims.

Roger looked at me helplessly. 'Do we have to?' he whispered.

I laughed. 'Of course not. I'd much rather hear what your plans are – for the future.'

'Next year, all being well, I'm off to Shelton Park. I don't suppose you've heard of it – it's a place for aspiring curates, near Oxford. And then' – his eyes lit up – 'I'm hoping to work somewhere like Liverpool 8, somewhere really challenging.'

'Teaching Boy Scouts to knot?' I suggested.

He gave me a curious look. 'I'm not a great knotter,' he said.

Despite that unlikely beginning, Roger and I continued to meet occasionally, usually for a drink in the Union bar after choir practice, and once for a trip to the cinema to see *Dr Zhivago,* which we'd both of us missed first time round. We had little enough in common apart from the choir and Dr Treadgold, though the shared experience of campus life gave a spurious feeling of kinship: we both disliked the refectory menu on Wednesdays, and preferred the older buildings of the university to those put up in the Sixties. None of this was the basis for more than an easy friendship, though later events made me wonder if Roger viewed our minimal time together as courtship, a notion which never once entered my head. The best thing about Roger was that he saved me from the attentions of Engineers, and from the serial sexual couplings favoured by my fellow students.

During the summer term, the Choral Society was temporarily disbanded, Roger was busy with Finals, and everyone, students and staff alike, spent as much time as possible out of doors. Once my own exams were over – piffling events compared to Roger's – and my evenings free of study, there was nothing to keep me inside, and during the long calm twilights of early June I began to explore the more distant parts of the campus. Clustered at one end of the site behind a screen of poplars were the houses of the teaching staff, a seemingly self-contained enclave, remote and unsullied by students. How the staff spent their evenings at other times of the year I cannot say, but that summer whenever I passed there was always a party afoot, brash, cheery and noisy, spilling out from the houses into the garden. To those in the know, each party was probably different, but from the outside they looked and sounded alike, the same ingredients in various mixtures and groupings, any novelty as illusory as the patterns formed by the random arrangement of coloured fragments in a kaleidoscope.

One balmy June evening I was making my way along the path that skirted the back of the staff gardens when just such a party was in full swing. Down by the house, sounds of jazz mingled with bursts of brittle, braying laughter from couples gathered together at the top of the lawn, everyone bent on enjoying themselves in the loud, carefree manner of people who know each other well and have spent the evening drinking together. But as I approached closer, I became aware of two figures near the bottom of the garden standing silently together, separate from the rest. At the moment I passed, one of them touched the other's cheek with a tentative gesture of great longing and tenderness. Embarrassed, I looked away and tried to slink silently past, but in that fraction of a second I'd seen that this couple were two women.

That touch was the slightest action, yet it moved me profoundly. I felt absurdly and wildly excited, elated even, that such passion could thrive in the adult world of the university. It seemed to me an affirmation, an assurance that life truly had more to offer than the casual sexual dalliance of my fellow students. As I made my way slowly back across campus, I thought of Terry and Jo, of how gentle and loving their embraces must be. I thought, too, of the way that intense and urgent desire is content with discreet expression, so different from the blatant all-out fondling endemic among the undergraduates. Most of all I wanted to be touched like that, tentatively and deliberately, by someone for whom it meant everything.

When I arrived back at my room, it was not quite ten o'clock. Still tinglingly alive with the feelings aroused by my walk, I was irritated rather than pleased to find a note from Roger pinned to the door. It read: '8pm. Sorry to miss you. There's something I'd like to discuss. Shall be in the bar until closing – hope to see you there. Roger.' I was certainly not in the mood for tricky theological debate, but felt so guilty that the poor chap had spent almost two hours waiting that I set off at once, back the way I'd just come. Apart from Roger the bar was deserted; half a glass of flat-looking beer was on the table beside him. He leapt to his feet when he saw me.

'Bobbie, you got my note? Of course, yes, you must have. That's why you're here. Silly me. Would you like a drink? What can I get you?'

His manner was jumpy, not at all like his normal self; his Finals, I thought, must be taking their toll. I asked for a vodka and orange. He brought it immediately, then sat gazing silently into his beer glass, seemingly having forgotten entirely the threatened discussion. This again was unusual; he was generally an easy talker, not prone to anything as unproductive as silent gazing. I realised I would have to break the ice.

'How are Finals going?' This seemed a safe enough topic, and snapped him out of his reverie.

'They've gone. All over. The last paper was this afternoon. In fact . . .' He turned to face me, looking more anxious than

I'd ever seen him. '...that's why I wanted to have a chat. I'm going home tomorrow, Bobbie, and I wondered...' Here he paused to swallow a mouthful of flat beer. '...I wondered whether you'd like, whether you'd be able, to come and stay for a bit in the holidays. At home. At my home. With my parents.'

'With your parents?' I had the confused impression I was being invited to act as temporary housekeeper, or perhaps companion, for Roger's parents, who had somehow heard of my motherless state and wished to offer a safe summer refuge. I must have looked bewildered, for Roger went on to explain.

'Ha – yes, with my parents, but I'll be there too, of course. It's just that I've told them about you, mentioned you in my letters you know, and they would so like to meet you. And as I won't be around here for a bit, I thought I'd ask you now, and you could think about it, and let me know when I get back. If you'd like to meet them, that is.'

Having disburdened himself of these unexpected remarks, he visibly relaxed, gave one of his most boyish grins and addressed himself to the duty of swallowing the remains of his beer.

Clearly it was now my turn to respond. How little I actually knew about this eager young man who'd just nerved himself to invite me to stay with his family! Yet was not the offer itself evidence of great kindness, his own no less than his parents'? The little that Roger had told them – and it must have been little, given the meagreness of our acquaintance – had somehow predisposed them in my favour, and that in itself was a flattering thought. But it was Roger's extreme nervousness in conveying the invitation that was the really decisive factor: it had meant a lot to him to ask me, and, in my highly charged state that evening, this was sufficient to sway me.

'I should love to meet them,' I said.

'Would you?' He grinned a second time. 'They *will* be pleased. Now – when can you come?'

We agreed on the first week of August.

That summer the dovecote at Hendre attracted a trickle of visitors. All were made welcome, for you never knew, according to Terry, who might prove a useful contact.

'And once the *Compendium*'s published, it'll only get worse.' She seemed to relish the prospect. 'Tourists by the coach load, I shouldn't wonder, all longing to see for themselves the biggest, most ancient, most splendid dovecote in Britain. Someone rang up today about coming later this month – a couple, I think, from some Preservation Society or other...'

'SPAFS,' put in Jo, 'which stands for Society for the Protection of...'

'Aging Female Smallholders? suggested Terry. 'Or am I expecting too much?'

I offered 'Anything Faintly Sexual,' which I immediately had to justify. 'According to Jung...' I began.

Terry gave an exaggerated groan. 'Can't we leave him out of it? And Freud too, if possible?'

'But you've got to agree it's female in form and function – a circular, dark enclosed space, dedicated to procreation.' I gradually warmed to my theme. 'It's packed with reminders of pain and disappointment, of so much devotion that ended in nothing. As a building it's fantastic, I'm not denying that, and the atmosphere inside is extraordinary, busy and peaceful all at once, like a fugue. But when you remember that doves are the symbol of love, doesn't it strike you as barbarous and unfeeling, a monument to cruelty and manipulation and everything hateful and male?'

'Yes,' Terry said quietly. 'It's all that and more – the paradox at the heart of things. But our visitors don't see it like that.'

'Exactly! They just gawp and say, 'Isn't it big, isn't it old', then dash indoors for the homemade cake. They don't think about what it *means*.'

Terry patted my arm. 'Don't worry, we won't make you meet the tourist hordes. You can find somewhere quiet to hide.'

'In any case, you're both of you wrong.' Jo had been rummaging through some papers. 'The people at SPAFS protect

Ancient Farmyard Structures. And the tea'll be worth it if they decide to preserve our lovely old building. You never know – they may bring with them a big fat donation.'

We were drinking homemade wine at the time, and were in the mood for believing all sorts of nonsense.

Having toasted our mythical donors, Terry said, 'Before I forget, Bobbie, I'd like you to help me change a wheel on the Traveller tomorrow, and if you're exceedingly lucky, I'll let you in on some of the secrets I've learnt on my Car Maintenance course. Jo knows them already...'

'Oh, the hours we've spent under the bonnet! You wouldn't believe how absorbing an engine can be! Now, is anyone ready for more?' Jo waved the bottle in my direction. 'It's Elderberry and Blackberry, one of our best. I've put two aside as an offering to Roger's parents.'

'You're giving them *two* bottles of E and B?' This was consummate generosity indeed. To this day I've not tasted a headier brew. 'But what if they're TT? I really don't know much about them, except that they'd despaired of ever producing a child when Roger came along. I gather he's the much-adored fruit of somewhat elderly loins.'

'Tell them it's an old Welsh remedy for something or other,' suggested Jo.

'And that after a few glasses they will experience a great feeling of well-being,' added Terry, who was evidently experiencing this particular feeling herself. After a few more glasses, her sense of well-being gave way to anxiety. 'You will come back to us, won't you, Bobbie? You won't go off for ever with this young man?'

'Of course not!' I'd have got up to give her a hug, had the room not developed an alarming tendency to spin unpredictably if I moved. 'Roger's just a friend. His parents are simply nice people who...'

'...are looking for a vicar's wife as a daughter-in-law. I'm serious, Bobbie,' for I was unable to stop myself laughing. 'Don't let them bamboozle you. We'd never forgive ourselves if you were bamboozled, would we, Jo?'

'We certainly wouldn't,' said Jo.

'I won't be bamboozled,' I promised .

But when I met Roger's parents, I began to think Terry might well have been right. The Trevelyans lived in a very pleasant part of suburban south-west London, where the roads were lined with cherry trees and the houses had well-kept gardens back and front. As happily married couples go, they were a perfect example of the species: their world centred unashamedly around Roger to the extent that they rejected each other's Christian names in favour of the terms Mother and Father, something I'd thought only occurred in the more senti-mental pages of Mrs Gaskell and Dickens. At the same time they took pride in their late parenthood, as though they'd never fully recovered from the astonishing birth twenty-one years earlier.

'Of course, Father and I never thought we'd have children,' Mrs Trevelyan confided to me the moment she got me alone. 'We'd hoped and hoped for years, but it just didn't happen. And when I realised – well, you could have knocked me down with a feather. 'You must be mistaken,' I told the doctor. But he wasn't. I was forty-two in the September, and Roger was born in the October. And now look at him, taller by a long chalk than Father, and wants to be a vicar. You go to church regularly yourself, I expect, Robina?' She managed to make the question sound almost casual.

'Oh, please call me Bobbie; everyone does. I went to an Anglican school and was in Chapel almost every day there. It's something I really miss. The chapel isn't the same at University. For one thing, it's almost aggressively inter-denom-inational, a sort of 'one size fits all' you know.'

I was bluffing a bit here. Of course I knew about the chapel set-up, but lacked the courage to experience it for myself, fear-ing it would not come up to school standards. As it happened, I seemed to have said the right thing.

'Oh, I do so agree. All this mixing together – where will it end, that's what I ask myself. Of course, they think the world of Roger at St. Silas',' Mrs Trevelyan continued. 'He was chris-

tened there, confirmed there, he's been in the choir and a
Sunday School teacher. It would be lovely if he were married
there. You live in Wales, I think?'

At such moments even I could hear the distant clanging of
alarm bells, and tried to deflect Mrs T.'s train of thought by
telling her about the activities of my aunt at Hendre. As usual
I caught myself suppressing any mention of Jo. I hated myself
for this; such constraint made me feel like a traitor, yet I could
not overcome it. It was something of a relief when Roger and
his father returned from their manly tour of the garden and
Mrs Trevelyan slipped out of the room, saying she would just
see to the meal.

'I do hope you like chicken, Rob-Bobbie. The butcher had
such lovely plump chickens this morning that I simply could-
n't resist, even though it isn't Sunday.'

I assured her I enjoyed chicken on any day of the week and
handed over the wine from Hendre to Mr T., who spent a long
time admiring its rich colour and quizzed me about the ingredients. I think he suspected it was a kind of fruit cordial, in
which case he was in for a shock. He then looked carefully at
the label, and commented on the beauty of the italic script.

'So few people today take pride in penmanship, don't you
find, Robina? And what does the illustration represent?'

It was the dovecote, rendered in exquisite detail by Jo,
whose script it was also. I launched into a description, and
father and son both expressed great interest which showed no
sign of waning even when I mentioned the *Compendium*.

'The book covers all aspects of doves and dove keeping,' I
enthused. 'There's a whole section on dovecotes and their
history, and there are recipes too, but the parts I like best are
about doves in history and literature and art,' I said, sounding
to my own ears more and more like an amateur salesman.

At this moment we were summoned to the dining room to
partake of the plump chicken, and what with all the movement this involved, and the settling down at the table, and the
saying of Grace (pronounced by Roger in strangely clerical
tones), and the passing and admiring of vegetables, and the

pouring of wine, I thought we'd probably left the topic of doves well and truly behind. But this was not so.

'Robina has just been telling us something most interesting, Mother,' Mr T. began when the carving was safely over. 'Her aunt has written a book about doves. Now tell me, Robina, which aspect of doves do you yourself find most fascinating?'

How could I admit to being absurdly and hopelessly fascinated by every aspect of doves for the last nine years? Instead I said the first thing that occurred to me.

'I've always felt rather sorry for the dove that Noah sent out from the Ark.'

'Was it the dove that found dry land, or was that the raven? I always get them confused,' said Mrs T. 'But Roger will know.'

Roger did know. 'At first the dove came back empty handed, so to speak. But later she came back with the olive branch – isn't that right, Bobbie?'

'Yes. The first time there was nowhere for her to land because of all the water. It says: 'she found no rest for the sole of her foot'. I've always liked that line; it makes the dove sound like a very weary person, not a bird. And then, yes, Roger's right, she did come back with the olive branch, seven days later.'

'But you said you felt sorry for this dove,' pursued Mr T. 'Why is that? She did a good job in my book, bringing back the very thing that Noah wanted.'

'Oh yes, she did, but he kept her in the Ark for another seven days, and then let her go again. And this time she didn't return.' I looked up expectantly. Surely they could see the problem?

Mrs T. couldn't. 'But by then the Flood was over, and she could find herself a nice tree or a rock or somewhere else dry to perch. More peas, anyone?'

It was up to me to explain. 'But there'd be no other doves. They'd all have drowned in the Flood along with everything else. She'd be quite alone, on dry land admittedly, and in the open air again, but without her mate, who was still in the Ark. And doves, as you probably know, pair for life. I think it's such a sad ending, being all alone like that,' I concluded, feeling by now extremely foolish.

Roger came to my rescue. 'Perhaps she's a symbolic dove, not a real one. And symbols, you know, can't feel lonely.'

It was exactly the conclusion I had come to myself.

'A symbol, eh? But a symbol of what?' asked Mr T., helping himself to more gravy.

'Of Love, of course,' I said, before I could stop myself.

For a moment, everyone paused in their eating to stare at me, and I knew I had to go on. Feeling the need for outside help, I swallowed a large gulp of wine.

'Well, we're told the Flood happened because of all the wickedness and evil and violence and suchlike in the world. And the worst wickedness, and the greatest evil, and a great cause of violence is the absence of love. It's possible that when Noah sent the dove out the first time, and she came back, it was a sign that the world was still attached to its bad habits and wasn't yet ready for love. But when the dove brought back the olive branch, that was an acceptance of the need for all the violence to stop.'

'Just as holding out an olive branch means wanting peace,' put in Roger. He was enjoying the wine, and had drunk more than anyone.

'Exactly. And finally, when it was the right time, the dove could go out into the world and fill it with love.'

'Even without her mate?'

'Perhaps she had to sacrifice that particular love for an altogether bigger one,' I hazarded. The wooliness of my theory was becoming increasingly obvious to me, but Roger seemed to like the idea of sacrifice.

'You know, Bobbie, I think there's a great deal of truth in what you say. You and I should talk about things more often.'

'And now, who's ready for plums and custard?' asked Mrs T., effectively banishing further talk of any kind just then.

For the rest of my stay I did my best to avoid such topics at the dinner table, and managed never to mention doves again in the Trevelyans' hearing. This wasn't hard, as there was so much else to talk about at meal times once Roger and I embarked on the series of outings he'd lined up for me, each one calculated to charm a first-time visitor to London. Together we went by train to Kew and Richmond, and cruised the Thames from Putney to Hampton Court; one day we went to the National Gallery, Whitehall and St. James's Park, and another to Piccadilly and Bond St. After a day spent at the V & A, we joined the queue of promenaders at the Albert Hall for a performance of *The Dream of Gerontius* conducted by Colin Davies and walked back to Hammersmith tube station deep in a discussion of Newman's theology. For Roger turned out to be not only an energetic and thoughtful host, but also an ideal listener; I found I could talk to him and be taken seriously, yet without having my ideas of one day held against me the next.

As my visit drew to an end, Mr and Mrs Trevelyan each contrived to catch me alone and tell me how much they hoped to see me again before too long. Both conveyed the same message, but Mr T. used considerably fewer words than his wife, who became quite prolix on the subject.

'Father and I are so pleased to have met you at last, Rob-Bobbie. Now that Roger's off to Shelton Park, you won't be seeing so much of each other, but he tells me you'll be keeping in touch. I do hope so. He hasn't had a lot of girlfriends – he's always been too busy for that sort of thing – but I told him it's not too soon to think about settling down, especially as there won't be any young ladies where he's going. So we're very, very pleased. Like I told the Vicar, it's not every day you come across a girl who knows her Old Testament. And Rob-Bobbie, you will come and see us again, won't you, now that you know where we are? Father and I would love to see you, and there's always a spare bed. Do give our regards to your aunt. Perhaps Father and I will meet her too, one day?'

I explained that my aunt left home only rarely, due to the exigencies of her livestock, but rashly committed her to a visit if ever she found herself in the area.

When I left, Roger accompanied me to Paddington, and as we sat together for the final journey through London on the Number 10 bus, he apologised if anything his parents had said or implied had upset me.

'They're feeling old, Bobbie, especially now the old man's retired, and they want me to start producing grandchildren while they're still able to enjoy them. Based on their own experience, they imagine this might take me anything up to twenty years. It's no wonder they think I should settle down with a good woman as soon as ever I can. And they rather hope that good woman will be you, Bobbie.'

This was exactly the kind of conversation I'd desperately hoped to avoid, especially on a Number 10 bus. It was no time for prevarication.

'Then you must tell them I'm not a good woman, Roger, just an average sort of overgrown schoolgirl who is certainly not planning to settle down and produce babies in the near future. Surely they'll let us remain friends without actually frogmarching us down the aisle?'

Roger smiled and shook my hand theatrically. 'Agreed. Friends it is then. And you'll write to me, Bobbie, and come and see me sometime? But no settling down just yet.'

'Only with a good book,' I said.

It was seven months before I saw Roger again, although we wrote to each other regularly during the autumn and spring term, a dutiful correspondence which my friends in the Psychology Department insisted on regarding as a touchingly quaint courtship. Of course it was nothing of the kind. We exchanged news of our studies, and I kept Roger up-to-date with Dr Treadgold and the Choir (Vivaldi's *Gloria* this year, after distressing flirtations with Poulenc and Harrison Birtwistle). But these letters were really rather a chore both to read and to write, and only when engaged in one or other activity did I ever, if I'm honest, have Roger in mind at all.

Thankfully there was no question of my repeating the visit to London over the Christmas holiday, but one of Roger's letters in February contained the surprising and repeated request that I be at Shelton Park on the fourth Sunday in Lent, when he would be preaching at the College Eucharist. Preaching practice was a trial every theological student endured as part of his training. No-one actually failed the sermon element of the course, but the hapless preacher faced a bombardment of helpful advice and suggested improvements from his peers and mentors the following day, just too late to be useful. The Eucharist started at a quarter past nine in the morning, an hour at which Shelton Park was inaccessible by public transport, but there were a few guest rooms available for visitors who needed to stay overnight. Roger wrote that he'd already reserved one for me, and had booked a table at a local restaurant for the Saturday evening.

Whether it was the lure of proper restaurant food that decided me, or simply that it would be a way of filling a dreary Sunday, I cannot say, but I accepted Roger's invitation. In the intervening weeks, I suffered considerably over whether to wear a hat, which proper churchgoing always seemed to require, but Dr Treadgold, over a timely cup of chamomile tea, advised me against hat wearing, saying it was no longer necessary in the modern church. This was welcome advice: I had never owned a hat, and rather hoped I never should.

The weekend started promisingly. Roger met me at the station and seemed utterly unchanged; even the duffle-coat was familiar. On the short walk to the College we talked together as easily as we had in London, and I began to feel ashamed that I'd found our correspondence such a burden. Roger was enjoying his time at Shelton Park, and spoke particularly warmly of one of his tutors, the Reverend Archibald Bunt, a man very highly thought of, apparently, in the world of Apocryphal studies. The room in which I was to spend the night was part of a separate, and otherwise empty, guest annexe, and exactly matched my idea of a room in a Club for clerical gentlemen. Amply proportioned and possessing its own bathroom, it was unrelievedly sombre, with dark oak everywhere, even cladding the walls. I expressed surprise at the presence of a double bed, but Roger explained that, as most guests tended to be parents who needed accommodation as a couple, it was a sensible arrangement.

'Were your parents not able to come?' I asked, for I had a sneaking dread that Mr and Mrs T. might pop up at any moment, and I would become Rob-Bobbie again.

'I didn't actually invite them.' He sounded rather sheepish. 'I thought it would be best if it was just you and me, Bobbie. I so wanted you to see the College, and this seemed a good opportunity. If you like, I can show you round a bit before we go out to eat. I've booked us a table for half past seven. I hope that's alright?'

It was alright, but only because the tour of the College started in Roger's room, where we had coffee and biscuits. Without this sustenance I would undoubtedly have fainted by the wayside somewhere between the Library, where we duly admired the Burne-Jones stained glass, and the Chapel, one of Pugin's lesser-known creations. Had I so collapsed, I'd have missed the extraordinary Gothic Refectory – empty, alas, of food at that hour – and the undistinguished Master's House, about which even Roger could find nothing to say except that the College Master lived in it. Nearby was a small lake, home to some early-nesting coots and one solitary moorhen, who made her way cautiously round the water's edge on her comically feathered feet as we watched. Massed armies of King Alfred daffodils lined the path back from the lakeside. In sunshine this might have been pretty, but under the leaden sky of early March, and in a chill wind, it was merely bleak, and the daffodils, far from tossing their heads in sprightly dance, seemed more like victims of St Vitus. It was a relief when we arrived back at my room and I was able to warm up in the bath while Roger went off to change into a suit.

The restaurant, 'The Shelton Arms', was just outside the College gates, and, to judge from the menu, relied heavily on clerical patronage, for all the dishes sported names like Churchwarden's Pie and Bishop's Dumpling. I settled for Curate's Casserole on account of the alliteration, while Roger opted for Parson's Rump because it seemed mildly irreverent;

we both chose Cathedral Pudding to follow. Roger ordered wine which the waiter brought with exemplary speed, and while waiting for the food we drank enthusiastically and set about inventing more and more unlikely clerical dishes of our own. By the time our meals actually arrived – mine turned out to be nothing more exotic than chicken stew, and Roger's a predictable steak – we were deep in a discussion of the proper way to prepare Rector's Ragout, and were not, I fear, entirely sober. At some point we must have ordered a second bottle of wine, for when the Cathedral Puddings appeared – disappointingly solid mounds of sponge topped with lemon sauce – Roger deftly removed the remaining half-full bottle from the table and placed it between my feet, gesturing that I should conceal it in my bag for drinking later. This proved impossible, and when we left I had no alternative but to pick the bottle up and blatantly walk out with it.

Back in my room Roger took off his jacket and loosened his tie. As we sat together on the bed drinking the last of the wine out of the tooth glasses from the bathroom, he put his arm around me and placed several kisses here and there on my neck and cheek.

'I'm so glad you're here, Bobbie. May I stay a while?'

'Of course,' I said, at the same time trying to think of reasons against it. 'But what about tomorrow? Don't you want to go through your sermon one last time?'

'Let's not think about tomorrow just yet. I'd rather think about now.' And his arm tightened its grip, bringing more of my face within kissing distance.

'But what if anyone finds you here?' Surely, I thought, Shelton Park must have its moral equivalent of Dr Treadgold?

'Don't worry about that. There are no rules about visiting here. As we're all men, it's assumed not to be necessary. In any case you're my guest. You could be my cousin or my sister – though I must say I'm glad you're not. Come on, Bobbie. You do like me, don't you?'

'Yes, of course I like you, and I have enjoyed the evening. It's been – very Trollopian.'

He looked puzzled.

'Like Anthony Trollope,' I explained. 'Victorian and churchy.'

'Oh.' He sounded relieved. 'Trollope with an 'e'. For a moment I thought you meant...' And he laughed.

By now we'd finished the wine, which had left my mouth feeling dry and puckery. I disentangled myself from his grasp and picked up a glass. 'I need a drink of water. How about you?'

He shook his head. 'Don't be long.'

In the bathroom I turned on the tap and let the water run for a long time until it was icy cold, then sat on the side of the bath to drink it. No doubt, in view of the double bed and the absence of anyone else in the guest annexe, I should have anticipated an amorous end to the evening, but I had not, and now it was happening I had no idea how to stop it. I drained the glass and returned to the bedroom.

To my astonishment, Roger had used his time alone to undress completely and get into bed. His shirt hung from the back of the chair with his trousers folded carefully underneath, and his shoes, each containing a sock, sat neatly side by side. None of this suggested that here was a man in the throes of uncontrollable passion. I took comfort from the thought.

Roger raised himself on one elbow. His chest was startlingly hairy, and thick tussocks like paint brushes stuck out from under each armpit.

'Do come and join me, Bobs. I've had a great idea for Deacon's Delight.'

The use of my pet name and the apparent return to the playful mood of the meal were enough to disarm me. I switched off the light, undressed and got in beside him. Immediately he began to kiss me, this time on the lips and with such ferocity that I could feel the edges of his teeth. Simultaneously his hands located my breasts and he began to pump them rhythmically, like someone kneading dough.

'Oh Bobbie,' he murmured when finally he unclamped his lips from mine. 'You are lovely. Don't go away – I won't be a minute.'

He swung his legs out of the bed and went over to where his jacket hung on the back of the door. There was a crackling noise, as of paper being torn, then indeterminate fumbling. He returned to bed and climbed on top of me.

'No need to worry about accidents,' he said, as he resumed the kneading. 'I promise I'll be gentle. I don't want to hurt you. Just relax, Bobbie, and enjoy it.'

As well might a gaoler tell a prisoner to relax as he places him on the rack. Beneath Roger's hirsute torso I soon became hot and uncomfortable and was quite unable to move, despite my best efforts to wriggle free. Whatever was happening was happening to Roger alone; I felt like a grotesque doll brought out specially for the purpose. Until, that is, there came an extended stretch of pain as Roger drove himself into me. The soreness as he moved in and out with increasing speed made me gasp repeatedly, but just when I thought I could bear it no longer, he shuddered and moaned and collapsed on top of me, where he lay like a dead weight, seemingly unaware I was still beneath him. I thought he must be sound asleep, but eventually he stirred and I was able to release myself from his imprisoning embrace.

'Oh Bobbie, I'm so glad we did that, aren't you? You enjoyed it too, didn't you? I could tell.'

'What makes you think that?' I tried to keep the amazement out of my voice. Enjoyment was the very last word I'd have chosen to describe the experience.

'The way you moved and the sounds you made. You were very, very exciting.' He now lay quite apart from me, not touching at all, his hands linked together behind his head. 'After that, I'm sure everything will go well tomorrow.'

I'd completely forgotten the sermon. I wondered if all vicars view the act of sex as a way of ensuring success in the pulpit. 'You never did tell me what you'll be preaching about. I know I'll be there tomorrow, but can't you give me a hint now?'

'Well, as it's Mothering Sunday, I decided on the subject of The Family. How important it is, you know, and how very central to the Church.'

'But is it?' I asked.

'Is it what?'

'Central to the Church. I don't remember there being much in the New Testament about the importance of families. In fact, wasn't Jesus rather prone to overlook family ties when he chose his disciples, dragging all those fishermen away from their homes. Zebedee must have been really miffed when James and John just waltzed off like that – and Simon too, who worked with them. There was no thought for the family then, was there?'

I was feeling cross and argumentative, and Roger seemed so smug lying there, distant and remote, despite our fleshly encounter.

'But the family *is* central to the Church, Bobbie. Think of marriage and baptism, both key parts of the Christian life. Marriage in church is a commitment before God, and a sort of promise to bring children into the world. The Church and Family go hand in hand – surely you can see that? It's only within the family that love can truly flourish.'

I was suddenly back in Mrs Gallagher's class, facing a similar lie. 'Two of the most loving, caring people I know have lived together for years but are not married, and will never have children. They are real Christians in every sense of the word – kind and thoughtful and helpful to others.' I could hear myself making Terry and Jo sound like overgrown Brownies. 'Yet according to you, God has no time for them or their life together. Is that what you're saying?'

'Well, yes it is – theirs, and every other unsanctified union. I think you'll find that's pretty much what everyone in the Church thinks. If we turn our back on the Family, there's no telling where we'll end up. There'd be no sanctions at all – anything could happen.'

'But that's nonsense!' I was thoroughly roused by now. 'You're speaking as though we're all savages. Commitment, respect – even physical love – aren't exclusively found in the family. Surely you must admit that?'

'No, no, Bobbie. Love only means anything within marriage

– a man and a woman coming together in Holy Matrimony in order to have children. Take marriage away, and there'd be anarchy. It will all be clear tomorrow, in my sermon. You'll see. And now I'd better be off if I'm going to have a good night's sleep beforehand.' And with that he got out of bed and started dressing. As he bent to put on his shoes, he asked, 'Shall I see you at eight tomorrow in the Refectory? They do quite a good breakfast on Sundays – sometimes there's boiled eggs, and I've even known there to be kippers.'

'I often skip breakfast,' I lied. 'Have yours without me, and I'll see you after Chapel.'

'I'll see you there, then – there's a sort of bun fight afterwards, when I can introduce you to people. Archie Bunt will be there, and one or two others I'd like you to meet. Night-night, Bobbie. Sleep well.' He gave me a peck on the cheek and departed.

I lay in the bed for a long while after he'd gone, deciding exactly what to do. Then I had a very deep bath, put on all my clothes and lay down again on top of the bedclothes. I dozed on and off until it started to become light, then I walked out of the annexe and out of the College and did not stop walking until I arrived at the station, where I settled down to a very long wait for the train.

Thank goodness I hadn't wasted money on a hat.

6

Hampstead 1975

Con bravura

Friday 23 May. Alex's fortieth birthday. She wakes up alone in the flat. On her way, naked, to the bathroom – now that Maggie's left home, she no longer bothers with nightclothes – she catches sight of herself in the full-length mirror. Her birthday suit. Not bad. No sagging breasts or spreading hips. Not yet. And all her own teeth. A hundred years ago she'd be chewing gummily by now, a toothless wreck. Oh, the miracles of modern dentistry!

The post brings birthday cards, mostly of the humorous kind. As though being forty were some sort of huge cosmic joke. Rather an unforgiving number, forty. 'In her late thirties' suggests youth and 'in her early fifties' maturity. But forty's neither one thing nor the other. A mean, sneaky, ill-defined decade. Alex vows then and there to enjoy every year of it.

Over breakfast she writes out a shopping list. These days she shops for choice at the Italian delicatessen on Heath Street. Salami, yes – and paté – she'll make French toast. And salads. Coffee beans. White wine and plenty of it. Then across to the fishmonger's for the salmon she's ordered – she's got a fish kettle somewhere. Eggs, milk, cream. She'll make her old standby, crème caramel, an infallible favourite. But she'll get some rich dark chocolate cake from the delicatessen too, in case it proves fallible today. And flowers, lots of flowers. If she goes out now, she can get the cooking done this morning and prepare the mayonnaise later.

Was it madness to think of giving a dinner party this

evening? Or a way of ensuring she wouldn't spend the evening of her birthday alone? At any rate, it's done. Invitations issued and accepted. She can't turn back now. There'll only be six of them – there's no room at the table for more. The Hope-Pattersons, naturally, Piers and Drusilla. They've been marvellous with Maggie over the years. She just wishes she could like them a little more – all that heartiness is so depressing somehow. And Richard and his wife, up from Cambridge. He rang out of the blue last week. Coming up for the Chelsea Flower Show. Could they possibly meet? Yes, dinner would be lovely. Wife – Maureen? Eileen? Kathleen, that's it – a very keen gardener, it seems. Alex plans to put her next to Piers H-P, who's been known to drone on for hours about fuchsias. Or was it freesias? Some sort of plant, at any rate. And Crispian Helmsby, her producer at Radio Three. She's been to a party at his flat, and this is a chance to reciprocate. Mind you, the party was perfectly dire. Some very dull people pinned her in a corner and talked non-stop about ballooning, and when she finally made her escape, it was only to fall into the hands – literally – of a drunken radio presenter, who chatted her up quite fruitlessly but with nauseating vigour. Still, she doesn't often entertain, and it never hurts to flatter Crispian. She can rely on Drusilla H-P for that. Old Drusilla's desperately impressed by anyone in broadcasting. Even by those on Radio Three.

By half past twelve the poached salmon and crème caramel are cooling safely in the fridge, and Alex is getting ready to meet Maggie for a birthday lunch. She has to nerve herself to do this. Since moving to a flat in Earl's Court and starting her job in advertising, Maggie's become dreadfully dogmatic. And judgemental. Her father's genes rearing their ugly heads, no doubt. Looking through her wardrobe, Alex rejects Laura Ashley in favour of Jaeger. Crisp and cool is the effect she's after. Elegance with competence. These days she meets her daughter in a restaurant near Finsbury Circus, conveniently close to Maggie's office in Liverpool Street. Convenient for Maggie, that is. Alex takes the Northern Line to Old Street then hails a taxi. Other ways of getting there would all involve walking. And she needs the confidence that stepping out of a taxi gives her. With Maggie, she needs all the confidence she can muster.

She's a few minutes late. Maggie looks pointedly at her watch as they sit down.

'Got to be back in the office by two. Big meeting... major client... worldwide sales... if this campaign takes off...'

Alex stops listening and picks up the menu. She preferred Maggie in her 'love, light and peace' days. All those candles and joss sticks. So comforting, somehow, so dreamy. This fast-talking stranger's much harder to like. But still Alex tries.

'Lasagne for me, I think. And a glass of house white. What about you?'

'The mushroom risotto. But no wine. I'll need a clear head for the meeting. We're actually very busy just now. I don't usually stop for lunch.'

'Then it was very good of you to stop today on my account.'

'Actually, Mum, there's something you ought to know.'

Oh God – what's coming now? Alex prepares herself for whatever it is by imagining the absolute worst. Pregnancy. Illness. Eviction. Though not perhaps in that order.

The food arrives. Maggie pokes about in the risotto, eats some, then begins. 'You remember Nick?'

'Your friend from Gainsborough Gardens? Yes, of course I remember him.' She's never warmed to Nick – real name Dominic Scott-Ridley, if memory serves. Father in the Foreign Office. Rolling in money. Nick a spoilt and sneery teenager. Must be twenty-two or twenty-three now. Please, please, not my future son-in-law. Not him. Anyone but him.

'Actually he left home ages ago. Bad scene with his parents. His father's a terrible bully. He won't accept that Nick doesn't want a career in the diplomatic service.'

Alex tries to look as though this might be considered a loss to diplomacy in general.

'So he's moved in with me.'

'Ah.' Alex keeps her voice deliberately neutral.

'I said he could, actually.'

'Well, in that case . . .'

'And there's plenty of room.'

'I suppose there must be.' Since Alex has never been asked to this flat, she's hardly in a position to judge its size.

Maggie scowls between mouthfuls. 'I knew you'd object.'

'I'm not objecting!'

'You are – I can tell. You never liked him.'

Alex takes a stab at the lasagne and a desperate swig of her wine. She wasn't expecting such perspicuity, not from Maggie. 'And what's he doing? Nick? At the moment?'

'He's busking, actually. At Earl's Court tube. He's very good at it. Makes a bomb.'

'That's alright then.'

'Yeah. It is. I just thought I'd tell you.'

'Well, yes – thank you. I'm glad you did.' She finishes off the wine. 'How's your risotto?'

'OK.'

Alex has burnt the roof of her mouth trying to eat the lasagne. It hardly seems to be cooling at all. And it's obvious Maggie hasn't remembered her birthday. Well, she's damned if she'll let her get away with it! She signals to the waiter for another glass of wine. 'By the way,' she says casually, 'I heard from your father a few days ago. He must think the post from Australia's much slower than it is. His birthday card arrived far too early.'

'Oh Christ – your birthday! I completely forgot. Sorry, Mum. Many happy returns.'

'Thank you. You'll be interested to know that your father's talking about marrying again.'

Maggie says dully, 'Good for him,' before shovelling up more risotto.

'If he's serious – and you never can tell with your father – I imagine he'll want a divorce.'

'Yeah – well, he'd have to.'

'I just thought I'd tell you.'

'Right.'

'So now you know. And I know about Nick.'

'Yeah. Actually, Mum, I'd better be going if you don't mind. Gary'll have a fit if I'm late. He needs me to see to the visuals.'

'I'm sure he does. No – I'll be fine. This lasagne must cool down sometime. You go, sweetheart, if you must. It's been lovely to see you.'

'OK then. Bye, Mum. And have a great birthday.'

'I'll do my best.' And Alex signals for a third time to the waiter and asks for another glass of wine and the bill.

She takes a taxi home, and tries not to dwell on the unsatisfactory lunch with Maggie. Instead, she thinks about Matt and his news from Australia. A pregnant girlfriend, apparently – one of his former students. That's no surprise. Who else would admire him sufficiently? Or so uncritically? Of course there've been other women – it's his fifteenth year on the loose – but no-one he's talked about marrying. Maybe he's finally met his match, despite his diminished allure. No longer a Big Shot from what Alex has gathered – not that he mentioned this on his occasional cards, but the newspapers carried the story. Unfortunate episode at a first performance. Drunk in charge of an orchestra. Problems staying on the podium. Passed off as illness, but the end of his public career. Teaching music nowadays at a minor institution. No need for Maggie to know. Not that she seems very interested. Gary and the visuals and Nick, the busking Nick. Nothing else is real for Maggie. Not Alex. Not yet.

Back at the flat, she resists the urge to fall into bed – three glasses at lunchtime perhaps a mistake – and makes strong black coffee instead. This keeps her going through the rest of the preparations. She arranges the flowers in the drawing room, Matt's former studio. The Bechstein's still in place. She plays quite often, now that Maggie's gone. Her upstairs neighbour, an elderly Jewish lady, is delighted. 'Play', she says whenever she meets Alex on the stairs, 'with your heart and with your soul. I can dream I am back in Vienna. But play only good Viennese music – Mozart, Schubert, Beethoven. No French nonsense.' And Alex duly saves Debussy for when she hears her go out.

By half past six the food is ready in the kitchen, where they will eat. Alex has never owned a dining room. Apparently it's become quite chic to eat in kitchens these days, in an inverted *déclassé* sort of way. Or so the colour supplements try to make out. She puts some Gershwin on the record player, pours herself a large glass of wine and takes a long bath. By the time the first guests arrive – the Hope-Pattersons, predictably – she's elegant once more in a silk Jaeger dress and is prepared to enjoy the evening as best she can.

Drusilla H-P, hearty and zestful as ever, in a long blue skirt and cream blouse, presses a vast and incredibly heavy package into her arms on arrival.

'Piers told me you were looking for something to sit in the bay window, and when I saw this I just couldn't resist. I do hope you like it.'

'If not, just tell it to hop it.' Chortle, chortle, chortle from Piers.

Alex unwraps a hideous china frog, green with black markings. Incredibly ugly and monstrously large. It's unspeakably ghastly. And she'll have to keep it sitting here, in case Drusilla or Piers ever drops in. Impossible to disguise it or pretend to have lost it. My God, who makes these things? It probably cost a fortune.

'How very unusual. And so big. It will certainly fill the space.' She can't bring herself to thank them.

Clutching the loathsome object to his chest, Piers staggers across the room – Alex can barely lift it; she wonders how Drusilla ever carried it up the stairs – and places it on the floor in the centre of the bay where it squats malevolently. All three stand and gaze at it in silence. Alex wonders how she'll live with it crouching there, seemingly ready to pounce. Then she pours them a drink and enquires after Beverley, Maggie's erstwhile boon companion, now doing VSO in a clinic somewhere in Africa. Full account of appalling working conditions from Drusilla. The hygiene, my dear, the sanitation. Absolutely no equipment to speak of. Some of the cases you wouldn't believe. Piers takes over with detailed account of one such unbelievable case. Primitive eye surgery graphically described. Alex wills herself not to listen. She thinks instead of the *Adagio* of the Schubert Quintet and waits for his lips to stop moving.

'Dear me,' she says when this blessed moment arrives. 'How gruesome! And when do you expect her back?'

Now it's Drusilla's turn. Long preamble about the rest of the staff at the clinic. Alex fails to see relevance to question. Never hears complete answer, as doorbell mercifully rings, and there are Richard and a stranger she takes to be Kathleen, and Crispian with them. Such a coincidence – they arrived at the block simultaneously. Introductions all round. More drinks. Crispian hands over his gift with a flourish – a new recording of Bach's cello suites. Richard and Kathleen had no idea they were coming to a birthday celebration, but have brought a gardenia – straight from Chelsea – and two gloriously expensive bottles of wine.

Richard seems well. A little older perhaps, but that's not surprising – it's been nearly six years. Hairline beginning to recede, waistline a little thicker. But as good looking and charming as ever. Kathleen is smart, brisk and very, very County. She drinks fruit juice and collapses elegantly into a chair. At Chelsea Show all day. Positively dead on our feet. Had no idea of its size. Huge crowds. Terrible crush. Saw absolutely everything. Couldn't bear to miss a single plant. Piers quizzes her about the gardens. Which was her favourite? Alex puts on one of Crispian's records, turns the volume low, and slips out of the room to make the French toast.

When she returns to summon them to the table, Piers and Kathleen are discussing the work of the American Fuchsia Society, and Richard and Crispian are lamenting the poor reception of Radio Three in various parts of the country. Drusilla is gazing at Crispian with undisguised lust. He's generally thought to be deeply attractive to a certain sort of woman, though Alex can't for the life of her see why. Not her type at all. Too soft around the edges, too pliable, too eager to please for her taste. But not, it seems for Drusilla. Perhaps that's understandable – life with Piers can hardly be the fulfilment of any woman's dream. He must be pushing sixty, but behaves like an eternal Boy Scout. Even down to the baggy shorts in summer.

Drusilla's drooling becomes even more pronounced over the meal. Alex puts Crispian at the far end of the table opposite herself, with Kathleen on his left and Drusilla on his right. Much opportunity for playfulness over the passing to and fro of butter, the offering and accepting of French toast. Piers still pursuing gardening topics with Kathleen. Alex picks out the words 'mulch' and 'top dressing'. She and Richard discuss the musical scene in Cambridge. Dull compared to London, of course. Nothing like the range or quantity, but standard impeccably high. Exquisite choral singing. Some interesting early Renaissance programmes. Quite the thing now, Early Music. Personally, would rather hear a big romantic symphony orchestra any day of the week. Me too, says Alex, as she manoeuvres the first course out of the way and brings out the salmon. She doesn't say she'll be hearing the Brahms *Requiem* at the Festival Hall on Sunday. Too much salt, too big a wound.

The salmon and salads are much admired. Drusilla briefly wrests her attention from Crispian to discuss various healthy dressings, mostly involving yoghurt. Kathleen gives amusing account of salads eaten in obscure French hotel, acquired surreptitiously by the chef each evening from neighbouring garden. Owner finds out. Salads disappear from menu. Piers launches into a list of varieties of lettuce successfully grown in his Hampstead garden, but is neatly interrupted by Drusilla, who asks Crispian about Alex's new radio programme.

'We're all longing to hear about *Schneider's Showcase*. Such a divine idea. Were you the one who thought of it?' She gazes as one besotted.

Crispian modestly admits to being part of the team responsible. Concedes that it's Alex's imprint which makes it such a success. People like to listen to a woman talking authoritatively about the arts, he says. Not as threatening, somehow, as listening to a man.

Alex grips her chair to stop herself from throwing things at him. Patronising sod. If they only knew the trouble she had getting him to agree to the format! He'd wanted a regular magazine programme. Lots of short items from his male cronies, which she'd link dully together in the studio. A spider at the centre of a web she hadn't spun. She was the one who'd insisted on doing it alone. Showcasing something different each week. A conductor. An orchestra. A composer. Even a musical instrument. So far it's gone down better than expected. Listening figures remarkably high. Sizeable postbag each week. All appreciative.

Drusilla continues to address Crispian, as though Alex has no say at all in the matter. 'And what can we look forward to soon? Do give us a teeny clue.'

Crispian gestures to Alex. She refuses to take the hint. He ploughs on unaided. 'Well, I think I can safely say there'll be the festival showcases. Aldeburgh. Cheltenham. Edinburgh...'

Alex seizes the opportunity. 'Of course, I'll need a car. Hopeless to rely on public transport these days.'

Richard, an old campaigner where expense accounts are concerned, nods sagely. 'Good heavens, yes. They can't expect you to stand around on station platforms at all hours of the day and night. Out of the question, eh, Crispian?'

'Absolutely. Goes without saying.'

Soft at the edges, just as she'd known. She begins to fanta-size about life with a car. Hasn't driven for years. Not since Manchester. Perhaps she'll take a refresher course. Richard gives her a sly wink when Crispian isn't looking.

Over the crème caramel – no-one opts for chocolate cake – the question of Alex's car is taken up by everyone. Richard suggests a Ford Capri. Stylish, smooth, sexy, handles superbly well. Excellent torque, whatever that is. Alex responds to the flattery in this and feels absurdly grateful. Such a *nice* man, Richard. Drusilla says she likes Volkswagen Beetles on account of their comically droopy shape. Piers apoplectic at thought of foreign car. Or possibly at notion of droopiness being amusing. Alex knows men see cars as extensions of their penis. Strange creatures, men. Can't beat an Austin 1100, Piers says. Just the car for a woman. Solid and easy to park. Crispian suggests something sleek and sporty. An E-type Jag, perhaps. Alex wonders if she should find this flattering, but doesn't. Competitive, somehow, and vaguely challenging. Soft at the edges but hard in the centre, our Crispian. Not, Alex feels, the nicest of men. Kathleen admits to longing for a Porsche but actually driving a Mini. Alex surprises everyone, including herself, by announcing that she knows exactly what she'll buy. And she does. A purple Ford Escort. She saw one on Heath Street this morning. Wished it were hers and that she were in it. Soon will be. A fortieth birthday present to herself.

She ushers them back to the drawing room, still discussing cars. Back in the kitchen she's rustling up coffee when the telephone rings. She answers, but there's only a husky, moaning noise. Heavy breathing, she decides, and is about to put down the receiver when she distinctly makes out her name.

'Alex? Al – are you there?'

'Matt?' She's astonished. 'Is that you? You sound dreadful.'

'She's left me, Al – gone off and left me.' The moaning resolves itself into Matt's drunken sobbing, all the way from Australia. 'The bitch says the baby's not mine.'

With her free hand Alex measures out the coffee beans. 'If that's the case, then you're well out of it. Though why you think I should care about this...'

'I loved her, Al – I really did. And all the time she was screwing around.'

'You're drunk, Matt. You must be very drunk indeed to even think of ringing here.' She slams down the switch on the grinder and misses his next few remarks. 'Get yourself to bed, Matt,' she says when the grinding's finished. 'It'll not seem so bad in the morning.' As she puts down the phone, she realises it probably *is* morning on the other side of the world. 'The bloody nerve,' she says aloud, pouring water into the pot. 'To ring today of all days, when he's never rung before.' And she promptly dismisses all thought of Matt from her mind.

Back to the drawing room to offer coffee and brandy. Only Kathleen refuses both. Piers is well away now. Traffic jam sagas. Calls on Drusilla to confirm precise details of hold-ups in recent years. The Oxford ring road, Birmingham in general and the A38 beyond Exeter. Much venom at wanton parking all over Cornwall. Alex vows to avoid such trouble spots. She pictures herself driving fast and unhindered, mainly at night, not always alone. She looks round the room and catches sight of the wretched giant frog. Averting her eyes, she intercepts a look between Richard and Kathleen. Tender, loving and – yes – proud. Of course – she's pregnant! That explains the lack of alcohol all evening. And their eagerness for the Chelsea Show this year. So Richard's about to start life as a parent just as her own mothering days are over. She hopes he'll enjoy the early part. After the first twelve years, it's downhill all the way.

Crispian's been trawling through her record collection, vast now, after all those years of reviewing. She hopes he's impressed. Then he leafs through the pile of music on the Bechstein. Picks out Chopin's *Nocturnes*. Begs Alex to play. Another challenge. She's sufficiently drunk to respond, and chooses the one in E flat, Op. 9 No. 2. Her fingers find the notes with very little effort. This is what I can do, she thinks. This is what I am good at. She wonders what her Jewish neighbour thinks of Chopin's wistful melancholy. As she lets the last *ppp* chord die away, she notices tears on Drusilla's cheeks, and hastily offers more coffee. But with one accord they decide that it's time to leave. A lovely evening. Delightful company. So civilised. She kisses Kathleen and tells her to take care of herself. She even kisses Drusilla, dry-cheeked now, but not quite restored to full heartiness, she's pleased to see.

'Oh, Alex!' Drusilla pauses in the doorway. 'I've been meaning to say I've booked in with your dentist at last. The Clapham man. First appointment next week. The Receptionist sounded a bit snooty, but I mentioned your name and that seemed to smooth things a bit.'

'I bet it did. I must have handed over a fortune by now. But he's definitely the best I've found. Almost no pain at all. Do let me know what you think of him.'

'I will. And thanks again for a lovely evening.'

'We'll be listening on Wednesday,' Piers promises, and plants his damp, fleshy lips on Alex's cheek. It's all she can do not to shudder.

Crispian seems to take himself off. She's not involved in his departure at all.

And that's it. Fortieth birthday successfully navigated. Now that it's over, the day takes on a balmy glow. Let the new decade do its worst. Ignoring the mess in the kitchen, Alex undresses and goes to sleep, alone, in the flat.

7

Tempo comodo

'And here is Robina Sinclair, who is come to join our team.'

It was my first day at the Institute of Aural Studies in Gordon Square, and the introduction was made by Dr Helga Grossmann, plump, bespectacled and unmistakeably Teutonic. I'd come across her pioneering research into musical memory during my final year at university, and was sufficiently intrigued to write and ask about her research methods. She replied at some length – I suspect she was unused to fan mail – in a style that was quaint and endearing.

'To promote our researches,' her letter informed me, 'we write the tunes of controlled difficulty, for the people to hear. When they return, we record the remembrances and analyse. We see what they forget and what they remember. So we write a new tune, and wonder will they remember this more? Always we ask the question: What does this tell of the way the brain concerns itself with sound? One day perhaps we write a tune that no-one ever forgets. Until then, there are many experiments and much analysis to perform.'

I was totally charmed. After a further exchange of letters came the offer of a research post. I accepted, installed myself economically in a bedsit in Camden Town, and looked forward to a useful life unlocking the secrets of musical memory.

'The spaces that we have are not so good,' Dr Grossmann told me on my introductory tour, apologising for the cramped underground room in which five of us had to work. Her own office, an ill-disguised cupboard, was tucked away in a corner.

'Upstairs there are bigger departments, but it is here that we do the work of the bigger importance. Is that not so, Greg?' she asked of a young man who was busy comparing a series of graphs.

'I won't have you casting aspersions on the lovely secretaries upstairs, Dr G.' was the amiable reply. 'They're all of them jolly good sports. And I'm Russell, not Greg, as it happens. Greg's the less handsome one – over there.'

I followed his gaze to a remarkably similar young man who was also comparing a series of graphs. He looked up and waved in acknowledgement.

Dr Grossmann shrugged. 'Russell – Greg – I confuse them always. It is safest to call them both Grussell. But the women I never confuse. Here is Paula and Kate,' she said, introducing them in turn. 'They also studied Music and Psychology. In England today I think we need many women researchers, to balance the number of men.'

'Dr G.'s determined to do her bit for Women's Lib,' Kate explained. 'She's kinder to us than to Grussells, all on account of our sex.'

'Except when it comes to planning experiments,' put in Paula. 'If your design's the slightest bit sloppy, she'll be down on you like a ton of bricks – won't you, Dr G.?'

'But of course.' Dr Grossmann wagged an admonishing finger. 'I am a very good leader, and you are a very good team. But suggest to me something not scientific, and you will find I am a monster! Often,' she said, turning to me, 'I cannot be here. I go to many conferences, and must also beg for grants of money from rich businesses. Then you discuss and you plan, but you must not, not, not' – again the admonishing finger – 'do any research without me. Now I must get back to work. Paula and Kate will explain to you what they are doing. I hope you will be happy here, Robina, and stay for a very long time.'

'I'm sure I shall,' I said. 'And please call me Bobbie; everyone does.'

To say that our progress was slow would be an exaggeration: we barely moved forward at all. The secrets of musical memory resisted our merciless probing, though we groped for them daily with patience and circumspection. Often we'd abandon a particular line of enquiry in favour of something more promising, only to discover that this, too, led nowhere, and back we would go to a new and suggestive beginning, certain that this time we'd arrive at a concrete, if tiny, conclusion. When we repeatedly didn't, I began to believe our work could continue for ever; indeed, it was Dr G.'s intention that it should. Each stage of our research was duly written up in the *Journal of Aural Studies*, and each of us earned a Ph.D. in the process. I was the last to win mine, for a provocative piece of work entitled '*A paradigm for the study of musical memory: what we can learn from tonal response.*' Though it hardly set the world on fire, I enjoyed being able to call myself Doctor, and, most importantly, Dr G. was pleased with it.

'Now that we all have been doctored,' she announced one morning, 'I propose a celebration – a picnic on Hampstead Heath. Come to my house at midday on Sunday. If it rains, we stay indoors. If not, we shall picnic.' She beamed at us all before adding, 'I shall supply the wine,' which instantly made it desirable. Alas in this instance her planning was logically flawed: though not raining when we set out from Willow Road, it bucketed down the moment we started to eat, and we ended up drinking her very fine Mosel under the sheltering trees.

With our research at the Institute promising to amble on indefinitely, it seemed sensible to stop paying rent on my unlovely bedsit and invest instead in a flat of my own. Thanks to my father's allowance, I'd saved what I thought was a competent sum, but it failed to impress the local estate agents, who all dismissed me with the same withering comment: 'For anything at that sort of price, you'll need to look south of the river.' South of the river I went, and discovered the joys of the Commons. Streatham, Wimbledon, Wandsworth, Tooting – I toyed with them all before finally falling for what in estate agents' jargon was a 'garden annexe' in one of the roads leading directly off Clapham Common. Originally the kitchen and scullery of a four-storeyed house, this semi-basement was now a one bed-roomed flat and did indeed open out on the garden, though only a small rockery and sitting area belonged to me; the rest was the property of the people upstairs. It lay, as vast swathes of south London are doomed to lie, under the Heathrow flight path, which explained why those on the Middlesex side held it in such contempt. But I loved my flat from the moment I saw it, and when Terry and Jo were able to bring my records and books and some spare furniture from Hendre, I bade farewell to Camden Town for ever. With the flat-warming cheque from my father I bought a patio table and chairs, and there I would sit for breakfast during the long hot summer of 1976, looking out on the single black poplar which towered at the end of the garden. I even grew to love the sight of Concord passing overhead at predictable times of day, an elegant, powerful bird.

My love life at this time was patchy. I hadn't been long at the Institute before Russell waxed very insistent. In the end it seemed kinder to yield than to spurn him continuously, but the affair was never quite serious, and he soon returned to haunting the upstairs corridors, where bevies of glamorous secretaries could be had, it seemed, for the asking. After Russell there were occasional men in my life, but the only one who moved me – and the very best lover by far – was a Greek I met at a party. His name was Stavros, and he *might* have been a ship owner, though his imperfect English left this delightfully vague. His first words to me were, 'Do you like bananas?' When I said that I did, he disappeared, only to return half an hour later with two carrier bags full of the wretched things: he must have searched for one of those all-night shops which flourish in parts of London, and bought their entire stock.

'Now you come to my house and we eat them,' he said, and in the absence of Dr Treadgold to consult on Hellenic behaviour, I tamely agreed. We did, it is true, eat bananas, but he also introduced me to slow, thoughtful lovemaking which involved far more than the rubbing together of our genitals and was unexpectedly and totally satisfying. I was never to see my Greek again: over our third banana, he confessed he was leaving for Pireus the following day, and I wondered later whether his imminent departure was one of the reasons I let myself go so completely. But I never forgot that evening, nor my introduction to such physical pleasure as I'd previously only imagined.

After Stavros, I lived in a permanent state of waiting. For what, and for whom, I had little idea, though I fully believed that London would supply whatever it was I was waiting for. I kept my flat immaculate, ready for any encounter. There was always a bottle of wine in the fridge, and, from a superstitious dread of being found domestically careless, I hoovered and dusted regularly: if one lives in the hope of entertaining an angel unawares, one cannot risk alienating the heavenly visitor by shoddy housekeeping. All winter I waited, and throughout the whole of the spring. It is possible, in London, for the seasons to pass by unnoticed, so bound does one become to the routines imposed by living and working in a crowded city. The walk to the station, the teeming platform, the airless, tightly packed train and the seething pavements do not vary substantially summer or winter, and are there to endure, not enjoy. But sometimes the song of a blackbird on an April evening, or the sight of a clump of celandines on the Common, would puncture my urban indifference. Then I would notice that time was indeed moving forward, and feel a renewed upsurge of hope that whatever I was waiting for was moving inexorably closer. At such moments the possession of a clean and tidy flat seemed an irrelevance, a presumption, as though Destiny alone were insufficient and needed a helping hand. In this mood I would drink the bottle of wine and ignore the crumbs on the carpet, in the certain assurance that what was approaching was bound to occur without my intervention. But a few days later I would replace the one and remove the other, a prey once more to superstitions which I could not entirely abandon.

'There's nothing else for it,' said Greg philosophically. 'We'll have to pack up and go home.'

'But it's not yet half past three.' Kate seemed mildly shocked. 'Won't Dr G have a fit?'

Greg gave her a pitying look. 'At the moment she's safely in Hamburg, and isn't due back till tonight. You know what will happen. She'll spend the weekend writing a detailed account of the conference, and on Monday morning she'll read it to us. It's bound to be full of exciting news of what our colleagues in Germany are up to. If we ask some well-judged questions, she'll happily spend the morning explaining. It won't enter her head to ask what we did in her absence.'

'And we've finished those graphs that she wanted,' Russell added. 'There's really no more we can do.'

'Except plan the next stage,' I pointed out tentatively.

'Oh, not in this terrible heat!' Paula objected at once. 'It's so stuffy in here. I hate this sultry weather – it gives me a permanent headache.'

It was the third Friday of June, and the week had been marked by spectacular thunderstorms, with lightning and rainbows in turn transforming the London sky. The air was reluctant to clear, and our basement was even more oppressive than usual.

'Perhaps we could take the latest set of results home with us to look at over the weekend,' Kate suggested.

And that, without too much reluctance, was what we decided to do. We left in very good spirits, with the pride of successful truants. It was sunny as I walked from Gordon Square to Warren Street tube station, but when I emerged into daylight again at Clapham Common, there were threatening dark clouds overhead. Clearly another heavy storm was on its way.

Parked on the opposite side of the road from my flat was a purple car I had not seen before. By now the neighbours' cars were familiar to me, by shape and colour if not by make and model: they were part of the immutable landscape, and like hedges and trees, occupied the same spot each day. As I drew parallel with the interloping vehicle, a woman, wearing sunglasses and a soft cream suit that swung from the hips as she walked, crossed over and got in to the driving seat. She must have been following me down the road. At the same time I noticed that the rear offside tyre of the car was flat. She started the engine and was about to drive off when I managed to attract her attention.

'Flat tyre,' I mouthed, gesturing madly at the rear wheel.

She switched off the engine and got out to look. At the sight of the wheel hub resting on the ground she groaned. 'Oh God! How on earth did that happen?'

'There'll be a spare,' I said.

She looked round vaguely, as though hoping a convenient fifth wheel might suddenly appear from somewhere.

'It'll be in the boot.' I added helpfully. 'With the jack.'

She seemed not to believe me. 'But the boot's empty.'

'It'll be cunningly hidden – probably under the floor.'

She took off her sunglasses and looked at me closely. Then she smiled. 'You seem to know all about it.'

'Well, I've helped to change the odd wheel in my time. And none of them has ever fallen off. It's not difficult, as long as you can get the nuts undone.'

'Do you mean you can do it? I thought I'd have to get hold of a mechanic.'

'There's no need for that – I can do it. And you'd have to wait ages for anyone to come out on a Friday afternoon.'

'Can I do anything to help?'

'Not unless you want to ruin your suit. Look, I live just over there, in the basement flat. If you take my things in, you can wait for me there. It looks as though it might rain any minute.' I got out the key to the flat and handed it over, along with my handbag, briefcase and jacket. 'I promise I won't make off with the car.'

'I know you won't do that. This is terribly kind of you. Are you sure...?'

'Yes, I'm sure,' I said.

The nuts were a bit tight, but I managed to undo them by

a combination of jumping on the spanner and kicking it vigorously. Terry had shown me this trick when we'd changed a wheel on the Morris Traveller together. The rest was straightforward. I retightened the nuts as well as I could. The car keys were still in the steering column. I took them out and locked the car. Crossing the road, I felt the first heavy drops of rain.

'All done,' I shouted, as I entered the flat. My voice struck me as too loud and hearty, an actor making an obvious entrance.

She was standing by the bookcase in the living room. 'Finished already? That was quick. You must be quite an expert.'

'I just missed the rain. I'll have a wash and then put the kettle on. Or perhaps you're in a hurry?'

'No, no, not at all. I have to get back to North London, but there's no rush. A black coffee would be lovely.'

In the kitchen I ground up the last of my coffee beans, and found some biscuits I hoped weren't too stale. When I returned to the living room, my guest was staring at one of the pictures on my wall. It was a drawing, done by Jo, of the dovecote. I'd always liked it, and they'd had it framed for me when I moved to the flat. She did not look round when I came in, and seemed to be addressing the picture.

'About five or six years ago – it was in August, a Tuesday, I think – I visited that dovecote. With some friends. We had lunch on the way, and got there in the afternoon. Somewhere in Wales. It was very, very hot and very, very quiet. There was no-one around. Then someone came out of the house and said she'd call her aunt. That was you, wasn't it? You're Bobbie. I thought I recognised you outside, but when I saw the picture I knew for certain.'

She turned round and held out her hand.

'Hallo, Bobbie. I'm Alex. Alex Taylor.'

*

It's after eight o'clock by the time Alex finally arrives home. She's barely aware of having driven across London. What she is aware of is an immense elation, like yeast rising within her.

Never before has she felt so – *possessed* is the only word for it. She pours a large whisky and carries it to the drawing room. Playing the piano might help. But after the first few chords she can't bear to sit still any longer, and breaks off. She moves to the window and looks at the houses opposite, roofs and pavements dry now after the earlier rain. Still the restlessness won't leave her. She finishes her drink quickly, pours another and takes a long, hot shower, as though she can physically rid herself of the tormenting agitation by washing it away. And true, she does feel calmer afterwards. Wrapped in a bathrobe, another whisky at her side, she sits in a chair in the window of her unlit bedroom, and as the June sky finally darkens, lets herself relive the time at Bobbie's flat.

They simply talked – not for long – for half an hour, perhaps. She tries to remember exactly what it was they said. It began with the dovecote. Bobbie had only the vaguest recollection of her visit – lots of people turn up, apparently – but remembered the panicky geese. Alex explained how she came to be in Clapham – check-up at the dentist's at end of the road. Mentioned the afternoon in Haslemere, and the harpsichord factory. Hence the car. Parking always tricky round the Common. Bobbie can drive, but doesn't have a car. Uses the Northern Line mostly. Asked Alex where she lives. Doesn't know Hampstead well, but has visited the Heath. Picnic there one Sunday with Dr Helga Something. Ruined by sudden downpour. Sheltered under trees. Alex has a vivid picture of the two women huddled together in the dry. Dismisses it instantly. Doesn't want to think of Bobbie with anyone else. Absurd. She barely knows her. The work at the Aural Studies place sounds interesting. Musical memory. Alex isn't exactly sure what it is they do, or why they're doing it. Didn't like to ask, in case she'd got it wrong. Kept on being distracted by her face, the eyes, the mouth. Forgot to listen sometimes. Hopes it didn't show. Boxes full of records. Mainly chamber music. Nothing much for harpsichords, she said. Cello in the corner. Obviously reads a lot – shelves full of novels, and quite a few scores. Easy to talk to. Trusting, too, to hand over all her worldly goods like that, to an absolute stranger. Seems to live alone. No sign of other occupant. No engagement ring. And all the time the rain poured down on Clapham, they were cocooned in the basement, comfortable together. So friendly, so familiar somehow. A recognition of someone known, or someone imagined. Oh – very important: she should have the tyre repaired and keep it as the spare. A garage would tighten the wheel nuts for her, just to be sure.

But when the rain stopped, she'd had to leave. There was no reason to stay any longer. She curses herself for not arranging another meeting. She could easily have suggested something. Lunch, perhaps, or dinner somewhere. But no, she'd said nothing. Nothing at all. The thought makes her feel suddenly desolate and in need of more whisky, which she drinks at the kitchen table. And there, in front of her, she sees the answer. Clipped inside a piece of paper on which she's written '21st June' are two complimentary tickets to the Queen Elizabeth Hall on Tuesday. She'll send one to Bobbie. Inspired now, and not a little drunk, she hunts for an envelope and writes the name and address. Inside she puts one ticket. No note. Just the ticket. She seals it and stamps it, pulls on trousers and a jumper and walks out of the flat to the pillar box, before she can change her mind.

*

I spent a miserable weekend after Alex Taylor left, alternating between hope and disappointment but chiefly tormented by the latter. On the one hand, the very thing I'd been waiting for appeared to have come about, so justifying my constant state of expectancy and the tidy state of my flat. At the same time, thanks to my boorish dullness, it had been a most unsatisfactory version of the encounter I'd so often imagined. As I replayed the conversation repeatedly, over and over again, I thought of all the witty replies I had failed to make, all the amusing comments I had not uttered. In retrospect, I seemed to have talked at tedious length and learnt nothing at all about Alex. She was far and away the most fascinating, elegant and attractive person I had ever met, and precisely because this was so, my rage at my own poor performance was searing and intense. I had wantonly wasted the opportunity of getting to know her better. Nor did the encounter appear to have led anywhere. As soon as the rain stopped, Alex Taylor left my flat, eager, no doubt, to return to the more stimulating surroundings of Hampstead. In my most wretched moments, I imagined she'd forgotten me already, or had turned our meeting into an after-dinner anecdote, a funny thing that happened on the way from the dentist. Throughout the weekend, I tried not to catch sight of the bottle of wine in the fridge, for it reminded me too keenly of all I had dreamed of and all I'd so utterly failed to achieve.

Yet even while I entertained these punishing thoughts, I allowed a small thread of hope to keep itself alive. Alex had remembered me from Hendre, five or more years ago. She'd asked about my work and the music I listened to, and seemed quite interested in what I told her. Might not all this mean something? Most hopeful of all, she knew where I lived and might, at some future date, call again. I even worked out when her next six-monthly check-up at the dentist would fall, and, ignoring the improbability of a second flat tyre in identical circumstances, began to imagine another meeting, more lively and productive than the first.

Even when the ticket arrived in the post on Monday morning, all the misery of the weekend did not instantly vanish. There was nothing to indicate whom it was from, no sign, no message anywhere, apart from the Hampstead postmark. Dr G. lived in Hampstead: conceivably the ticket could have come from her. It was a while before I realised I could safely dismiss this unwelcome notion. Dr G. had been in Hamburg until Friday evening, and was hardly likely to have rushed out and posted a ticket to me immediately on her return – she'd have been far too busy preparing her Conference Report, and in any case she of all people had no need to use the post, since we'd be working together in less than two hours. And of course I knew her writing, whereas that on the envelope was unfamiliar. Only when I'd thoroughly rehearsed all these arguments could I allow myself the joy of knowing that Alex had sent it.

All day I could think of nothing beyond the fact that I would see her again at the concert, although certain other disobliging ideas naturally occurred to tarnish the rapture with which this thought filled me. She'd sent me the ticket because she could not be there herself. Or she would be there, but along with a crowd of friends and relations, like Rabbit, and would have neither time nor opportunity to speak to me. Worst of all, she'd be there with her husband. On that possibility I could not bear to dwell.

I scarcely slept on Monday night, and despaired of ever getting through Tuesday. At work I was distracted and unable to concentrate properly. My preoccupied state did not pass unnoticed.

'Our little Bobbie is not entirely with us today,' Dr G. announced as I lost the thread of something I was trying to explain. 'She must be in love, I think.'

In Dr G.'s eyes, being in love was tantamount to a crime, since it involved caring for something other than the workings of musical memory, and I hastily denied it. At the same time I wondered if she might not possibly be right.

When at last the working day was over, I made my way as slowly as I could to the South Bank. Though I dawdled on my walk to Warren Street and again on Hungerford Bridge, letting the stream of commuters pass me by as I gazed, unseeing, at the view of the City, I still arrived with over an hour to spare. Even so, the foyer of the Queen Elizabeth Hall was far from empty, and I looked everywhere, hoping to see the face which had haunted me since Friday. When I was certain she hadn't arrived, I bought a coffee and a programme and sat down at one of the small tables facing the entrance, from where I could watch the audience come in. I waited and I waited, not daring to take my eyes off the doors even to glance at the programme for fear of missing her. As more and more people arrived, they developed the annoying habit of standing about in large and noisy groups, blocking my view for minutes at a time, so that

I had to scan the crowd all over again, in case she'd come and I hadn't seen her. As the time of the recital drew nearer, there was steady movement from the foyer to the auditorium, but still I watched and waited. When a voice announced that the performance would begin in five minutes, the exodus increased; two minutes later, when the second warning sounded, I was virtually on my own. Convinced now that she was not ever coming, I finally stood up to make my way in to the hall, and at that very instant Alex appeared in the doorway.

'Bobbie!' She hurried over to me. 'I'm so sorry I'm late. Have you been waiting long?'

'No,' I said, 'not long.'

And we gave ourselves up to the ushers, who were busily rounding up stragglers so that the concert could begin.

*

It's a full house. Not a spare seat anywhere. Alex sits next to the aisle, Bobbie on her left. They're barely seated when the quartet walk on stage, tune up briefly and launch into the Beethoven. Soothingly familiar, but no less potent for that. Alex begins to relax. The harsh edges of her day become smooth under the influence of the music. All her recent worries – that she'd be late, that Bobbie wouldn't come, that she should have put a note with the ticket – have turned out to be groundless. What she's most aware of, what affects her more than the music itself, is the presence of Bobbie beside her, so close that their arms could touch. She's sitting in absolute stillness, wholly absorbed by the playing, a perfect listener. Ever since posting the ticket on Friday, Alex has pictured this moment, and now that it's actually happening, can scarcely believe that it's real. She wants it to be the start of something, but doesn't yet know what that is; wants more than this evening, but cannot as yet see the future. For the moment, let this be enough. Beethoven, Mendelssohn, Schubert. And Bobbie. Most of all Bobbie.

*

By the time the interval arrived, I was just about capable of coherent speech once more. I'd barely heard a note of the Beethoven quartet, so drained had I been by the long wait for Alex and so filled with delirious delight at her eventual arrival. The delirium took a while to subside, but I was able to listen quite sensibly to the Mendelssohn. In fact, I was sorry when it ended, not just for the sake of the music, but because beyond it loomed the interval, and I dreaded a repeat of my disappointing conversational performance of the previous Friday.

I need not have worried. Alex suggested we stay in our seats instead of moving, as there'd be such a crush in the foyer, and once the people from our row had filed apologetically past us and we were left alone among the tiers of empty seats, there was somehow no strain between us.

'I'd forgotten how much I enjoy that Mendelssohn quartet.' Alex leant slightly towards me. 'It's a long while since I heard it. What did you think of it, Bobbie?'

'It made me think of Beethoven all the time.' I said. 'Not the early quartets, like the one we just heard, but the late ones. Especially during those rather bare fugues. But perhaps it should have made me think of Bach? Wasn't it Mendelssohn who popularised Bach's music?'

'It was indeed. But he was also the first to take Beethoven's late quartets seriously, if I remember rightly. Everyone else said they were unplayable. Can I borrow your programme for a moment? It might say when Mendelssohn wrote that quartet.'

I handed her the programme, realising as I did so that I hadn't so much as opened it myself.

'Ah yes,' she said, pointing to the programme notes. 'Look, it says here – 1827.'

'And Beethoven died in March that year, not knowing his work had been so well understood. How sad!' Alex looked at me with surprise. 'It's a date I remember from school,' I added quickly, hoping she didn't think I was showing off. 'How old was Mendelssohn in 1827? Twelve-and-a-half, or thereabouts?'

Alex smiled. 'Oh, he'd reached the grand old age of eighteen by then. So you know Beethoven's late quartets quite well, do you?'

'Quite well,' I admitted, 'though it took me a while to get used to them. My favourite is Opus 130, with that glorious *cavatina*. If I had to take one record with me to a desert island, that's the one I'd choose.'

'Which last movement would you opt for? The *Grosse Fuge*, or its later replacement?'

'Definitely the *Grosse Fuge*. And I'd want to take the score as well, to try to work out what's happening. At a recital like this, I tend to watch the cellist and ignore the other three parts, but with the score in front of me, I'm more even-handed.'

'There was certainly plenty for the cello to do in the Mendelssohn – lots of drama and passion. The other day I heard a marvellous young cellist at the Aldeburgh Festival, playing Bach and Hindemith – an unusually challenging programme.'

I could see a fifth music stand and chair being brought on to the platform, and was about to glance at the programme. But Alex's next words made this unnecessary.

'Now for the Schubert, Bobbie, and a double helping of cellos. Do you think we have enough strength? If we survive this, would you like to have dinner with me afterwards? We shall surely need some sustenance, and I should like it so much if you could.'

As a result, I enjoyed the Quintet more than ever. The slow movement seemed to mirror my last few days exactly: the calm peace of Friday, the turmoil of the weekend and the transfigured joy of the present, heightened, now, by the promise of yet more time together.

From the South Bank we took a taxi to Piccadilly – Alex had left her car at home that day – and found a small Greek restaurant where we were, after a while, the only diners. During the meal, Alex told me that she worked for the BBC, but did not say much about it. For this I was grateful: I had never owned a television set, and neither had Terry and Jo, and programmes which were the stuff of life to other people meant absolutely nothing to me. She asked about my colleagues at the Institute, and I fear I must have made them out to be more amusing than they actually were, for she laughed a lot, especially when

I described Dr G.'s ruthless devotion to the cause, and the awful power she wielded over us. By this time it was dreadfully late, and the waiters, clearly hoping we would be shamed into departure by their presence, began to stand idly about, looking bored and yawning noisily; two of them even sat down at a table and started a game of cards. Eventually, though, we had to leave. Alex was surprised to discover it was past midnight, and as we walked down Haymarket towards Trafalgar Square, she suddenly hailed a passing cab and spoke to the driver.

'Quick, Bobbie. After midnight they often won't go south of the river, but this one will. Get in.'

For a wild moment I thought she was coming with me. But no.

'Thank you for a lovely evening,' I heard her say, as she shut the door on me and gave the driver some money. And away I was whisked to the depths of Clapham, and to my solitary, tidy flat.

I spent Wednesday in a state of high excitement. To stave off the depressing thought that our second meeting, like our first, appeared to have led nowhere, I managed to convince myself that Alex would ring me at the Institute. Each time a phone rang anywhere in the building, I thought it must be her. Each time I was mistaken, and when, by the end of the day, I'd heard nothing from her, my earlier excitement gave way to near despair. I still didn't know what to make of our relationship, if relationship it was. Perhaps, after all, the concert and the meal were no more than a way of thanking me for changing the wheel. What could I do to make sure that I saw her again? On the tube journey home, it dawned on me there was indeed some action I could take. Back at the flat, I pored over the London telephone directory and, using my *A to Z*, located the addresses of all the A.Taylors listed. There were eight in the vicinity of Hampstead, and I wrote them all down, thinking I could ring each in turn and ask to speak to Alex. It then occurred to me that I could ring her at the BBC. Feeling not quite powerless after all, I decided to have a bath before eating, and took my radio in to the bathroom with me, hoping that music would help cheer me up.

To my intense astonishment, what I heard was Alex's voice. It was unmistakable; her impeccable diction with its slight northern overtones was particularly pronounced on the radio. Moreover she was talking to a man who made harpsichords – apparently he had in his possession an instrument made by his grandfather and decorated by Burne-Jones. As the bath water cooled around me, I listened in stunned stupefaction. At the end of the programme, the announcer informed me that the next edition of *Schneider's Showcase* would feature the Aldeburgh Festival.

To say I felt embarrassed would do scant justice to the agony of shame and confusion that engulfed me. I'd heard of Alexandra Schneider, though I'd never before heard her programme. I'd even read about her, on the Arts pages of *The Times*. Dr G. often left articles of musical interest lying about the office, in the hope that they might, by some process of osmosis, inspire us in our work. The Alexandra Schneider I'd read about – there'd been no photograph – was hailed as one of the most influential reviewers of our time, especially in the field of chamber music, and her move to radio was deeply regretted as an incalculable loss to the world of musical criticism. This was the woman to whom I had voiced my superficial opinions of Beethoven's string quartets. This was the woman I had tried to entertain by describing our ridiculous research on musical memory. This was the woman I had foolishly, oh so foolishly, hoped might be interested in me.

I did not blame Alex for not letting on who she was, but I did blame myself for not giving her more opportunity to talk about her life. Feeling that I'd blundered in every possible respect, and profoundly ashamed of the hopes and dreams I'd entertained, I vowed there and then to banish Alex from my thoughts, as I guessed by now she'd rid herself of any thought of me. By day I did this relatively successfully, but forgetting her at night was not so easy. My body, as though prepared for something which it then had been denied, refused to let her go, and for two consecutive nights I was plagued by images which both aroused me and amazed me by their strength.

After a third night of erotically disturbed slumber, I was woken early on Saturday morning by a ring of the doorbell. Assuming it was the postman, I put on my dressing gown and went to the door. There stood Alex, a paper bag in each hand.

'Bobbie, I'm sorry...I couldn't bear it any longer. I had to see you. I do hope you're alone. And feeling hungry. Look, I've brought our breakfast.'

And clutching a bag of croissants and a packet of coffee beans, she stepped inside my flat.

*

If Alex were entirely honest, (which, of course, she isn't. How can she be? Who, even at forty-two, dares to be completely honest about something so important, so utterly perplexing? Not Alex. Not quite yet.) she would greet Bobbie like this:

'I'm here at this hour of the morning because I can't bear to be apart from you a moment longer. I've done everything I can to stop thinking about you. I tried to lose myself in work, played the piano, listened to music, watched Open University programmes when I couldn't sleep. I even started reading *Madame Bovary* in French. None of it has been the slightest use. I can't get you out of my head. You're there when I wake in the morning, and every time I'm alone. For a week now, you've obsessed me. I don't understand what's happened, but I know I want to see you and to be with you, and for you to want it too.'

Of course she says none of this. Instead, she and Bobbie get plates and mugs from the kitchen, and set out breakfast on the table in the small sitting area – estate agents would call it a patio – at the back of Bobbie's flat. The sun's not yet hidden by the black poplars at the bottom of the garden. It's going to be another cloudless day. While Bobbie warms croissants, finds butter and jam, Alex boils the kettle and grinds the coffee beans. Bobbie disappears to dress, and when she returns there is Alex sitting in her garden, at her table, asking what she'd like to do for the rest of the day. And neither of them can really believe what's happening, but each is too full of happiness to want anything to be different.

'What about Kew Gardens? I've only been there once, and went by train, but with the *A to Z* we could find our way in the car. I've left it on the table.'

Alex goes indoors to fetch the *A to Z*. Inside it she finds a slip of paper with the addresses and phone numbers of eight A. Taylors. At first, she's puzzled; then she understands. Now, wonderfully, finally, she's absolutely sure.

8

Con amore

We spent the day at Kew. From Brentford Gate we strolled down to the Rhododendron Dell, now past its flowering best, and on to the lake, where we watched coots and moorhens, mallards and various other breeds of duck, many with their brood of young. Sometime in the afternoon we came across the Pavilion Restaurant and ate outside, along with hosts of sparrows who appropriated each empty table in turn to scavenge for leftover crumbs. While I watched the birds, Alex watched the people around us.

'Look at the married couples, Bobbie. You can easily spot them. They're the ones not talking.'

It was true. Husbands and wives were conspicuous by their silence, while pairs of women together – friends, sisters, mothers and daughters, perhaps even lovers – were all deep in conversation. I felt it incumbent upon me not to break the pattern.

'I happened to hear your programme on Wednesday – by accident, really. I was in the bath at the time. It gave me quite a surprise.'

Alex smiled. 'It must have done. I hope it was a *pleasant* surprise. I'm sorry I didn't tell you before. I nearly did in the restaurant. It was one of the reasons I insisted we stay in our seats in the concert interval – I was afraid if we went to the foyer, we'd bump into someone who knew me. And I didn't want it to get in the way, to make a barrier between us. You don't think any the worse of me for it, do you?'

Now it was my turn to smile. Think *worse* of her, for being Alexandra Schneider? How could I? ' Of course not. Though if I'd known, I wouldn't have wittered on as I did at the concert. You must have thought me full of ridiculous notions.'

'I'd hardly be here now if I'd thought that.' She patted my hand. 'As it happens, I agreed with everything you said. And it was lovely to know you weren't trying to impress me. That's what people do when they know who I am. And I don't want you to do that.'

'I'll try my best not to,' I promised, as we set off again on our stroll.

It was glorious weather, and Kew that day was a popular destination. On the main paths and avenues we were constantly having to leap aside to avoid hordes of tourists, French, German, Japanese, all with their guidebooks and cameras, but when we chose instead to wander across the grass, it was quite easy to lose sight of other people completely. And that is how I remember that day, the two of us alone in the sunshine, Alex's arm slipped through mine, with the beauty of Kew all around us, but nobody else at all.

On our drive back to Clapham, Alex stopped at a licensed grocers on the Upper Richmond Road, where, not wishing to risk culinary failure, we bought food of an undemanding nature and some bottles of white wine. Back at the flat, we spread our purchases on the table and I fetched the bottle of wine from the fridge, thoroughly chilled now after its long incarceration. We both drank more than we ate, and soon needed a second bottle. We talked all the while: Alex told me of concerts she'd been to, and I described life at Hendre, but part of me was constantly dreading the moment when Alex would say it was time to leave. I suggested she put on some music while I got rid of our debris. Coming out of the kitchen, I opened the back door and looked out into the late June evening. A tawny owl was calling from the black poplar, but otherwise all was still. No music disturbed the silence. I turned back in to the passageway, and there was Alex facing me.

'Bobbie, I've something to ask you.'

'The answer's yes,' I said.

She laughed. 'How do you know what I wanted to ask?'

I looked at her steadily. 'Because I feel exactly the same.'

'I can, then?'

'You can.'

And I took her by the hand and led her into my bedroom.

*

It's the softness of Bobbie's body that takes Alex by surprise. Familiar only with the hard, unyielding flatness of men, she finds the roundness and smoothness of the breasts, the gentle curve of the buttocks, the soft suggestion of hips, delightful. As they lie curled together, their bodies touching at last, she finds the courage to tell Bobbie all that she couldn't say earlier. She hears Bobbie say, 'You haven't been out of my thoughts for a moment, but I hardly dared hope...' and she thinks, 'This is meant to be. I'm safe. I'm home. I've arrived.' Later, Bobbie says, 'Tell me all about yourself. Everything there is to tell.' And she does. Things she's told no-one else. About her parents. University. Matt. Maggie. Even about Miss Kettle. Bobbie lies on one elbow, and listens, looking down at her, and when the words finally stop, she kisses Alex gently on the mouth and traces the side of her face with her finger. Alex stirs, her mouth searches for Bobbie's, and their kisses become bolder, exploratory, questioning, surprised and surprising. Later still – perhaps they dozed, though neither wanted to; it would be such a waste – Alex says, 'I'll have to go home tomorrow. There's work I must do. Will you come with me?' And Bobbie smiles and says, 'Today, you mean today. It's tomorrow already. Yes, I'll come.' And they lie together in perfect content- ment, made for each other, like spoons in a drawer.

*

Late on Monday evening, Alex rang me at home. We'd spent Sunday together in Hampstead, but I'd caught a late tube back to Clapham. Now as soon as she spoke I could sense her excitement.

'I'm going away at the end of the week – it's all been arranged in a rush. As run-up to the Three Choirs Festival, I'm off to Gloucester to chat to all sorts of people – choral directors and landladies and Cathedral staff – to see how it's all put together. I was thinking – I don't suppose you could come as well? Would Dr G. let you?'

'Gloucester?' I must have sounded doubtful, but in fact I was hatching a plan.

'I know.' Alex was instantly apologetic. 'Hardly glamorous, is it? Not like Rome or Verona. I'd quite understand if you didn't . . .'

'No, no.' She'd got it all wrong. 'Of course I can come. Dr G.'s not an out and out Tartar – she does let us take the odd holiday. I was just wondering whether we could combine it with a visit to Terry and Jo. It's ages since I saw them, and I'd love you all to meet.'

'I've met them already, remember? And eaten their splendid tea.'

'They do even more splendid breakfasts and dinners.'

'You certainly know how to tempt a girl.'

'And I want them to know. About us. How important you are to me.'

'Do you? I'm flattered. In that case . . .'

'When are you due in Gloucester?'

'Friday, from eleven o'clock onwards.'

'Could we go down to Hendre on Wednesday?'

'It would have to be after the programme. And I'm often not up to much then.'

'I could drive, if that's what you mean. You could surely cope with being a passenger. And at that time of day there won't be much traffic. If I meet you at the BBC . . .'

And so it was arranged. I'd take two days off work, we'd spend the whole of Thursday at Hendre, and go together to Gloucester on Friday. I rang Terry, who declared herself delighted, and insisted on postponing the evening meal until we arrived, though I warned her we'd be very late. Avoiding all mention of gender, I said I'd be bringing a friend called Alex, and left her to draw what conclusion she liked.

It was half past ten when we pulled in to Hendre's yard. So quiet was the Escort engine that nobody heard our arrival. There was only the tiniest sliver of moon, but the shape of the dovecote was unmistakeable, outlined against the remnants of daylight still lingering far to the west. Alex had dozed in the car, but was now quite sprightly again.

'Let's go in there first,' she whispered. 'Last time I came, I was stuck with some very dull people. I'd like to see it again with you, in the dark.'

We crossed the yard in silence. The minute I entered the building, I was struck by its air of ineffable peace. Tonight it had lost the taint of betrayal that lay at its heart like a scar. Forgetting the way they'd been plundered and pillaged, I gazed at the tiers of nest holes and saw them only as emblems of love and fidelity, home to innumerable unions and witness to life-long devotion. Could I ever explain to Alex all that the dovecote meant to me? I was about to try when I felt her hand on my shoulder. I turned towards her and she pulled me close.

'Shh,' she whispered. 'Don't say anything. There simply aren't the words. It's a magical place and I love it here. But most of all I love you. You do know that, don't you? I've never felt this way with anyone before. I had no idea it was possible to feel such love. You won't ever leave me, will you? I don't know what I'd do without you.'

I could just see her face in the darkness. 'I promise I'll never leave you.'

'Is that by any chance a troth you are plighting?'

'Consider it plighted,' I said.

We went back to the car and removed our luggage with sufficient noise to bring Terry to the door. If she was surprised at the sight of Alex, she gave no sign. They introduced themselves to each other without any help from me.

'We were wondering when to give you up for lost,' Terry said, hugging me warmly. 'If you're anything like us, you both must be famished. Come through to the kitchen. Jo's made a spectacular quiche.'

'You've fed me once before,' Alex told Terry as we followed her indoors, 'though I don't suppose you remember. Four of us came to see the dovecote and you gave us tea, one August afternoon.'

'It was the week we got Arthur and Guinevere,' I added, knowing Terry would recollect the difficult pair of geese.

'Yes – yes, I do remember. A chatterbox wife, if I'm not mistaken, and a rather distinguished man. Well, well – Jo, we have standards to maintain! Our food has already been sampled.'

Over the meal we talked of London and concerts and books, and I tried to give an intelligent summary of our latest work at the Institute. We got through several bottles of home-made wine, and when we'd finished eating I handed over the new novels I'd brought for Terry and Jo.

'There's the new Penelope Lively, *The Road to Lichfield*, and Paul Scott's *Staying On*.' I explained, while Terry delved into the bag. 'I remember how much you enjoyed the *Raj Quartet*, and this is another of the same. You haven't got it from the library, have you?'

'No such luck. I never remember when they're open these days. No matter when I go, they're always shut. Nothing's the same now we're Powys, not Radnorshire. I suspect they've changed their opening hours, just to fool me. Oh, Bobbie, the new Iris Murdoch as well! I'll be the envy of all my friends.'

This was a standing joke with Terry. She and Jo had no friends, at least no-one with whom they could share the delights of Iris Murdoch. I used to wonder how they managed with no-one but each other to talk to; only now was I beginning to understand how it is possible to find everything one needs in a single person.

To Alex she said, 'Bobbie thinks that we love her on account of her wit, intelligence and natural charm, but actually it's because she brings us books from time to time.'

'It's the same with me,' responded Alex. 'I like to keep her close by me in case the car ever has a wheel that needs changing.' And she described to Terry and Jo my skills as a car mechanic.

When we left the kitchen table to sit by the inglenook with our coffees, Alex produced a bottle of Chivas Regal. Jo had seemed thoughtful all evening, but once the drinks were poured and Alex had proposed a toast to 'the Guardians of the Dovecote', she suddenly snapped her fingers and said, 'I've got it!'

'Got what?' Terry was clearly as puzzled as the rest of us.

Jo directed her words to Alex. 'I've been asking myself why your voice is so very familiar. It wasn't until you pronounced the toast just now that I realised. It's all the more shaming, as I'm one of your greatest fans. Every Wednesday without fail – including this evening. Isn't that right?'

The penny must have dropped for Terry too by now. 'Glued to the wireless she is. We both are. We have to be, otherwise our brains would atrophy and die from lack of use. Why didn't you tell us, Bobbie? We could have got out our phonograph and sharpened a few needles.'

'I wanted you to meet Alex as Alex, not as someone famous,' I said.

'Then I'm glad we didn't know. But we should really be toasting you.' She raised her glass. 'To *Schneider's Showcase*.'

'*Schneider's Showcase*,' Jo and I slurred back in unison.

Later, as I was unpacking, Terry came and sat on my bed. She motioned me to sit next to her.

'I'm afraid Jo owes me rather a lot of money.'

I didn't believe this for a moment. 'How can that be?'

'Gambling, Bobbie, gambling.' She shook her head in mock disapproval. 'She bet me a sizeable sum that Alex was a man.'

'But you knew better?'

'Yes, I did. Of course there was Roger...'

'My salad days,' I said, embarrassed by the memory.

'But I guessed Alex was quite a different kettle of fish, as you gave me so little to go on. Silence is often a sign that something's important.'

'I thought you might have a suspicion, and really didn't know how to tell you. It was all too...'

'Not 'too rash, too unadvised, too sudden' I hope. We all know what happens in cases like that.'

'No, no – though it has all been rather quick. It was simply too…overwhelming. There are times when I hardly believe it myself, and as for explaining to somebody else…'

'You don't have to, my sweet. I remember it all too well. It was just the same for Jo and me. And anyway, it's written all over you. Both of you.'

'Is it?' This was exactly what I wanted to hear.

'Oh yes – as plain as a pikestaff. It's there in the way you look at each other, the way you walk together. I could tell the moment you crossed the yard from the car. It's as though you've known each other all your lives.'

'It's been barely twelve days,' I said, 'but it feels like much longer.'

' Of course it does.' She patted my arm. 'I've often thought we should measure time by depth and not length in certain circumstances, and this sounds like one of them. I want you to know that you have my blessing – and Jo's too, of course. But a word from the wise. We can take it for granted that Alex adores you and would never want to cause you pain…'

'I know she wouldn't.' I had no idea where this was leading.

'But it might not always be easy for you.'

'Not easy? What do you mean?'

'I mean that when Jo and I fell in love, all those moons ago, we decided to bid the world farewell and move here, where no-one would bother us or care about how we lived. But Alex is very much *in* the world. She's well known. Famous, you might say, in certain circles.'

I decided to spill the rest of the beans. 'And she's married, too, in a way – though the husband's not around. Matthew Allardyce, the composer. He's been working in Australia for years and years and isn't likely to come back now. There's a daughter as well, five years younger than me, but she's already left home.'

'Allardyce? Allardyce? No – the name rings no bells. But a husband *and* a daughter – that might be a lot for you both to cope with. What I was going to say is that people can be hurtful, cruel and thoughtless. People who knew her before she met you. Who may not understand what's happened. Or like it very much.'

'That may have been true in the past, but not now, surely? And not in London?'

'There's darkness in people whenever and wherever they live, my poppet. Ignorance, prejudice, fear. And the greatest of these is fear. I know you like to think that everyone in London's enlightened and liberal, and maybe you're right. But there may come a point where you have to...make choices. I want you to know that if you ever, either of you, need to get away for a while, you'd be more than welcome to come here. You know that, don't you? This is your home, Bobbie, and you'd be safe here. Both of you.'

I thought at the time she was probably exaggerating, imagining problems that didn't exist. But I thanked her and hugged her and told her she was the best aunt a girl could have.

'And now,' she said briskly, 'you'd better go and see Alex. She probably feels like Catherine Morland at Northanger Abbey, shut up in this gloomy old house. She'll be glad to see a friendly face. Look after her, Bobbie. She needs you just as much as you need her, and she doesn't have a foolish, fond old aunt on the premises.'

They'd put Alex in the guest room at the front of the house, and when I crept in she was looking out through the open window, over the yard and the dovecote. She turned when she heard me come in. 'I was just about to let down my hair, so you could climb up it. Or build a balcony. I couldn't decide which.'

'The door was a great deal easier,' I said. 'Anyway, it would take years for your hair to reach the ground. I couldn't wait that long.'

'Nor could I,' she said, shutting the window. 'I've waited long enough as it is.'

She took off her bathrobe and got into bed.

'I didn't bring any nightclothes,' I said as I undressed and got in beside her.

'Nor did I, as it happens.'

'What about the hotel? Won't we need some there?'

'If you insist, we can buy some in Gloucester. Though I've no intention of wearing them.'

'I've been talking to Terry. She gave us her blessing and said I should come to you. Of course I'd have come anyway.'

'I was certain you would. What else did she tell you to do?'

'This,' I said, as I kissed her.

On our previous night together, kisses were all we'd exchanged. Fierce or tender, ardent or playful, gentle or passionate, we used them in place of language: they said what we didn't, and that, at the time, was enough. Tonight they were just a beginning. Any lingering doubt as to how to proceed now vanished entirely; we followed the best of all guides, and let our own desires teach us the other's needs. We learnt how to touch from the touch of the other, to caress from the way we were being caressed. As urgency grew in us both, we knew what would bring satisfaction, for our longings were one and the same. Fused in each other, giving and receiving in equal measure, we lost all sense of self. And when the frenzy was over, we lay tangled in absolute stillness, no longer quite sure who we were.

'Now you possess me totally,' Alex breathed in my ear, and fell asleep in my arms.

*

Alex wakes in the morning and knows she's never felt so complete. So utterly, indubitably happy. She wonders how she'll get through the day, wanting only Bobbie again beside her. Some time in the night – perhaps it was early morning – she'd been aware of Bobbie leaving her. Not to upset the aunt, she said. Though heavens, Alex doubts if she's fooled. Now, in the morning sunshine, she looks out at the yard, past the dovecote. Jo is milking the goat. And there, coming out of an outbuilding, a basket of eggs in her hand, is Bobbie. She looks up and waves. Alex showers, dresses and all but runs downstairs, ashamed that she's missed so much already.

It's a day that she'll never forget. Terry and Jo go off in the car – it's not often they have the chance – saying they won't be back until after the evening milking, and if Bobbie's forgotten all she once knew about goats, there's a book about it somewhere. Alex forages for a picnic and Bobbie takes her through fields and down footpaths to secret places she's known for years. They eat by the side of a brook and later lie on the bank in the late June sunshine. They're alone and in love; never before has Alex known such exquisite and perfect contentment. They watch swallows and martins swoop down to the water for flies. They talk and they laugh or they're silent together. And Alex wants this day never to end, this new peace never to leave her.

Back at the house, she watches Bobbie milk the goats and chivvy the geese and the ducks. Together they find eggs, pick lettuce, chop herbs. They make salads of surpassing splendour, open a bottle of wine and wait for Terry and Jo. Alex holds Bobbie in her arms and says, 'I'd like to live with you here.' And Bobbie replies, 'One day, who knows – maybe we will.' For anything and everything is possible in their life together, the future they both will share.

Too soon, it seems, they hear the car, and Terry and Jo, laughing like schoolgirls, return to take charge of their homestead.

9

Andante cantabile – poco a poco un più agitato

We drove back along the M4 on Sunday evening, sated from four nights of love.

As our distance from London lessened, so I became more subdued. Our time together was over, and the thought of returning to everyday life filled me with something like panic. Alex by contrast seemed keen to be home: she was speeding along in the middle lane, humming snatches of Stainer's *Crucifixion* which the choir had sung that morning in Gloucester Cathedral.

After a while she noticed my silence. 'What's the matter, darling? I'm not driving too fast for you, am I?' As though to challenge me further, she pulled out to overtake a minibus and stayed in the outside lane. The speedometer nosed up to seventy. 'This is the best way to drive – very fast, at night, with my lover beside me. It's not often I'm able to do it. But we'll tootle along in the inside lane if you'd rather.'

'No,' I said. 'It's not that. I was just thinking you won't have much time for me, once we get back.'

'Of course I will, darling – all the time in the world!'

'Only when you're not busy at work, or not away interviewing someone, or not off at a festival somewhere. And that could be barely at all.'

'The summer's always hectic – there's so much going on. But the programme stops in November. I'll have oodles of free time then. And it's only *work*, after all. It's not as though I'm planning a string of affairs...'

'But your work's a full-time commitment, and it really matters, not only to you but to all those people like Terry and Jo who tune in week after week. In terms of importance, you've got to admit I'm a pretty poor second.'

She took a hand off the steering wheel to fondle my knee. 'My work doesn't make me feel like you make me feel. You're streets ahead of the competition there.'

'But you'd never give it up, would you?'

'Give it up?' I could tell the idea had never occurred to her. 'Why should I?'

'Well, people do – give things up, I mean, for other people.'

'I'm not sure how my giving it up would make things better. In fact, I'd been thinking quite the opposite – what fun it would be if we could work together, if you worked for the programme too.'

This wasn't the solution I was looking for. 'I couldn't do that,' I said.

'Why not?' To my great relief she was driving more cautiously now.

'Oh darling,' I put my arm on the back of her seat and let my fingers play with her hair, 'I couldn't work *for* you. I love you, for heaven's sake. I know things about you that no-one else knows. I couldn't be one of your team. And it would still be your programme. Anyway, it would mean leaving the Institute.'

'Aha!' She sounded almost triumphant. 'And you don't want to do that? Not even to work with me?'

I knew I had caught myself out. I'd suggested Alex give up something of genuine significance, but couldn't bring myself to consider giving up a job I'd never taken completely seriously.

'Leave the Institute? It wouldn't be easy. I've been a main member of the team there for almost six years. Only five other people in the world know as much about it as I do.'

'But what does your research actually achieve in the long run? I know you won't mind if I say it seems a little...' – she searched for a word – '*reductionist* to me.'

Did I mind? Not at all; I was glad she'd thought of nothing worse to call it. 'You're right – it is reductionist. That's *exactly* what it is. Because when we've broken things down into little pieces and tried to understand those, we can put them back together again and maybe understand the original big thing a whole lot better.'

'As a general rule, I'd agree – with machines perhaps, or even the human body. But it's *music* we're talking about here. How does your work help me to understand or enjoy a piece of music more fully?'

'Sing me something. Sing me the opening of Mozart's Clarinet Concerto.'

She sang the opening eight bars.

'Now, doesn't it strike you as utterly amazing that you can *do* that? Think of all the processes it involves. How does your brain store and remember that tune so that you can reproduce it so exactly?'

'I haven't the faintest idea! I'm just glad that it does.'

I laughed. 'I don't know either. Not yet. But if anyone's going to find out, it'll be us, at the Institute. Little by little we're getting there. Give us, say, ten more years and we'll be able to start to answer that question.'

Alex gave me a puzzled look. 'But it's not a question I ever ask.'

'That's like saying you don't ever ask how electricity works, but are happy to use the light switch.'

She nodded. 'Yes – that's me to a T.'

'But someone, somewhere, *does* know how electricity works. That's the difference. What we're doing is at the very cutting edge of knowledge. Nobody knows the things we are trying to find out. Nobody in the whole wide world.'

Now it was Alex's turn to laugh. 'OK, you've convinced me. At least, I'm convinced that you believe you're doing work of the utmost importance.'

'How strange!' I said, surprised by how strongly I felt. 'I think I might even believe it myself.'

All too soon we were back in Clapham: the moment I'd

dreaded had come. Alex pulled up outside my flat, switched off the engine, turned to face me and took one of my hands in both of hers.

'No, my love, I won't come in. If I did, I know I wouldn't have the strength to leave. And if I stay tonight, then why not tomorrow as well, and the night after that? You see how it is. But there is an obvious solution.'

'What's that?' I asked, though I guessed what was coming.

'Will you live with me, Bobbie? I don't mean now, or even next month, but sometime soon. Can I think of us living together in the abstract, and know it will certainly happen?'

'Yes,' I said firmly. 'You can count on it absolutely. I don't mean to settle for anything less.'

It is pointless, I know, at this distance in time to harbour regrets: behaviour is part of the moment, and only with hindsight seems wayward or blind. But I often wish we'd acted on impulse, silenced our scruples, been recklessly, hastily bold. Instead we were culpably cautious. How Atropos and her hideous sisters must have gloated to see us thus wasting the thread of our lives, wilfully postponing opportunities for happiness until they became remarkable by their very rarity.

As it was, we compromised: we delayed making plans till November, when *Schneider's Showcase* would take its winter break. Alex remained firmly attached to her Hampstead flat, not only through familiarity and custom, but also because she saw it as Maggie's home. Certainly her bedroom was still as she'd left it, and the flat contained an awful lot of her belongings: this was one of the reasons I felt uncomfortable there. Even more off-putting was the fact that Alex had lived there with Matt. That I found hard to accept. If he one day returned, I felt he could step straight back into his former life and find his way unerringly from bathroom to fridge to grand piano, as though nothing had changed in his absence. Of my Clapham basement I remained impossibly fond, partly because it and its contents were the first things I'd properly owned, but also because it was where Alex and I had met and spent our first night together. As such, it was sacred territory. Had I lived anywhere else, I fully believed we might never have met, let alone become lovers.

Thus we muddled along with things as they were. I spent the odd weekday evening and night at Hampstead when Alex was free, and from there travelled to work just as easily as from Clapham. The Northern Line became our lifeline, the umbilical cord that linked us together. I grew to love the names of the stations going north from Euston – Mornington Crescent, Camden Town, Chalk Farm, Belsize Park – for each one brought me closer to Alex. Even on the return journey my fondness remained, because of their role the previous day. But 'home' to me meant my flat in Clapham, the place I returned to regularly. Alex sometimes spent part of the weekend with me there, but only when she had no work commitments, which gave it a holidayish feel, quite unconnected with everyday life.

Then, at the end of August, this makeshift arrangement was brought to an end. It was a Friday, and I'd gone straight to Hampstead from the Institute, because Alex had tickets that evening for Mozart's *Requiem* at the Royal Festival Hall. She'd been working at home all afternoon, and was more than usually glad to see me.

'You won't believe what a miserable time I've been having! Nobody's in when I ring them, which means I've not been able to do any of the things I'd planned. I've wasted the whole afternoon. And I've missed you, darling, missed you dreadfully. I always do when I work at home.'

'Poor you,' I said, for she did indeed seem despondent. 'I'd have been here much sooner, but we all had to get out at Camden Town. It was ages till the next train arrived, and then it was packed to the hilt. Perhaps we should set out early for the concert, in case the same thing happens on the way to Waterloo. If we leave in about half an hour, we should be all right.'

This was a further disappointment. 'And there was I, hoping we might go to bed.'

'We still might, if I came back here afterwards.'

'That's what we'll do, then.' She cheered up instantly. 'There's some wine in the fridge – we can save it for later. Meanwhile, I'll heat up some soup and some rolls, and you, my sweet, can pour us a drink and tell me about your day.'

It had been rather a good day as days at the Institute went, for Dr G. had read us a paper she had presented at a Neurological Sciences conference earlier in the week. It was really a shameless begging letter, asking for partnership funding with a neurology department. But to have our modest pieces of research described in such grandiose terms, and to hear Dr G.'s vision of what we might achieve if only we could continue our work alongside real clinicians, had rendered us all quite light-headed.

'I'll say this for your Dr G.,' was Alex's comment as she cleared away our dishes. 'She certainly understands psychology.'

'She should do,' I laughed. 'It's what she's qualified in.'

'And she puts it to very good use, sending you off on a Friday afternoon with a song in your heart and a spring in your step. None of you will be looking for another job *this* weekend, that's for sure. Shhh...' She stopped dead in her tracks. 'What on earth is that noise?'

We both listened. There was a dragging sound, as of furniture being moved, which seemed to be coming from the hall.

'Could it be burglars?' I whispered.

'Burglars don't usually have keys,' Alex whispered back. She motioned me to stay where I was and went to investigate, shutting the kitchen door behind her. I could make out the sound of voices, and picked out tones of shock and surprise, though none of fear or alarm. Not burglars then, I decided.

After several minutes, Alex returned. 'It's Maggie,' she whispered quickly, looking at me with appalled horror. 'She's come home!' And in a louder voice, 'Maggie, do come and meet Dr Sinclair. We're just on our way to the South Bank, I'm afraid. Bobbie, this is my daughter, Maggie.'

I'd seen photographs, of course, but they were all of a younger, confident, smiling Maggie, and hadn't in any way prepared me for the disdainful young woman who made her reluctant entry into the kitchen. Alex, I knew, was decidedly ill at ease with her daughter since she'd left home and started her job in advertising, and now, confronted by her aggressive stance, her cool, appraising look and her tight, almost shrewish features, I could understand why. Maggie terrified me instantly.

'How nice to meet you,' I said with what shreds of charm I could muster. 'Did you come by tube? I was wondering if they're running normally now.'

Maggie gave me a withering smile, or perhaps it was a sneer. 'No way could I get all my things on a train. I came here by taxi.'

'Right,' I said. 'Yes. No. Of course not. I'll just – er – the bathroom, and then perhaps...?'

In less than two minutes she'd reduced me to total imbecility.

In the hall I just managed to avoid tripping over Maggie's luggage, a soft, sprawling collection of black canvas which lay there like a geological intrusion. In the bathroom I thought of our plans for the evening, of Alex's look of horror, and how another bottle of wine was destined to spend an excessively long time in the fridge.

*

They walk to Hampstead tube station in silence, arm in arm. Their footsteps ring on the pavement in unison, equally paced. At the station entrance, Alex turns to Bobbie and says, 'It's no good, I couldn't concentrate now. Would you mind if we didn't go?' Bobbie nods, and asks for one single and one return ticket to Clapham Common. In the lift, Alex wants to weep on Bobbie's shoulder, to kneel and beg forgiveness, but does none of these things. Instead, she takes Bobbie's hand and holds it tightly. She keeps hold of it all through their noisy, racketing journey, and only lets go when the train lurches to a halt at their station. As they walk along the platform, Bobbie says, 'That's the loneliest sound in the world, an underground train leaving an empty platform at night.' Alex feels a renewed impulse to burst into tears. From the station, they take the path across the top of the Common, hand in hand. Before they reach North Side, Bobbie stops, draws Alex to her, kisses her and says, 'Yours isn't the only fridge with wine in it.' And they do not speak again until they are lying together in Bobbie's bed, a glass of wine each beside them.

'If only she'd told me – let me know she was coming. You'd think it would have occurred to her that it might be inconvenient, not to say bloody awkward.'

'At least we weren't in bed. We very well might have been.'

'That's what I mean. Bloody awkward!'

They each take a mouthful of wine.

'How long is she planning to stay? Did she say?'

'For ever, it seems. She's given up the flat in Earl's Court. She must have planned that, told people, organised things. A new tenant's moving in tomorrow, apparently. How could she do all that and not say a word to *me*?'

'What about Nick?'

'I didn't dare ask. She'll tell me when she's ready. Or not, as the case may be.'

'What about us?'

'I don't know, Bobbie. I don't know.'

'There's here and now.'

'Yes, there is. How fortunate. I've wanted you all day.'

'Me too.'

'More than Dr G. and her vision of the glorious future?'

'More – so very much more.'

Later, Bobbie says, 'She doesn't know about us, does she?'

'Who?'

'Maggie.'

'No, she doesn't.'

'But you'll tell her?'

'Yes, I'll tell her.'

'When?'

'I don't know. Soon. Sometime soon.'

They both take another mouthful of wine.

Alex asks, 'How did she strike you?'

'Well – you know – I only saw her for a moment. And it must have been hard for her. To be coming back home in the first place, and then to find me there.'

'She used to be such a sweet little girl. So loving and open.'

'Yes, I know. You showed me the photos.'

'And now – I don't even know if I like her any more. Isn't that awful? If she was someone else's daughter, I probably wouldn't like her at all.'

'But she isn't.'

'No, she isn't.' Alex sighs. 'She's mine.'

'And Matt's, don't forget. She's not only yours. There are bits of Matt in her, too.'

'But he buggered off when she was four. It's simply not fair, is it? I stick around and do my best with her, and she still ends up being more like him than like me.'

'You can put it all down to her genes. It isn't her fault.'

'No, it isn't her fault. It's mine, for getting involved with Matt in the first place. Whichever way you look at it, I'm the one to blame.'

'Nonsense! I bet you were a fantastic mother.'

'I tried to be – I really did.'

'Well, there you are. I don't think my mother even tried. And life's not like an exam. It's not the result that matters, but how much effort you put in.'

Alex looks at Bobbie miserably. 'Even if you fail?'

'*Especially* if you fail. If you succeed all the time, where's the merit in that? When you try and know that you're failing, but refuse to stop trying – that's what's really hard. And that's what you did. She came home to you, didn't she? The idea of living with their mother just wouldn't appeal to most twenty-five year olds.'

'Twenty-two year olds. She's twenty-two.'

'There you are then – she's still very young. She'll grow out of it. Look at me. At twenty-two I was still sleeping with men. See how quickly people can change.'

'I'm glad you did.'

'What – change? So am I.'

'No – sleep with men, I mean. If you hadn't, you wouldn't be sure this was what you wanted.'

'And I *am* sure. Dead sure.'

'I know. So am I.'

'And I've never wanted babies – not for a moment. Do you think that's odd?'

'No, not odd. Just sensible.'

Alex leaves in time to catch the last train north. Bobbie goes with her to the station. Alex says again that she'll tell Maggie soon. She won't give Bobbie up. Nothing will make her do that. She promises to ring when she's done it, asks Bobbie not to ring her at home. It might interrupt the very act of telling. Alex stands on the escalator and concentrates on the descent, not daring to think of the future.

Next morning she wakes with a sense of oppression. She cannot immediately think why. Then she remembers. For the first time in four years, her daughter's in the room next door. She hunts through drawers for nightwear, fails to find any, and makes do with a dressing gown firmly tied. Surely Maggie won't be shocked at the sight of maternal flesh? She creeps about the flat, not wishing to wake Maggie so early. The longer she can postpone their encounter, the better. She makes coffee and toast, collects the post and settles down to read it at the kitchen table.

Three hours later, she's showered, dressed and has done a useful couple of hours' work at her desk. Still no sound from Maggie. She decides to take her a breakfast tray – there's a limit to how much creeping about she's prepared to do. She makes more toast and coffee, then remembers Maggie drinks only herbal tea. Luckily there's an unopened box at the back of the cupboard. She's uncertain how long the sachet should steep, and fills a jug with boiling water. Feeling like a maid in a French farce, she takes the tray to her daughter's bedroom. Knocks. Knocks again. No answer. Surely Maggie can't still be asleep – it's nearly one o'clock? Stealthily, noiselessly, she turns the handle and opens the door.

There's no sign of Maggie. Her luggage is there, but no

Maggie. Foolishly, Alex looks everywhere, even calls her name. Then she sees that her bed's not been slept in. So certain was she that Maggie would be there, she can't understand what's happened. She's about to return to the kitchen when she catches sight of a note on the bedside table. What a damn silly place to leave a note. Doesn't the girl have any common sense? 'Going to Bev's. Back around lunchtime tomorrow.' She doesn't know whether to laugh or cry. The irony of it. Bobbie could have been there all along.

It's mid-afternoon when Maggie finally appears. She refuses Alex's offers of food and drink, says she's 'shagged' – a word Alex abhors – and retires to her room. At seven she's ensconced in the bathroom preparing to go out, a process which takes an inordinate time. When she emerges, she says she must dash, she's meeting some friends up in town. Tells Alex not to wait up. That may be a joke, though Alex can't be certain. At five in the morning, the unfamiliar sound of her heels on the hall floor – surely she used not to clomp? – wakes Alex, who is slow to go back to sleep. For the next two hours she lies wakeful, rehearsing exactly what she'll say to Maggie – she, who interviews total strangers with consummate ease – and only drops off again as daylight is breaking. She wakes feeling thick headed and snappish. After breakfast, she leaves a note clearly visible on the kitchen table and takes a walk on the Heath. She finds a seat with a view over London and tries to work out where Clapham might be. She wonders what Bobbie is doing and has a fierce impulse to go and see her. But she knows she can't: she promised to speak to Maggie first. With a palpable sense of girding her loins, she returns home to do just that. When she finds that her note has been replaced by one from Maggie ('Gone out – back later'), she finally weeps with frustration, sobbing, head down on the kitchen table.

It's Tuesday evening before mother and daughter are both in the flat together. After a good day at work, Alex feels buoyant and ready for anything. Even for a talk with Maggie.

'Would you like something to eat? I was thinking we could have omelettes.'

'Are the eggs free range?'

Alex hasn't a clue. She picked them up in Sainsbury's in a hurry. 'Of course,' she says with assumed confidence.

'OK then. Is there any cheese?'

'Of course.' This time she's certain. She gets a piece of Double Gloucester out of the fridge and puts it on the table in front of Maggie, along with the grater. 'Perhaps you could grate some while I do the eggs?'

Maggie holds the piece of cheese gingerly with the tips of her fingers and passes it a few times across the grater. Then she swears. 'Damn. I've broken a nail. I'll just go and fix it.'

Alex completes the grating in her absence. Maggie returns to find a tomato salad, warmed crusty rolls and two cheese omelettes on the table.

Alex starts off bravely. 'Well, this is nice. I can't remember when we last ate together at home. Is the omelette alright for you?'

'It's fine.'

'How's work these days?'

'Oh, you know. Just work.'

'Any big campaigns at the moment?'

'We're working on one for dog food. It's rather good, actually.'

'I'm sure it is.'

Maggie looks at her mother quickly. 'And before you ask, no, I'm not pregnant.'

'I never thought you were.' It's true, it hadn't occurred to her. She knows Maggie's far too much in control to let such folly befall her. But she mustn't be sidetracked. 'I suppose things just didn't work out with Nick?'

'Nick?'

'It was Nick who was sharing the flat with you, wasn't it?'

'Yeah, it was. But he was just a friend. He left in June, actually.'

'Ah – I see. I didn't know'

'That's why I decided to come back home. It got far too expensive without him. The rent and everything.'

'I suppose it must have.' Barely two months, thinks Alex. She can't have tried very hard.

'You've no idea, Mum, how much it all costs these days.'

'Well, I think I probably do know . . .'

'I thought I could save some money by coming home. But if you don't want me here . . .'

'Of course I want you, sweetheart.' Was Maggie always so defensive? 'It's just that things have changed a little here. For me.'

Now that the moment's arrived, Alex feels terribly nervous. She collects up their plates and takes them to the dishwasher, but does not put them inside. Instead, she speaks carefully to the draining board. 'You see, I've fallen in love.'

She waits. The world does not shatter. Perhaps it'll be all right.

'Great.' Maggie speaks dully. 'Who with?'

'You met, actually. On Friday.'

Now Alex can't bear not to look. She needs to see how her daughter's responding.

'On Friday?'

'Yes. When you came home. She was here.'

'That doctor person? You're in love with *her*?'

Is there disgust in the pronoun, or is it just incredulity? Alex goes back to the table, sits down by Maggie and turns to look at her.

'I know it must seem strange. It was strange for me, too. I can't really explain it. But it happened – it's real, it won't change. We both fell in love – and she means the world to me,' Alex finishes quietly.

'Christ, Mother!'

'I wish I could make you understand. How she makes me feel. I've never been so happy as when I'm with her. She's funny and kind and clever and makes me laugh. We like the same things. She brings me such joy, Maggie. No-one's ever understood me the way she does.'

'Do you screw each other?' She spits out the question.

'Oh Maggie! What an awful word to use.'

144

'Well – do you?' The look she gives is hostile, disapproving.

'We sleep together sometimes, yes.'

'Christ, Mother! You mean here, in this flat?'

'Sometimes here, sometimes not. It depends. Does it matter?'

'Christ, Mother!'

'Will you stop saying 'Christ, Mother'!'

'What else do you want me to say?' She's almost shouting now. 'I come home after four years and find my mother's turned into a dyke!'

'I haven't turned into anything. I'm exactly the same, Maggie. I haven't changed. It's just that for the first time in my life I know what it is to be in love, to feel completely happy with someone.'

'And what about Dad? You are still married to him, aren't you?'

'Your father's done his fair share of screwing, as you call it, for the last fifteen years – all over Australia. He was planning to marry one of his students not so long ago, if you remember.'

'But he didn't.'

'As it happens, he didn't – but not out of loyalty to me. Only because she dumped him.'

Maggie stands up, scraping the chair legs on the kitchen floor. 'I don't want to hear any more.' At the kitchen door she turns and shouts back at Alex, ' I'm not surprised Dad stays away if he's any idea what sort of woman he married!'

'He doesn't ... That's not ... Maggie! Where are you going?'

'D'you imagine I want to stay here? I'll be out. At Bev's. At least her family's *normal*.'

And Alex lets her go, hears her clomp to her room and out of the flat, slamming the door behind her. She sits there knowing she's failed, that she's made things worse, not better. A few minutes pass. She pours herself a large whisky, drinks it quickly, then goes to pick up the telephone on her desk in the drawing room. She's about to dial when she changes her mind. Instead, she finds her car keys, gathers together what she needs for work the next day, and sets off to drive to Clapham.

She doesn't leave a note.

10

Molto movimento

During September, things started to change at the Institute. Dr G.'s address to the Neurological Sciences conference failed to produce any response whatsoever, and she had nowhere else to turn for extra funding. Without it, we could continue our work for three more months; after that, the team would be disbanded. Dr G. told us this in her usual bluff, forthright manner, but it was clear she was desperately upset. She spent more and more time shut away in her office, muttering to herself and typing up reports which no-one was ever now likely to read. I felt increasingly sorry for her. The whole idea of research into musical memory had been hers, and to it she'd devoted every moment of the last eight years. I could only imagine how she must feel, knowing it was doomed to extinction.

One Wednesday, when Alex was busy as usual, I hung around after work with the idea of asking Dr G. out for a drink. I did not imagine that a drink with me would in any way cheer her up, but I did think it would give her a chance to unburden herself of some of her terrible sadness. She gave my suggestion brief consideration.

'You are a kind and thoughtful girl, Bobbie, and I know you mean well. But I do not drink, at least not in English pubs.' I was about to leave when she pulled open the bottom drawer of her desk. 'However, if you wish to share this bottle of wine with me, I should be very pleased.'

To my astonishment she produced two glasses and a

corkscrew, with which she deftly removed the cork from a bottle of *Trockenbeerenauslese*.

'I was saving this to celebrate our new fundings but, since that will not be necessary, we may as well enjoy it now. You might find it a little sweet, but I like to imagine that the nectar of the gods tasted something like this.'

She was probably right. It was the sweetest wine I'd ever drunk, but I knew enough to recognise its quality, and to know that sharing it was an act of great generosity.

'I shall miss our work,' I said, when I'd savoured a couple of mouthfuls.

'I know you will. At first, perhaps, you were not quite – fully committed, shall I say? But lately I believe you have come to understand its value. Am I right?'

'You are,' I said. 'Recently I had to justify it to a friend, and was quite surprised how passionately I felt about it.'

'Ah – but you are the passionate type! With you, I think, there is no lukewarm or tepid, only hot and cold.'

She laughed, and I laughed with her, though whether at the flaws in my personality or simply as a result of the wine, I did not know.

'What will you do?' I asked.

'I shall offer myself to the universities, or, if they do not want me, go back to my old work. I used to be a music therapist, you know. It will not be such a change. But what about you, little Bobbie?' Her use of the epithet, I'd come to realise, was in no sense derogatory, but simply a sign of affection.

'I don't know.' In fact I hadn't thought about it at all. 'I suppose I shall have to apply for some other research post somewhere.'

'If I did return to music therapy, I would interest myself for using music in a clinical setting. And if I did that, I should probably need a research assistant. Perhaps not full time, but for three days a week. Is that something you would consider?'

'Would that be in Hampstead?'

She looked at me with her head on one side like a curious bird. 'Would that make a difference?'

'It might. I'm not sure at the moment.' Now that Hampstead was home to Maggie as well as Alex, it was no longer the blissful location it once had been.

'Well, think about it, little Bobbie. I have trained you well, and you know my methods. You can even read my writing. We could work well together, I think. And it would make me feel less guilty.'

'Guilty?' Her use of the word surprised me.

'I failed to keep our researches going, and for that I shall feel always guilty.'

'But you shouldn't,' I protested. 'You've been such an inspiration to us all. And everyone knows you've done all you possibly could. It's not your fault there's no money around at the moment. Feel angry if you like, but not guilty.'

'You are right, little Bobbie, as always. I shall try to remember – not guilty but angry. It's not as if our team is specially picked out for misfortune. Many, many other projects are having to close, not just ours. A friend of mine who is investigating musical response in the very deaf people, she, too, finds herself without funds. A group recording tribal chants in Africa has had their work stopped before time, and a team who investigates the use of music to help the schizophrenics has also had its funding very reduced. And these are only some of the projects that I know of, based here in London. Across the country there are many, many more. Gone, gone, all gone.'

As though to suit the action to her words, Dr G. divided the last of the wine neatly between our two glasses. She had clearly reached that maudlin stage of intoxication which heralds violent action in some and inertia in others. Feeling ill equipped to deal with either, I suggested we ring for two taxis. Her roll-call of dead and dying research projects seemed likely to last all evening, and I could only offer the banal consolation that there was nothing we could do about it.

'Perhaps not. But perhaps . . . if only someone could tell the world what is happening,' Dr G. said as we made our way to the front of the building to await our transport. 'We should not sit by and let it happen, wagging our heads and saying how wrong it is. But who could voice our anger? Who could do that for us?'

'I think I might know someone who could,' I said, as I helped her into a taxi, and on my own journey home I sketched out a plan for a radical edition of *Schneider's Showcase*, which I described to Alex on the phone the following day.

She took some persuading. It would be a departure from her usual format, and she didn't want to risk alienating her regular listeners, who were used to informative programmes with a strong musical content. She was afraid that such a programme as I was suggesting might turn into an explosive, even acrimonious, discussion about funding for the arts. She did, however, agree to put the idea to Crispian. He mulled it over, told her he thought it had considerable potential, and was unwise enough to use the word 'anodyne' in reference to Alex's existing style of work. This roused her to fury, and when furious she was capable of anything, even of agreeing to chair a live discussion on the regrettable demise of arcane aspects of musical research. Through Dr G., who was touchingly awed to be rung up by the famous Alexandra Schneider, she obtained details of other fundless researchers. Once contacted, nothing could stop them from taking part in her programme too, and Alex found herself caught up in their combined tide of anger. A date was fixed for the second Wednesday in November, and Alex even persuaded a government spokesman and someone from the Department of Education and Science to take part as well. The closer the day of the broadcast drew, the more cheerful Dr G. became, and I felt I ought to remind her that the programme was only a way of making her voice heard. It could promise nothing further.

'I know, little Bobbie, I know. But to think that Alexandra Schneider had heard of our work and wishes it to continue! That will show to the world how important it is! You were right when you told me that anger is more powerful than guilt, and I will be so very, very angry when I speak about our work on the wireless.'

I may have been successful in assuaging Dr G. of her guilt, but was busily amassing plenty of my own. Having omitted to mention *how* Alex knew of our work, let alone that she regarded our analytical approach with deep suspicion, I was finding it impossible to tell Dr G. the whole truth now.

On the evening of the broadcast I went with Dr G. to the BBC but did not enter the building. Though I wanted to be near by, I couldn't bear to witness the event at close quarters, and had arranged with Alex that I would listen on her car radio. I settled down in the passenger seat, and, as the programme began and Alex introduced her guests and her topic, I felt a great sense of satisfaction. Countless people across the country would now hear Dr G.'s anger, and all because she'd been kind enough to share a bottle of wine with me.

The programme was a triumph. Each of the contributors spoke engagingly about their threatened research, and to the representatives of the Establishment Alex was charming and provocative by turns, lulling them into believing she might actually share their point of view before lunging for the jugular with a crisply phrased question. She guided the discussion unobtrusively but doggedly, and covered a range of issues concerning anomalies of funding, the future of musical research and the commitment of the educational world to the promotion of music and the arts. All in all it was a *tour de force*, and at its end I gave a solitary round of applause, which I tried to imagine was being echoed throughout the homes of Britain.

It was a while before Alex appeared. Dr G., at her side, looked rather as the King of the Visigoths must have looked while defeating the mighty Attila and his band of Huns, Vandals and Ostrogoths on the Catalaunian Plain. Alex looked simply exhausted. She opened the passenger door.

'Darling, will you drive? I don't think I've got the strength. Helga's coming back with us for a bite to eat. I warned Maggie that I might be bringing one or two people home, and she decided to spend the night elsewhere, so we won't be disturbed.'

Dr G. got in the back seat and I drove us to Hampstead. Once at the flat, Alex poured us each a glass of wine and sank into an armchair in the drawing room. I went to the kitchen to find us some food, and was met by a scene of unusual chaos. Dirty saucepans, dishes and bowls covered most of the available surfaces, and the sink was blocked with what looked like a mixture of pasta and tomato. Hanging over everything was the powerful smell of fried onion. Clearly Maggie had eaten before she'd gone out. I opened the window, loaded what dishes I could into the dishwasher and was in the act of clearing the sink when Dr G. – I could never think of her as Helga – came in.

'Alexandra asked me to tell you there's a quiche and plenty of salad in the fridge. But perhaps I should not be here at all? Perhaps I am the intruder?'

'Oh no!' I said. 'It's perfectly fine. I'm very glad you're here. Alex will be feeling better in a while. I expect you've gathered that we know each other quite well. Very well, in fact.'

I looked at her. She was smiling.

'I always thought it was possible for you to love a woman, Bobbie. Indeed, I sometimes hoped...but let us not speak of that now. Where is this quiche and this salad? We will have a nice meal, the three of us, and then I will leave you alone. Tomorrow I do not expect you at work before lunchtime. And thank you, Bobbie, for what you have done. I realise now that this evening's programme would not have happened without you.'

'You're wrong,' I said. 'It was you and that bottle of wine that made it happen.'

And with my hands still covered with grease from the sink, I gave Dr G. a hug.

*

Alex wakes with Bobbie beside her in her own flat. It's almost twelve weeks since they've spent the night there together. Alex whispers, 'I've missed you' to the sleeping Bobbie. 'I love you and I've missed you so very, very much.' Bobbie stirs, turns, and wraps her arm around Alex, who feels enfolded by love and protection. Bobbie murmurs, 'You were magnificent last night' and Alex, mistaking her meaning, says, 'So were you.' They lie together, half sleeping, half wakeful, as the sun rises on yet another London morning. From the distance come sounds of traffic and movement. They sense that around them the world is busily turning. But here, at the heart of things, is peace and contentment, the still point of the turning world. And neither wishes to break it.

Eventually they get up, shower together, dress, make breakfast and start the new day.

'I like your Dr G.,' says Alex, wiping splodges of tomato sauce off the kitchen floor. 'I saw these stains last night, but hadn't the energy to shift them. How does Maggie do it, do you suppose – spill things everywhere?'

'She must have been practising. It probably takes years. She's become really good at Not Clearing Up...'

'...and has mastered the art of Messing up a Bathroom...'

'...and is proficient in How To Block up the Sink.'

Alex groans. 'Oh God, was it that bad?'

'Worse, much worse. What can her flat in Earl's Court have been like?'

'I dread to think. Nick probably left when he couldn't wade through the debris any more.'

'So she came back here, to sabotage her mother's home.'

'Oh, Bobbie – what else can I do? I can't turn her out on the grounds of excessive untidiness. I'm hardly a paragon of domestic virtue myself. It's months since I dusted.'

'A patina of dust, evenly distributed, merely enhances a room, I always think. Whereas piles of dirty dishes and abandoned underwear tend to have the opposite effect.'

'Please don't be cross, darling.'

'I just hate to see you running round after her.'

'I don't run round that much.'

'You shouldn't have to run round at all. She's not a child, even if she sometimes behaves like one. She still doesn't mention me, I suppose?'

'No, never. If I so much as say your name, she walks out of the room, or puts the radio on, or covers her ears and says she's not listening.'

'Poor you.'

'Poor me.'

'Poor us. What shall we do?'

'We could always elope.'

'She'd probably find us...'

'...and bring me her washing...'

'...and a few dirty dishes...'

'...and her dreadful thumpy music...'

'...and Bev.'

'Oh God, no – not Bev! The washing and the dishes I could cope with, but definitely not Bev.'

'Let's not elope, then. Far too risky. There's always my flat.'

'Thank God for that! And the telephone.'

'I sometimes hate the telephone – it's so horribly distancing. You're there and you're not there at the same time. I love the sound of your voice, but it's you that I want – all of you – not just your voice. And there's always that awful moment when one of us has to put down the phone...'

'I know, my love. It's the same for me.'

'What about Christmas?'

'Christmas?'

'It's only six weeks away. I thought we might spend Christmas at Hendre together.'

'I'd love to, darling. But it's Maggie's first Christmas back home. I can't just waltz off and leave her. Think of the terrible mess she'd make...

'...the mountains of washing up – days of it...'

'...the burnt frying pans...'

'...ashtrays overflowing...'

'...and wine on the carpet.'

'The stains would never come out. You'd better stay here, then.'

'Can you bear it?'

'At Hendre alone? I don't know. I'll try. Can you?'

'With copious doses of whisky and wine I probably can.'

Bobbie catches sight of the kitchen clock. 'Look at the time. I've got to go.'

'I know.'

'I'm glad you like Dr G. So do I.'

'Give her my love.'

'Absolutely not. I want it all for myself.'

'You've got it all. But as there's so much, we could spare her a little, perhaps?'

'Do you think I should work with her – next year?'

'Is that what you'd like?'

'Yes, probably. Music has got to be better than pills, and that's what she wants to do – make people better through music. You wouldn't mind?'

'Why should I mind? And she knows about us, which helps. Now go, before she sacks you for unpunctuality. But kiss me first.'

And Bobbie willingly does as she's asked.

It's the first day of December. Outside it's cold and raining, but Alex is safely at home. *Schneider's Showcase* is off the air for two months. Last night was the end of the series. The next programme won't be until the eighth of February – a special edition for Ash Wednesday, Allegri and his *Miserere*. Alex can't think so far ahead, prefers to deal with the here and now. At the moment, she doubts if February will ever come. All the bits of time in between, all those weeks and days and hours and minutes, have to be navigated first. There's plenty to do, of course: programmes to plan, appointments to keep, letters to answer. She'll do it all; the time will pass. But the one thing she longs for, the one thing she wants – Bobbie's daily presence in her life – seems as far away as ever. And without it she knows she's not fully alive.

She works, makes phone calls, fills the day. By three o'clock it's so dismal and dark that she puts on the lights. She almost hates these long evenings. Maggie will come home from work, they'll eat together and talk about this and that. But never about what's on Alex's mind. No, never at all about that.

Tired of inactivity, she decides to make a stew, a *Boeuf à la Bourguignonne*. There are two rump steaks in the fridge, which she planned to have grilled. Now she cubes and flours them, fries them in oil, chops carrots, leeks and onions, prepares mushrooms and shallots. Just as she's browning the vegetables, the doorbell rings. A wild hope that it's Bobbie surges through her. She turns down the heat and all but runs to the door.

It's not Bobbie, of course.

'Drusilla! This is a surprise.' She tries to look pleased. 'I'm in the kitchen. Do come through.'

'I was just passing and saw your light was on. I thought it might be a good time to catch you.'

To catch her? Alex feels well and truly caught. 'Well, yes. I suppose it might be. I'm making a stew.'

Given the ingredients and pans that surround her, nothing could be more obvious. But Alex knows it's best to start with the obvious with Drusilla.

'A stew – golly, how clever! I haven't made a stew for years. Piers and I like our meat grilled. So tasty, you know, and so healthy.'

Alex ignores the implication that the meal she's embarked on will be neither of these things. 'It doesn't need all of this wine,' she says, sloshing cheap Burgundy on to the meat and vegetables. 'Would you care for a glass? Or some tea or coffee, perhaps?'

'A glass of wine – how deliciously wicked! Though the sun must be over the yardarm by now.'

Alex doubts if any local yardarm – whatever that might be – has caught a glimpse of the sun today, but doesn't feel up to pursuing it. Instead, she pours two glasses of wine and puts her stew in the oven.

'I really just popped in to invite you to dinner. I know it's short notice, but I wondered if you'd be free tomorrow evening, or Saturday?'

Alex tries to think of reasons why she might be unavailable

two nights in a row, but invention fails her. 'Tomorrow's no good, I'm afraid,' she lies.

'Saturday, then? That'll be super. Piers' youngest brother, Cyril, is coming tomorrow for the weekend, and I thought it would be lovely if you and he...'

Alex's heart sinks. Drusilla the Matchmaker ploughs artlessly on.

'He's not been divorced long, and I know he's simply dreading Christmas on his own. Of course we'll invite him to stay with us. And then I asked myself who do I know who needs some excitement in her life? And I thought of you, my dear. He's frightfully well off and still quite handsome – for his age.'

'It's very kind of you,' Alex says firmly, 'but I'm not looking for anyone just at the moment. I wouldn't want to come to dinner under false pretences. Perhaps there's someone else who...'

Now Drusilla turns to face her and adopts what Alex can only imagine she considers to be an 'understanding' look. She merely succeeds in looking pained and anguished.

'Alex, I simply can't go on pretending. We know all about it. Beverley's told us everything. And it may surprise you to know this, but I do understand, I really do.'

Alex can't believe her ears. Thank goodness for the wine. She drinks deeply. 'And what has Beverley told you, exactly?'

'About your, your – *thing* – with the young lady doctor. Maggie's been very upset about it apparently, which of course upset Beverley. That's when she told us. Knowing that we're such good friends, I think she thought I could help. That's why I've come.'

'I thought you'd come to invite me to dinner.' Alex hopes she doesn't sound as angry as she feels.

'Yes, of course, that as well. I thought if you met a nice, attractive new man, then all that other business might stop. Though I can well understand how it started. Believe me, when Beverley was in Africa, I missed having her around. We both did. And if I'd been on my own and someone young and desirable, male or female, had come along then, who knows what might have happened. Of course I've got Piers, so the situation didn't arise. But I can quite see how it might. And I've felt things for women too, I do know how it can be. I remember the Games Mistress at school – Miss Gates, her name was, Catherine Gates. I had quite a pash on her for – oh, months. I've never told anyone this before, but I used to kiss her face on the school photograph every night before going to sleep. Silly old me! So you see, I do understand. And I'm sure you'll get over it. Look at me – I did.'

Alex declines the invitation to look at Drusilla. Instead, she holds the now empty wine glass and speaks firmly to it.

'I am not at the mercy of some adolescent crush, Drusilla, and am certainly not looking for a substitute daughter. I am simply in love with a younger woman. Maggie is finding this hard to accept. That, in turn, makes things hard for me, and this is something we will have to sort out between us. But nothing at all – no well-meaning neighbour – and I'm prepared to believe you mean well – no petulant daughter – nothing, nothing in the world could change what I feel for Bobbie. Who is not a medical doctor, by the way, but a doctor of philosophy. She and I are in love, and plan to remain so. I'm sorry if this goes contrary to your matrimonial hopes for your brother-in-law, or to Maggie's idea of what feelings are proper and fitting for a mother to have. Perhaps it would be best if you were to leave now. I'd be grateful if you did not discuss my private life with your daughter, though I can see it must be a great temptation to do so. And thank you for your invitation to dinner, but I'm afraid I must decline.'

Drusilla is speechless. She sees herself out. Alex sits at the kitchen table until her anger has calmed a little. Then she opens another bottle of Burgundy. After the second glass, the control she exercised with Drusilla finally deserts her. She finds she is crying, and through her tears, her head in her hands, she repeats over and over, 'I love her and I need her and I miss her so much.' When the storm of weeping subsides, she takes the heaviest object she can find – a poker bought for protection against possible intruders – goes into the drawing room and deliberately smashes the china frog.

By the time Maggie comes in from work, Alex has removed all trace of her vandalism, and has applied fresh make-up. Anyone who knows her well would see that she's troubled. Maggie notices nothing. Shallots and mushrooms have been added to the stew and Alex now adds parsley. Dried parsley, admittedly, but better than nothing. It is a stew done to perfection, rich, noble and delicious. Alex serves them both and pours the wine.

Maggie gazes at her plate. 'I thought we were having steaks.'

'We are, only they're cooked another way. I thought a stew would be nice for a change on a miserable day like this. Do you like it?'

'It's OK. Is there garlic in it?'

'Only a little.'

'I don't like garlic.'

'That's why there's only a little. How was work today?'

'Oh, you know. Just work. A group's going skiing at Christmas. From the office. They were telling me about it. Sounds good.'

'You hated skiing when you went with the school.'

'No I didn't. I just hated the people I went with.'

Alex seizes the moment. 'Talking of your friends . . . ,'

'They weren't my friends. That's why I hated them.'

'Right – OK. *They* weren't, but Beverley Hope-Patterson is. I want to have a word with you about her.'

'About Bev? Why? You don't even like her.'

Alex is surprised that Maggie knows this, but ignores it anyway. 'Her mother came to see me today.'

'Mrs Hope-Patterson? So? She's a friend of yours, isn't she?'

'After our conversation this afternoon, I wouldn't count on it. She came because of what Beverley had told her. About me. Things you had told Beverley.'

'Yeah – well, Bev's my friend. I tell her everything. She understands.'

'And I don't? I wish you would talk to *me*, Maggie. And let me talk to you.'

'We're talking now, aren't we?'

'You know what I mean. It wasn't particularly pleasant to be informed by Beverley's mother that you were upset – so upset, apparently, that Beverley asked her mother to do something about it. What on earth did you say to her?'

'Just about you and that girl. She understands. She thinks it's disgusting, too.'

'Then she doesn't understand at all. Not remotely. And neither do you.' She pauses for a moment to marshall her thoughts. 'Do you remember when I told you your father wanted to get married again? To one of his students – remember? He'd have been forty-two then, and she'd have been just twenty-one. Did you find that in any way disgusting?'

'No. But it's not the same at all. He . . .'

Alex interrupts. 'Wait a minute. Let's take one thing at a time. The age difference doesn't bother you?'

'No. I just said so.'

'Right. If I told you that I, at forty-two, had fallen in love with a young man of twenty-seven, how would you feel about that?'

'It would be kind of weird, but it would be OK. Loads of women have toy boys these days. It just means they're still attractive. And you don't *look* forty-two.'

'Well I am, I'm afraid. This is what forty-two looks like. But thank you anyway – I'll take that as a compliment. So, the age gap isn't the problem?'

'I never said it was.'

'True. Right. Do you know any people who are gay? Have you met any?'

'There's Mo's brother – I think he might be. And Charles, at work.'

'And what's he like, this Charles? You see him every day. You must know him quite well.'

'He's OK. He's quite funny, actually – makes me laugh. And he did some photocopying for me once, when I couldn't get the machine to work.'

'I see – he's a nice, kind, funny, gay man.'

'Yeah, he is. But he's a man. It's not the same.'

'No, it seems it's *not* the same. It's OK to be gay if you're a man, but not if you're a woman. Is that what you're saying?'

'Well, it's not, is it? I mean, lesbians – everyone knows what they're like.'

'Do they? They can be like me, Maggie. I'm one.'

'But you're my mother!'

'Yes, I'm your mother. And I am lesbian. I didn't *know* I was. I haven't been deceiving you all the time – nothing like that. But when I fell in love, really in love, it was with a woman.'

'But you do things together. In bed. That's what's disgusting. Bev knows – she told me. It's sick. At least you don't do it *here* any more. That's one good thing.'

'Is that how you see it? I'm afraid that only makes it harder for me. You see, I'd like it if Bobbie and I lived together. If only you'd try to get to know Bobbie, I'm sure you'd begin to understand what I . . .'

'No way am I getting to know her! No way is she coming here! This is my home, not hers.'

'But if you lived somewhere else . . .'

'Why should I? So that *she* can move in here? No thank you.'

'Bobbie. Her name is Bobbie, or Robina, or even Dr Sinclair. But not 'she'.'

'I don't need to call her anything. I don't need to think about her. And I don't need this conversation.'

'But *I* need this conversation, Maggie. You have to understand – I want to live with Bobbie. Like you lived with Nick in Earl's Court.' She notices Maggie flinch. 'How is Nick, by the way? Do you still hear from him?'

'His parents bought him a flat. Down in Wimbledon. He lives with Mo now. I think they might be getting married.'

'I'm sorry. I expect you were quite fond of him, when you were living together.'

'Yeah – well. I don't want to talk about it.'

'Right. Fine. But if you *do* ever want to talk, you can always talk to me. You're my daughter, Maggie. Nothing can ever change that. It's just that, now you're grown up, you might try to think of me as a person, not just as your mother. I have good days and bad days, just like you. And I want the same things you want. To be loved, to be needed, to be happy. We're not so different, you and I.'

'At least I don't want to screw a woman.'

Oh Maggie!

*

I'd been dreading December at the Institute. Throughout November we managed to carry on much as usual, but as soon as December arrived and our days as a team were numbered, we all began to feel restless. Greg was the first to make a definite decision, and without too much difficulty obtained a post in the Music Department of Aberystwyth University. He was thrilled at the prospect, and was even considering learning Welsh. At about the same time, Kate announced she was getting married and that she and her new husband would soon be moving to Bath. Russell and Paula, tempted away neither by matrimonial nor career plans, spent melancholy days with me, devising charts and graphs which summarised our work so far and would be part of our final submission to the *Journal of Aural Studies*.

Much to our surprise, Dr G. remained remarkably sprightly throughout this mournful period. She would greet us cheerily each morning and then closet herself away – to work, we imagined, on one of her endless reports, though now she whistled as she did so, and occasionally broke into song. We assumed this was a therapeutic measure designed to disguise her grief, but had to revise this view when she burst out of her office one Tuesday morning and clapped her hands, a sign that she wished to address us on some important issue. The five of us gathered around her.

'I have just been speaking on the telephone to someone from the Klopstock-Gneiss Foundation. You have not heard of it perhaps? Neither had I until two weeks ago, when I received a letter from a listener to *Schneider's Showcase*. This letter told me about the Foundation, which exists solely to encourage and promote new soloists, and contained the suggestion that I make an application to them for funds, because the Foundation has much money and is not at all well known. Therefore I sent them informations about us. Of course they are interested in our work, for do not soloists have to commit to memory long, long pieces of music? Our work can surely help all soloists do this. That, at least, is the decision of the administrative board of the Klopstock-Gneiss Foundation, who have just now telephoned me to say,' – and here she was obliged to sit down – 'that they will fund our research for the next five years, and perhaps for longer if certain rather trivial conditions are met. I am very sorry that Kate and Greg will not be with us next year, but at least there will still be a team here at the Institute, working on musical memory. They do not succeed to kill us off! That is what I came out here to tell you.'

And she scuttled back to her office, where she hummed to herself for the rest of the day.

*

Alex staggers out of Hampstead tube station, her arms laden with bags. She's been Christmas shopping – only two days left – and though her heart isn't in it, she's doing her best. She spent the morning in Harrods Food Hall, buying things she thinks Maggie might like. Crystallized ginger, stuffed olives, Turkish delight, peaches in brandy, duck pâté, pecan nuts, sugared almonds, bitter chocolate. The truth is she doesn't know Maggie's tastes at all, but surely something in this miscellany must suit, something will be deemed 'OK'. From Harrods she took a taxi to Bond Street. And it was there, in the window of one of the exclusive jewellers she'd never normally enter, that she saw the perfect present for Bobbie: a silver art nouveau dove, very simple and graceful, on an exquisitely worked chain. She bought it immediately, and now wonders when she can give it to her. Bobbie's travelling down to Hendre today, will be there for at least a week. It will have to be a New Year's gift. She completely fails to find anything suitable for Maggie, and has bought her record tokens once again. Yet more thumpy music blasting through the flat. Musical taste, *pace* the sons of Johann Sebastian, is certainly not inherited, she reflects, as she steps out from the shelter of the station into the rain.

She's barely gone a few steps when she hears her name called. She looks round, and there, emerging rather unsteadily from a none-too-salubrious pub, is Piers Hope-Patterson. Dear God, can she never avoid that family? He catches up with her and to her surprise and annoyance takes her arm. He bends his head so close that she can smell the alcohol on his breath – a mixture of beer and the sharper, cleaner whiff of spirits.

'Alex – how lovely. I was just thinking about you, as it happens.'

'Really?' She puts not the slightest note of interest in her voice. 'What a coincidence.'

She tries to move away from him, but he holds her arm in a vice-like grip.

'You're looking extremely attractive today, if I may say so.'

Alex can hardly deny him permission to say what he's already uttered. She makes another attempt to shake the loathsome man from her arm.

'These bags – so awkward. If I could just...'

'Yes, you really are a most attractive woman, Alexandra. I've always thought so. It's a funny thing. I was talking to some friends in there – all chaps together, you know how it is – about the sort of entertainment we johnnies enjoy. Strictly for the men, you understand.' He taps his nose slyly. 'You wouldn't believe some of the things... Anyway, it set me thinking.'

Alex senses he's going to say something unspeakably ghastly. Despairing of ever shaking him off, she comes to a dead halt there on Hampstead High Street and rests her bags on the wet pavement. She turns to confront him. 'Exactly what were you thinking, Piers?'

His damp, fleshy lips contort themselves into a leer. 'About you and your girlfriend. I know some of the chaps would be interested. Me too, of course. Just to watch. Strictly hands off. What do you say?'

Alex says nothing. Instead, she takes a deep breath and slaps his face as hard as she can. She hopes she' s bruised him, or better still, drawn blood, but doesn't wait to find out. She picks up her shopping and hurries on to the flat.

As soon as she enters the building, she knows Maggie's home. Thumpy music hits her from two floors above. She wonders briefly why the neighbours don't complain. Maggie's at home. Of course, the office stopped work at lunchtime. That's the trouble when Christmas falls on a Sunday. It leaks backwards into Friday and spills forwards into Tuesday. An endless festival.

Inside, Maggie is rushing from the bathroom to her bedroom. There's a jumble of clothes on her bed. Surely it's all more untidy than usual? Then Alex sees the canvas holdall. She has to shout to make herself heard.

'What's going on? You look as though you're packing.'

'Hi, Mum. Yeah. I haven't got long.'

'Really? What's all the rush?' Alex turns down the volume and sits on the edge of the bed. For once, Maggie looks happy – radiant, almost.

'One of the girls from work. She was going skiing, yeah? Well, she's got chicken pox. Or measles or something. Anyway, she can't go. So I'm going instead. The plane's at six. They'll be picking me up in about ten minutes. Turns out I was the only one with a passport who was free to go.'

'Free to go?' Alex thinks she might have misheard. 'But I thought you were spending Christmas here.'

'Yeah, well. This should be fun. You didn't think I'd say no, did you? It's got to be better than Christmas in Hampstead.' She bundles jumpers, sweaters and socks into the black canvas bag, then rushes back to the bathroom.

'Whereabouts are you going?' Alex shouts.

'Austria, I think it is. Or maybe Switzerland. Not sure.'

'How long will you be away?' She's back now, stuffing Alex's soap in the bag.

'Ten days, I think. Or maybe twelve. Not sure.'

'Right. Well. I'm glad I caught you before you left.'

'I would have left a note. I wouldn't have just *gone*.' She is struggling with the zip now, forcing the edges of the straining canvas together. The doorbell rings. 'That'll be them.' She picks up her bag, grabs her anorak and is halfway out of the door before she remembers Alex. 'Bye, Mum. See you next year.'

And slamming the door behind her, she takes the stairs at a gallop.

Alex goes to the kitchen and looks down onto the street. Below her she sees Maggie getting into a car. She raises her hand in a wave, but the car drives off and her daughter doesn't look up. 'And Happy Christmas to you, too,' she says to the empty flat.

It doesn't take her long to decide. She gets out the *Yellow Pages*, sits at her desk, and rings round local estate agents until she gets an answer. On the fourth try she's lucky. There's someone still in the office, thanks to a tricky, prolonged completion. She asks if he can do a valuation of her flat either tonight or early tomorrow morning. Later than that is no use, she says. She'll take her business elsewhere. The address she gives him is clearly an inducement: he agrees to come within the next two hours. She tidies away the fallout from Maggie, runs the dishwasher, pours away the milk. Her assortment of goods from Harrods she leaves where they are, for she'll need them tomorrow when she drives down to Hendre. A phone call is all it will take. She'll spend Christmas with Bobbie after all.

For the first time in weeks she feels truly triumphant.

11

Tempo libero

Is it always the case, I wonder, that occasions which ought to bring joy can be clouded by how they occur? That Christmas I'd had to steel myself to go alone to Hendre and leave Alex with Maggie in London. Never before had boarding the train at Paddington required such heroic effort, such quantities of self-control. All through the journey I told myself that if Alex could only join me for Christmas, I'd be the happiest person alive. Yet when she drove through the drizzle into Hendre's yard on the morning of Christmas Eve, it wasn't happiness I felt, but a niggling, carping resentment.

Alex for her part was hugely elated. 'Two hours and fifty minutes,' she announced proudly as she got out of the car. 'Doesn't that count as a record? I flew every inch of the way. If I'd left it till later, heaven knows how long I'd have been. I'll need a hand with these bags – but first let me say hello properly.'

I stood stiffly as she embraced me.

'What's the matter, darling?' She stood back and looked at me closely, her eyes filled with alarm. 'Aren't you pleased that I'm here?'

'Of course I'm pleased. It's just that you said you weren't coming...'

Alex looked at me almost coquettishly. 'Isn't a girl allowed to change her mind?'

'But you didn't,' I burst out. 'You *didn't* change your mind. You're only here because of something Maggie decided. If she'd not gone off skiing, you wouldn't have come.'

'You're right – I wouldn't. I'd still be in Hampstead, wondering how to get through the dreary old days till I saw you again. You've got to agree this is better.'

'It's better, yes – but still not the best.'

'Oh, darling, please don't be sulky. You've no idea how much I've longed to see you. And I've brought all sorts of lovely things for Terry and Jo – look.' She gestured to the back seat of the car, piled high with carrier bags and parcels. 'Come on. Let's go in.'

'No,' I said stubbornly. 'I'm not going in. Not till we've talked about this.'

'Do we have to? I'm not very keen on discussing things out in the rain.'

'Then let's go in here,' I said, and pulled her towards the dovecote.

She followed me, grumbling. 'For heaven's sake, Bobbie, I come all this way to be with you, and you won't even let me sit down.'

'Feel free,' I said, and taking off my jumper, I folded it up and put it on one of the low projecting stones.

Alex duly perched on it. 'Right,' she said, 'Now that I'm sitting comfortably, it's time to begin. Fire away. Only don't be too long, or we'll freeze half to death.'

I squatted down beside her. 'It's not that I'm not glad to see you – let's get that straight. I am – honestly. It's what I wanted all along. And if only you'd come here with me yesterday – come because *you* wanted to – I wouldn't be feeling like this.'

'But you know why I planned on staying. For Maggie. I explained it all, darling. I thought you understood.'

'Oh, I *understand* well enough.' In spite of myself, I couldn't disguise my anger. 'It makes perfectly logical sense. But that doesn't mean I like it. And what about next time? And the time after that? Will it always depend on Maggie?'

Alex spoke very quietly. 'Can't you just be glad at the way it turned out – for my sake?'

'You haven't answered me,' I said. 'Will it always be this way? When it comes to the crunch, will Maggie always come first?'

Alex stayed calm. 'Not always, no.'

I knew I must be causing her pain, but simply couldn't help myself. The resentment and hurt that had built up inside me insisted on tumbling out. 'You refused to come here with me, for Maggie's sake. And then look how she treats you – going off like that at the very last minute. What a terrible way to behave!'

'I know – I agree. She behaved very badly. It's how she is – thoughtless and selfish, just like her father. I'd been planning to talk to her over Christmas – talk about you and me. I thought I could make her change her mind.'

'But she's not going to change, is she?' I was shouting now, almost enjoying making Alex feel wretched. 'You've had months and months to change her mind, and none of it's done any good. Why should she change her mind *now*? She still won't accept me, won't even mention my name.'

'I know, and it hurts me as much as I know it hurts you. Which is why I made the decision.'

I was puzzled. I'd done my best to ruin Alex's arrival and make her feel guilty, and here she was smiling at me, positively glowing.

'Since Maggie won't change – and I think you're right: she won't – I realised it was up to *me* to change things. I've decided to do it, darling – sell the Hampstead flat. A valuer looked at it yesterday. By the time Maggie gets back from Austria or Switzerland or wherever she is, it'll be on the market. There – what do you think of that?'

She'd taken the wind right out of my sails. 'But…will she agree?'

'She'll have to.' Alex smiled grimly. 'She'll have no alternative. I thought if I give her a reasonable sum – she's earning quite well, and could easily raise a mortgage – she could buy a flat of her own. That should appeal, don't you think? It's what the Scott-Ridleys seem to have done for Nick, to get him off their hands.'

'Oh, darling!' I was now on the brink of tears. 'I'm sorry. I'm so sorry. There I was, going on and on, and all the time...'

She stopped me mid-sentence. 'No – I'm glad you said what you did. Obviously I've made you unhappy. For that there's no excuse.'

'You've really decided to sell the flat?' I still couldn't quite believe it. 'Because Maggie went off skiing?'

'Because of the way that she did it – yes. It made me so very angry. And this seems a happy solution – for her, for me and for us. Don't say anything to the others just yet. I'll tell them over dinner. You might have grown used to the notion by then. And now, my love,' she said, standing up, 'fond though you are of this venerable structure, its seating arrangements are less than ideal. Can we please go somewhere a little more cosy? My bones aren't as young as they were.'

Christmas Eve at Hendre is always the same. Rain or shine, we spend an hour or so in the afternoon gathering all the evergreens we can muster, then on the dot of three o'clock switch on the radio and, to the accompaniment of the carol service from King's College Chapel, decorate the house and the tree. It's always a merry occasion – Terry opens one or two bottles of their E & B wine to help the proceedings along – but this year it felt merrier than ever. As we draped ivy and holly over every available surface, Alex and I sang along with the carols, heard the familiar readings and recalled the wonder of Christmas. With Alex's news fizzing away inside me, my light-headedness steadily grew, and I became less and less able to concentrate on what I was doing. Once the decoration was complete, Alex went upstairs to wrap and label her parcels, and when the telephone rang and Jo disappeared to answer it, Terry looked at me gravely and asked was I perfectly well.

'I'm fine,' I said, grinning at her. 'Just excessively happy. It's Alex's fault, for turning up out of the blue.'

'And there I was, thinking Jo and I were the reason. Seriously, Bobbie, everything *is* all right between you? When she first arrived, I had the impression...'

'That's all sorted out,' I said hurriedly. 'I was grumpy and foul for a bit, but not any more.'

'If that's truly the case, can I ask you to do me a favour? I've bought Jo two feather-legged bantams for Christmas, the sort that look like they're wearing trousers. She's been longing to dabble in fancy fowl for ages, and I got them quite cheap from a breeder. You and Alex wouldn't drive over and collect them for me, would you? They'll be boxed up and ready to go. All you have to do is to carry them home and put them in the end stable without Jo noticing. I plan to distract her by roping her in to pluck the goose for tomorrow. How about it? Are you two birds game?'

'Game, setted and matched.' I was glad to have something to do. 'If you jot down directions, I'll gather up Alex.'

'Bless you – that's a weight off my mind. A bantamweight, admittedly, but a weight nonetheless. And when you return, there's the fatted calf to be eaten. Actually,' she added conspiratorially, 'it's a couple of ducks we killed earlier, now amply defrosted and tucked in the oven. One duck is never sufficient, but we thought two should be plenty for four.'

'But you can't have known Alex would be here,' I objected.

'Oh, can't I?' she said with a wink.

Negotiating unlit Welsh lanes in the dark is never straight-forward, farm entrances having so much resemblance to turnings, and vice-versa. But we located the breeder of bantams with only a handful of errors, claimed Jo's present, and were driving back to Hendre when Alex told me about her encounter with Piers Hope-Patterson.

'It was hideous, Bobbie – I don't know when I've felt so revolted. The very idea's disgusting. Do men really imagine that couples like us would perform for them – in public?'

'Piers must, to consider it worthwhile asking. But how very degrading! Does he think we're some kind of freak show?'

Alex shuddered with horror. 'It's simply perverted. Just hope that I never set eyes on the horrible man again, nor on his maddening wife. The sooner I'm gone from Hampstead, the better. Who knows what that pair have been saying, or whom they've been saying it to?'

I couldn't help smiling. 'Now I know for a fact you're deeply upset. You never normally end a sentence with a preposition.'

'Don't I? What strange things you notice. Yes, it was very upsetting. I could kill Maggie, blabbing away to Bev like that and listening to her nonsense.'

'Better not,' I said. 'To be sent to prison just now would be most inconvenient.'

'No female judge would convict me,' she replied staunchly. 'She'd understand the extreme provocation. In fact, she might even commend me for my long-suffering, patient forbearance.'

We'd been gone for an hour, just long enough for the goose to be plucked and have other necessary pre-cooking operations performed on it. Over time I'd grown used to such procedures, but wasn't too sure about Alex. It seemed wisest not to remind her that all of our meat dishes at Hendre were recently sentient beings, mostly familiar by name.

I need not have worried. As soon as we sat down to dinner, Alex asked cheerfully, 'And whom are we eating this evening? Have we met on a previous occasion?'

'Two Aylesbury drakes,' Jo answered. 'Quite war-like where mating's concerned, but otherwise tame and endearing. They always appear to be smiling, poor things – right to the very last moment.'

'Too many males, that's the trouble,' Terry put in quickly.

'Isn't that always the case?' said Alex, looking pointedly at me.

'It's to do with the temperature in the incubator, apparently,' Terry continued. 'With perfect adjustment, we could probably hatch only females.'

'But then we'd have no-one to father the ducklings the following year,' added Jo. 'One active drake and a harem – that's what we aim for, and until it's achieved, there'll be plenty of meals like this one.'

'I'm very glad to hear it,' said Alex, her eyes sparkling. 'A regular cull of redundant males is a thoroughly excellent plan. I've been making some plans of my own, as it happens...'

And she told them she'd decided to sell the flat, and her intentions concerning Maggie. 'I'm rather hoping Bobbie will follow suit,' she concluded, taking my hand and holding it tight. 'What about it, darling? Can you do it too?'

'Yes, Bobbie,' said Terry, leaning back in her chair and beaming round the table. 'It's down to you now. Will this winkle you out of your Clapham dungeon? Or shall we find you there in years to come, like Mariana in the moated grange, gazing at your mossy flower pots?'

'I've begun to feel,' I said, beaming back at her, 'that the Clapham air is somewhat less delightful than once was thought.'

'Ah – 'tis not so sweet now as it was before? A timely discovery. Perhaps you could force yourself to live in a proper house with a proper garden, instead of some old servants' quarters with a miniscule patio attached.'

I had no idea Terry thought so little of my flat, but knowing now that I'd soon be selling it, I did not mind her criticism.

'We'll do our best,' said Alex, 'to find the very prop – properest of houses . . .'

'. . . and to live there most improperly,' I added, since all the emotion of the last few days seemed to be overwhelming Alex, affecting her powers of speech.

'You'll be anxious to get back to London and set it all in motion,' said Terry thoughtfully, 'though I hope you'll stay here till New Year. As I understand it, three valuations are generally recommended, and no doubt you want everything organised before your programme starts again. We've been missing it dreadfully, haven't we, Jo?'

'Ah, I'd completely forgotten!' Jo smacked her forehead with the heel of her hand. 'Someone rang for you earlier, Alex – from the BBC. About delivering some notes you'd requested.' She looked at her watch. 'In fact, I'd have thought he'd have got here by now.'

Alex was instantly alert. 'What notes? What are you talking about? I haven't requested anything, nothing at all. Who was it who rang, Jo?'

Jo was obviously startled by Alex's tone. 'I didn't think to ask his name – I'm sorry, it sounded so plausible. Though it did strike me that driving down here on Christmas Eve was beyond anyone's call of duty.'

'It sounds as though you've been had, my love,' said Terry. 'Now tell us exactly what happened, and who said what to whom.'

'He asked if Alex was here, and I said she was. Then he said he was bringing the notes she'd asked for, and could I give him precise directions. He gave the impression it was all very urgent.' Jo looked at us all in horror. 'Oh God, I've done something stupid, haven't I?'

'You weren't to know it wasn't genuine,' Terry said soothingly. 'And what's done cannot be undone, as Lady Macbeth once remarked. It's probably some kind of hoax. Who was this man? Did he identify himself at all?'

Jo thought for a moment. 'Only by his accent. There was something odd about the intonation – it went up at the end of a sentence.'

'South African, perhaps?' prompted Terry. 'Or Australian?'

Alex drew in her breath sharply. 'Oh Christ! Are you sure?'

'At first he called you Alexandra,' Jo continued, still remembering. 'But at the end he called you Al. 'No need to tell Al I'm coming' – that's what he said. Of course I intended to tell you, but what with having the goose to see to and everything, it went clean out of my head.'

All colour had drained from Alex's face. 'It's Matt – it's my husband – it must be. No-one else calls me Al.' She turned to me in a panic. 'I don't want to see him – I can't. Not here – not now. Not ever, but specially not here.'

Terry suddenly became very commanding. 'Don't worry. We'll protect you. You're safe here with us. Jo, what time did he ring?'

'Just as the carols were ending – about half past four.'

'And he said he was leaving immediately?'

'That's what I gathered, yes.'

I'd never seen Alex so frightened. 'I did the journey this

173

morning in under three hours. Oh God, he'll arrive any minute!'

'But you know the route, and he doesn't,' Terry pointed out sensibly. 'He's bound to get lost on the way. And the M4's probably dreadful – bumper to bumper, with any luck. You two find yourselves a quiet corner somewhere. We'll keep him at bay, won't we, Jo? We'll say that you've gone and we don't know where. Better still, we'll say you set off for the ferry to Ireland – put him right off the scent.' She seemed to be relishing this bit of unwonted excitement. 'It'll all be fine, don't you worry. Remember, we're terribly good at despatching unwanted males.'

We took ourselves upstairs, and sat side by side on the bed. Alex was physically shaking. 'I left this phone number at the office once, when we came down in June. He must have got hold of it somehow.'

'But why?' I asked. 'Assuming it really is him, why follow you here? And why now?'

Alex stared blankly ahead. 'Maggie,' she said. 'She's behind this. She must have told him, told him about us. She knows his address in Australia – he sometimes remembers her birthday – and what better way of stirring up trouble than to get her father involved? On *her* side, of course. I doubt if he's coming to wish us both well.'

I tried putting the pieces together, to see if they'd fit: the letter from Maggie, stiff with disapproval, perhaps even requesting assistance; the flight to London for Christmas to confront the errant wife, not knowing of Maggie's absence; the empty Hampstead flat; the discovery of Alex's likely whereabouts from the BBC; the fabrication of a plausible story; the impulsive drive to Wales. Yes, it made possible sense. It was not at all fanciful to suppose that Matt would soon be at Hendre. He could easily hire a car . . .

'Your car!' I said, as an obvious oversight hit me. 'If he sees it he'll know you're still here. The dealer's address is all over it.'

We clattered downstairs. Terry and Jo were clearing away all trace of our meal. When they realised the problem, they told us to hide the car in the barn.

'It's wide enough, if you're careful,' Terry advised. 'There may be a few bales of hay at the very far end, but they won't do any harm.'

I got the barn doors open and guided Alex in. Terry was right: there was just enough room. From the neighbouring cowshed came the grumbling murmur of hens alarmed by this strange disturbance. We shut up the barn and were crossing the yard when we heard an approaching car. 'Quick,' I said. 'In here.' And for the second time that day I pulled Alex into the dovecote.

We only just made it. The headlights swept over the empty yard as the car swung round in a curve and stopped in front of the porch. Then there was darkness; for a long moment the driver stayed where he was. Alex, pressed up against the back wall of the dovecote, could see nothing at all, nor could she be seen. I stood nearer the entrance, and when the car door eventually slammed, peeped cautiously out. All I could make out against the light from the windows was the figure of a man in an overcoat, his collar turned up. He did not have to knock – the door must have been open. There was a brief exchange, too low for me to hear, then the visitor entered the house.

I edged round towards Alex. 'Hold me, Bobbie,' she whispered. 'Hold me and don't let me go.'

She was shaking violently as I wrapped my arms around her. 'Don't worry,' I said, my mouth to her ear. 'He wasn't ranting or raving. It'll all be completely civilised. Terry won't let us down.'

'I'm sorry,' she whispered, 'for spoiling your Christmas. You'll be wishing I'd stayed up in London.'

There was only one answer to that. What I did *not* say was that if I was right about the sequence of events, by coming to Hendre she'd avoided a meeting alone with Matt at the flat.

At last the car left.

After a decent interval, Terry appeared with a torch. 'Come out, come out, wherever you are,' she trilled. 'We've seen off the Demon King.' She laughed when she saw us emerge from the dovecote. 'So that's where you've been hiding! A good thing too – you'd not have been safe in the house. But you both must be frozen – come and get yourselves warm. Jo's stoked up the fire, and is making hot toddies as penance.'

Indoors she told us that Matt had been perfectly pleasant, if a little too insistent about hunting for Alex all over the house. 'He claimed he merely wished to see his wife during the festive season and wanted it to be a surprise – hence the earlier folderol about those non-existent notes. We were utterly honest with him, weren't we, Jo? We agreed you'd been here, but had no idea where you'd gone. All true, as far as it went – which admittedly wasn't too far. He's in London, he said, for another week, then heading back to Oz. If you stay here until the New Year, as we very much hope you will, you'll be quite safe. He won't have the nerve to return.'

'What was he like?' asked Alex, now a great deal calmer. 'He tends to be drunk and disorderly, from what I've been able to gather.'

'He was wholly sober tonight, and very determined. I should think he's a man who likes his own way. He trailed from room to room in search of you. There was no point in resisting.' She looked at us very demurely. 'After all, to find two double bedrooms in use is hardly suspicious – not in a house occupied by two maiden ladies.'

In fact we drove back to London on New Year's Eve, but only as far as Clapham, for three indulgent days in my flat. All told, this was the longest unbroken stretch of time we'd spent in each other's company, and while my feelings for Maggie were far from warm, I was nonetheless grateful then, as I still am now, that she gave us those days together.

*

8pm on New Year's Day. Alex and Bobbie are going dancing. Bobbie drives. She finds a parking spot not too far away, and they walk through the Chelsea side-streets. They have some idea of what to expect – they've both seen *The Killing of Sister George*, after all – but are unprepared for the volume of sound. The noise hits them as soon as they open the door. Vetted and allowed to enter, they descend into Stygian gloom. It takes a

176

while for their eyes to adjust. Alex knows her ears never will. She can just make out a bar at one end, the crowd around it four or five deep. Against the walls there are benches – the place doesn't stretch to chairs. They make her think of the church hall in Manchester, of Brownie nights huddled comfortably round her Sixer. To their right is the dance floor, the aim of the evening. Pairs of women, mostly disguised as badly-dressed men, clasp one another with varying degrees of intensity. There isn't a skirt to be seen. Thank God Bobbie insisted she wore trousers. They're Jaeger, admittedly, but no-one will know in this murk. And everywhere the deafening sound of music, the pall of cigarette smoke and the high pitched shriek of a crowd of women, all trying to make themselves heard. It's like being at a reunion of Old Girls who all share Maggie's taste in music. Only hotter.

Bobbie joins the scrum for drinks. Alex perches on a few free inches of bench. Next to her, a woman with all the allure and feminine charm of a bulldozer yells something in her ear. She has no idea what she's trying to tell her. Surely it can't be a chat-up line? She's only just sat down. She's trying to convey that she hasn't a clue what she's saying, when light suddenly dawns. She looks up and sees a woman built like a female wrestler scowling down at her, a pint of beer in each beefy hand. Clearly she's taken the wrestler's place, though she doubts whether those massive buttocks will fit in so narrow a space. She surrenders her perch and waits for Bobbie, who has somehow made her way to the front of the crowd at the bar. How she's done it is a mystery. She's half the size of the women around her, and far too polite to have pushed.

While she's waiting, Alex observes a group of women standing near by. There are five or six of them, all drinking beer from pint glasses. She wonders whether they will pair off during the evening, and tries to judge from their looks and gestures where their amorous interests lie. All have aggressively short-cropped hair and, she cannot help noticing, uniformly heavy and unsupported breasts. All wear trousers and T-shirts. Alex regards the T-shirt as the least flattering

177

garment known to woman, shapeless, bulky and concealing. On these shapeless and bulky women, it's perhaps the wisest choice. Just too late, she realises her stares have been misinterpreted. One of the group catches her eye and is about to make a move in her direction. Alex immediately looks away and sees Bobbie coming towards her, holding two glasses aloft. Double whiskies by the look of them. Beer's not compulsory then. Thank heavens for that.

'We'll have to make these last,' she shouts into Bobbie's ear. 'You're not to leave me again. Absolutely anything might happen.'

Thanks largely to the whisky, Alex begins to enjoy herself. She also feels possessive and proprietorial. Bobbie's by far the most attractive person in the room, and is, she notes with pride, a source of considerable interest to a number of other women. When they dance, holding each other with more than necessary closeness, Alex shuts her eyes and concentrates on the feel of Bobbie's body moving rhythmically against hers. She thinks she might faint with sheer pleasure. Then Bobbie's voice in her ear whispers, 'You're by far the most attractive person here, do you know that?' She laughs and says, 'Nonsense, you are', and feels insanely, ridiculously happy. They sway together for some time. There's little space to move, and the couples around them are all but static too. This is clearly the healthier end of the room. Their swaying neighbours appear to be of normal size, unlike the beer-drinking hefties near the bar. Only their manner of dressing strikes Alex as strange – she's seen several collars and ties on the dance floor. She finds it perverse that women who love their own sex should want to pretend to be men. There's nothing remotely masculine about Bobbie – she'd hate it if there were. Nor, she devoutly hopes, is there a tinge of the male about her own person. It's their femininity they love about each other. Isn't that the point?

Together they leave the dance floor to visit the cloakroom. Neither dares risk being left for a moment alone. Unused to graffiti in the form of dialogue, Alex puzzles over the inscription in the cubicle: 'My mother made me a homosexual. If I gave her the wool would she make me one too?' When she finally understands, she's irritated by its assumptions. That all mothers knit is nonsense for a start. She's never knitted anything in her life, apart from a lopsided kettle holder at Junior school – enough to put anyone off. And the idea that mothers could in some way determine the sexual orientation of their offspring strikes her as ludicrous. Her own mother definitely did nothing of the kind. And it would be madness to think she's had an effect on Maggie's sexuality when she's spectacularly failed to influence any other aspect of her life. Homosexual love, she's perfectly sure, is a possibility for some from the moment of birth. But if fingers have to be pointed, why not point them at men, who are so bloody hopeless at knowing what women desire? She wishes she'd thought to bring writing equipment with her. Then she'd change 'mother' to 'father'. That would show them.

Bobbie's waiting for her. It's quieter here in the cloakroom, cooler and less badly lit. Despite its appeal, Alex suspects they'd be ill-advised to linger. They decide to risk the dance floor again, and hope that a couple, or preferably two, will soon tire of swaying and yield them their space. Before this happens, a stranger approaches Alex and asks her to dance. She's tall, blonde and not unattractive. Alex catches the hint of an accent – Swedish, perhaps, or Finnish? She glances at Bobbie, sees her smile and nod, and finds herself held in Scandinavian arms, an experience far from unpleasant. She decides to enjoy it. They do not move far from where they started, and she therefore hears clearly the astonishing words, 'You're looking sad, Bobbie. Would you not like to be dancing?'

*

It was a terrible shock to meet Janet Forbes again. I wouldn't have recognised her, had she not used the very same words I remembered from the Leavers' Party at school. While most girls tend to lose their teenage puppy fat, Janet Forbes appeared to have acquired substantially more, and was decidedly podgy round the face, a feature only emphasised by her desperately short hair. She was wearing denim dungarees, known at that date as 'bib and brace', and stood in front of me with her hands in her pockets, looking for all the world like a plumber's mate, or even a plumber.

Once again I let her lead me on to the dance floor, where we swayed together much as we had done ten years before. Alex seemed to be enjoying herself with her blonde partner, who was certainly an elegant and rhythmic mover, unlike Janet Forbes, who stumbled even more clumsily now than she had in the School Hall. The unexpected strangeness of the situation reduced me to banality.

'Do you come here often?' I shrieked at her.

'Quite often, since I've been in London,' she shouted back.

'Are you still a vet?'

'Yes. I work for the PDSA. In Rotherhithe. Where I live.'

Few places in London, I thought with gratitude, are more geographically distant from Clapham than Rotherhithe.

When the music came to an end, we all four shuffled to the edge of the room. In the sudden silence I introduced Janet Forbes to Alex. Alex introduced the blonde as Dagmar from Denmark, and suggested we leave and find somewhere quieter to talk. Having briefly appraised one another, the two strangers agreed, Janet Forbes somewhat more enthusiastically, I thought, than Dagmar. The music was starting up again as we climbed the stairs to the blissfully cool and silent street. We were heading for a near-by café when Dagmar suddenly invited us to her flat. She lived near Harrods, she said, and true enough she did, in a series of vast and magnificent first floor rooms expensively furnished in the Danish taste. I began to see Dagmar in quite a new light.

I don't know in what light Dagmar saw me, but she was definitely smitten with Alex. She attended to her every need, plying her with food and drink, bringing her extra cushions and even offering to massage her feet when she learnt they were aching after all the standing around and dancing at the Club.

'That'll be the fault of those heels,' said Janet Forbes, looking critically at the shoes Alex had slipped off in order to recline on the now over-cushioned Danish sofa. 'You're asking for backache when you're older, wearing heels like that. I never wear heeled shoes. You can't run in heels.'

We all found ourselves gazing at Janet Forbes' footwear, which reminded me of the boots worn by miners in the 1930s. I doubted if they made her very fleet of foot.

'I rarely have cause to run,' Alex said amiably. 'So, Janet, you were at school with Bobbie. Did you enjoy it? I know Bobbie did.'

Janet scowled. 'I hated the place. Those terrible dried-up old women telling us how to be lady-like. I never wanted to be a lady then and I certainly don't now.'

'You feel yourself to be a man trapped in the body of a woman, perhaps? In Denmark there are many such.'

Having satisfied all of Alex's real and imagined needs, Dagmar was now content to sit on the floor and rest her back against the sofa. She had only to stretch her right arm a little to be within fondling distance of Alex's legs. As though she realised this herself, Alex at that moment tucked her feet gracefully under her. Danger successfully averted.

'That's *exactly* how I feel.' Janet Forbes looked gratefully at Dagmar. 'I've always wanted to be a man. At school, I kept on falling in love with other girls. I don't know if you realised, Bobbie, but I was once in love with you.'

'It's easily done,' said Alex, winking at me across the room.

'But you didn't know me at all,' I protested, feeling I should point out I'd done nothing to encourage this unwanted passion in Janet Forbes. 'We never even spoke to each other.'

'I know. It didn't matter. I worshipped you anyway. Then at university it happened again. I started to go to bed with girls then. But it was never right.'

'You were never tempted to go to bed with men?' Alex, I could see, was beginning to be curious about the case of Janet Forbes. I suppose it made a change. She never talked to musicians about their sex lives.

'Never. Why should I? I always wanted to *be* the man. But with girls I always felt incomplete, as though...'

'But it can be done,' Dagmar interrupted knowingly. 'In Denmark there are many things to buy. You tie them on and...'

Alex and I exchanged horrified glances.

'I've tried all those,' said Janet Forbes dismissively, thankfully cutting her short. 'They're better than nothing. But one day I want to have surgery. I'm on hormones already. They're working quite well. Look.' She proudly patted the breastless bib of her dungarees. 'That's why I came to London,' she continued. 'It's easier here. In Ayr everyone treated me like a freak.'

'In Denmark it is quite common. Man to woman, woman to man, it happens every day. I have been to bed with both – not at the same time, you understand – though that also would be interesting. I want to do everything that is interesting. In Denmark, anything is possible. You would like it there, Janet, I think.'

Janet Forbes seemed cheered at the thought, and Alex and I took this as our cue to leave. Perhaps Dagmar, for all her experience, hadn't met anyone quite like Janet Forbes before. I gave them both my telephone number at the Institute, knowing how easily messages could be mislaid there, and Alex endured a prolonged parting embrace from Dagmar. As I said goodbye to Janet Forbes, I asked her the question I had been dying to ask since I'd learnt Dagmar's nationality.

'Do you still breed Great Danes? I heard you were very successful.' I thought she'd see the funny side, but I was wrong.

'No,' she said, 'I gave it up. I find any kind of eugenics distasteful these days.'

Surely nothing she'd ever done as a dog breeder could be as extreme as the surgery she was contemplating for herself?

Driving back to Clapham, I apologised to Alex for the way the evening had turned out. Bumping into Janet Forbes seemed to me the worst possible way to end a New Year celebration.

'There's no need to apologise, darling. I enjoyed myself, really I did – I wouldn't have missed it for the world. And seeing all those women at the Club made me think about what Maggie said. If *they're* what she pictures when she hears the word 'lesbian', she has every right to be alarmed. There were some very alarming women indeed.'

'I suppose they go there to meet their friends and to drink and dance together. But isn't there something slightly odd about a club which takes members on the basis of sexuality alone?'

Alex looked at me quizzically. 'Instead of a shared interest in gardening, or slimming, or flower arranging, you mean?'

'Yes – that's how heterosexual clubs work, after all. Like-minded people getting together in pursuit of a common activity.'

'Or because of a shared outlook,' Alex suggested.

'I suppose that might be partly the case with those women. For all we know, they all share a lesbian outlook – whatever that might involve.'

'And if they're looking for a new partner,' Alex said brightly, 'where better to go?'

I shuddered. 'I'd never go there alone – not in a thousand years.'

'Nor would I. But perhaps it served that purpose tonight for Janet and Dagmar.'

'Poor Janet Forbes,' I said, remembering her plans for the future. 'Do you think Dagmar will be kind to her?'

'For a little while. Then she'll move on. I agree – poor Janet Forbes. Even with all the hormones and the surgery, she'll never be truly a man. She'll be a woman who became a man. Will that be enough to compensate for all those missed years of boyhood?'

'I doubt it,' I said. 'But perhaps she'll be nicer than most men because of it.'

Alex laughed. 'That wouldn't exactly be difficult though, would it? Men always want to assert themselves and prove to the world that they're right. Do you know, in all the years I lived with Matt, he never once shouldered the blame. If anything ever went wrong, it was always my fault, never his. No wonder so many women have such a poor view of themselves. It comes from constantly being put in their place by all those infallible men'

'Talking of Matt...' I ventured.

'Yes, my love, I've decided. I'll definitely get a divorce. I should have done it years ago, but since I knew *I'd* never want to marry again, there didn't seem much point. I had hoped Matt would start the proceedings, but he obviously hasn't got round to it. It's not as though being married to me is limiting his activities in Australia.'

'With any luck he's already back there,' I said. 'It was Saturday when he told Terry he was only in England a week longer, and that was eight days ago.'

'Nine, strictly speaking,' said Alex, consulting her watch. 'Tomorrow's already arrived.'

'And there I was, still enjoying today.'

'There's no need to stop,' was Alex's reply. 'Let's stick with today for as long as we can.' She gave me her most seductive smile. 'Who knows what yet might occur?'

12

Violamente – expressivo con amabilitá

Alex is back in Hampstead. Cursing Maggie's vagueness – ten days of skiing, or twelve? – she installs herself there irreproachably on the third of January. It feels strange to be home. The flat seems bleak and unfriendly. It also seems quite the wrong size, too cramped after Hendre, too large after Bobbie's basement. Among the post, a letter from the estate agent, confirming the price and requesting further instructions. She puts it aside, and mindful of Terry's advice, makes a note to contact two other agents. She turns on the heating, unpacks, puts unwashed clothes in a pile. Wood-smoky and muddy from Hendre, they remind her too keenly of Bobbie. She stuffs them into the Bendix, then opens a bottle of claret. The interview with her daughter looms horribly large in her mind. A meal, she decides. I'll explain it all over a meal. She opens the fridge and is faced with the need to go shopping. Not locally. From now on the High Street and Heath Street are strictly off limits. She'll go where she's certain she won't meet Piers or Drusilla, into unknown, anonymous Cricklewood.

The round trip takes fully two hours. And there's nothing exciting to show for it, only dull and dispiriting fare. In future she thinks she might risk eccentric forays in Hampstead – first thing in the morning perhaps, or when the shops are about to shut. Or maybe she'll wear a disguise. Just as she puts her key in the lock, the telephone rings. Convinced that it's Bobbie – who else could it be? – she rushes to pick it up and speaks headlong into the mouthpiece.

'How clever of you! I've been out, but now I'm back in. I was hoping you'd ring. How was your morning?'

Silence. No answer.

'Hallo?' she says. 'Are you there?'

She continues to hold the phone. If she wills it enough, with all of her being, surely she'll hear Bobbie's voice? But there's only the silence. Sinister, comfortless silence. Then, as she listens, a definite click. A receiver is being replaced.

'Wrong number,' she says aloud, forcing back disappointment. Of course it couldn't be Bobbie, who's beavering away at the Institute. She puts away shopping, eats fruit, pours more wine. Never before has the flat seemed so joyless. If only she'd thought to bring something from Hendre – for the three of the Twelve Days still left. Ivy, berried holly, anything green and uplifting. The place would seem livelier then.

As always when restless, she plays the piano – two Schubert *Impromptus*, some Brahms *Intermezzi*. She thinks of her upstairs neighbour, the Viennese lady, and hopes she's been listening. In twenty-one years of living above and below one another, they've only ever met by accident on the stairs. This strikes her as sad, now that she knows she'll be leaving. She decides to pay her a seasonal visit, picks up a bottle – the wine rack has plenty to offer – and climbs to the floor above. Knocks. Knocks again. No answer. The Viennese lady is out. In fact the whole block has a desolate feel. Is everyone else still on holiday, and she the only one home?

At six she'll ring Bobbie, but that's still two hours away. One hundred and twenty long minutes. And with every second that passes, Maggie's arrival creeps closer. If not today, then tomorrow. Or worse, in the middle of the night. Whenever she deigns to appear – possibly suntanned, certainly 'shagged' from the journey – she'll doubtless expect an immediate meal. There's chicken, onions, carrots – these Cricklewood had in abundance. Bowing to the inevitable, Alex pours more wine, switches on Radio Three and sets about making a casserole.

As she dices up breast, she thinks of meals at Hendre, with their ruthless and bloody beginnings. Do Terry and Jo ever long for anonymous, supermarket meat? She knows they kill their own poultry, but surely must need help with a pig or a sheep? She admires their down-to-earth living, wholly approves in theory, just refuses to picture the details: the plucking and gutting, the piles of unusable bits, the feathers, the mess and the gore. Bobbie, of course, takes it all in her stride; Alex guesses she's bumped off a cockerel or two in her time. There must be a certain technique, she decides, a knowing, infallible touch. The instant she thinks of Bobbie's touch, she's swamped by a lurch of desire. The knife slips on the chopping board and she grips it tight, waits for the feeling to pass, waits to be in control again before chopping up onions and carrots.

When Maggie arrives, she tells herself, she must try to look pleased to see her. Tricky, but hardly impossible. She'll tell her she spent a few days with some friends on a farm. Not that Maggie will think to enquire – she's certain of that. But the greater her claim to a life of her own, the stronger the reason for selling the flat, for breaking the tie with Maggie. She can see this might be the sticking point, and needs ammunition to hand. She could even imply that she's promised to return the hospitality. An invasion of wellie-clad farming folk. Maggie would run a mile.

The casserole's simmering gently. Glass in hand, she goes back to her desk to deal with the post. She's half-way through checking her bank statement when the doorbell rings. Ten days of skiing, not twelve, she thinks irritably. And why can't she just use her key? Remembering her vow to look pleased, she adjusts her expression to one of maternal delight and opens the door.

'Hallo, Al.'

She barely recognises him. The thinness of cheek, the sharpness of jaw, the sunken and bloodshot eyes. Raddled's the word that springs to mind. Raddled by drink and debauchery.

'Matt – Good God! I wasn't expecting...' She tries to conquer the rising panic. 'I thought you were Maggie. She's due home any time now.'

'Then I might be lucky and see her as well. Can I come in?' He pushes past her into the hall. 'You won't believe how often I've thought of you, Al. Pictured you here in our flat.'

'*My* flat,' she corrects.

'It was our home though, wasn't it? I've always thought of this place as home. We had some good times here, didn't we, Al?'

'Not that I recall,' she says icily. 'Actually, I was just in the middle of something. What was it you wanted?'

'A drink would be good for a start.' He's in the kitchen before she can stop him.

'Tea? Coffee?' she offers lamely.

'Wine would be less trouble,' he says, pointing to the open bottle. 'I'll have a glass of that.' She passes him a wineglass, which he fills to the brim and drinks in one go, then refills. 'You always did have expensive tastes,' he says, looking at the label. 'That's a nice little Saint- Emilion. Pricey, too, I imagine.'

'I can afford it,' she says. She's regretting leaving her own glass of wine on her desk, but is loath to pour another. Not in front of Matt. Dignity must be maintained.

'Oh, I'm sure you can.' He looks her up and down. 'The famous Alexandra Schneider, with her famous bloody showcase. Successful, are you? Listened to by millions?'

'The programme is popular – yes.' There's a dangerous note in his voice that she recognises, the sign of approaching violence. She tries to step away from him, but his left hand shoots out, grabs her arm and pulls her towards him.

'And how would the millions like it if somebody told them the truth? Where would the famous Alexandra Schneider be then, eh? I could do it, Al. I could end your bloody career. You'd only have yourself to blame. You're committing professional suicide.'

'I don't know what you're talking about.' In spite of her fear, she speaks with deliberate calmness. 'You're hurting me, Matt. Please let go of my arm.'

He grips even tighter. 'Of course you know what I'm talking about. You and your dykey Welsh friends. Oh, they covered up for you very nicely, but I knew if I waited you'd come back here.' One-handed, he pours more wine, drinks it and pours another.

'No, Matt – please. Don't drink any more. You've had quite enough as it is.' She won't respond to his reference to Hendre, won't admit that she knows he was there. If only Maggie were here now, she thinks, he wouldn't be acting like this.

He gives her a furious glare. 'I'll drink as much as I bloody well like. You seem to forget I've some rights here. This is the marital home, and you are still married to me. You're my wife, Al, for God's sake. In your lesbian frolics you seem to have overlooked that.'

'*I've* overlooked it? As I recall, the last time we spoke you'd just been abandoned by one of your students, who wisely decided the child she was carrying wasn't yours – though I gather it very well could have been. Weren't *you* overlooking something then? You were even planning to marry her. You haven't behaved like my husband for years. Don't try to pretend that you have.'

Too late she realises she's said the wrong thing.

'We can easily remedy that,' he says, leering drunkenly. 'A proper shafting by a proper man, that's what you bloody well need, not some grubbing about with a girl half your age...'

To her horror his hand moves to the zip of his fly. With all the force she can muster, she swings her free hand and smacks the side of his face. It's a feeble effort, but the best she can do. 'Get out, Matt,' she says. 'Get out now, or I'll call the police.'

An idle threat, and he knows it. Suddenly both his hands are at her throat and she's propelled backwards. Her head bangs once, twice, three times against the kitchen wall. She's choking now, struggling for breath, her eyes watering. She does what she can to fend him off. With both hands pressed against his chest, she kicks out wildly, but fails to make contact. Then she jerks her knee in his groin, not as hard a she'd like, but enough to take him aback. The instant he slackens his grip, she twists sideways, away from him, out of the kitchen and in to the drawing room, but she's too slow shutting the door and he leans heavily against it, forcing it open. She lets it go and Matt stumbles in, with a look of wild fury she's never seen before. He's demented, she thinks. Drunk and demented. Completely out of control.

'You bitch,' he snarls, following her into the middle of the room. 'You filthy lesbian bitch. Maggie was right when she told me you'd changed. She hates you – do you know that? Hates how you're choosing to live. She thought I could talk some sense into you, make you see how disgusting you are, how revolting it is, what you're doing. And *I* don't care for it very much either – my wife cavorting all over the place like some pervert. It's obscene, that's what it is. The thought of it makes me puke.'

'Don't think of it, then. Put it out of your head.' She's shouting now, and moving towards her desk, her only plan to get close to the telephone. 'Go back to Australia. Write your unplayable music. Make love to your gullible students. Don't give me a single thought. Maggie and I will sort something out. You'd have heard from me soon, in any case. I intend to get a divorce, and there's nothing you can do about that.'

'Oh, isn't there?' He moves suddenly towards her, punches her hard on the mouth, so hard that she staggers and falls backwards against the sofa. Then, as she sinks to the ground, he kicks her twice in the stomach, shouts 'Get up, you bitch!', yanks her upright and shakes her violently. There's blood on her face. Her lip feels swollen and numb and must be bleeding. Her stomach is tender, she can still feel the force of the grip of his fingers around her neck. She has no resistance to offer. When the shaking stops, she puts out a hand to feel for the arm of the sofa, and sits on it gingerly, eyes down, refusing to look at him.

He's spotted the wine on her desk and drinks it. He's in front of her now. She can sense his anger, knows that he hasn't yet got what he came for, but still won't look at him.

'Al...Al, say that it's been a mistake, that you'll give her up, this girlfriend of yours. I'll go away and leave you alone. Just say it, Al – for Maggie's sake, if not for mine. Promise you'll give her up.'

'Never,' she says quietly. 'Never. I'll never do that.'

He grabs her hair, pulls her head upwards. 'Look at me, damn you. Look at me and say that it's over. Just say it, can't you? It was fun while it lasted, but now you accept that it's wrong.'

She makes one final effort. 'It isn't wrong. Not for me. It's completely and utterly right. I love her, Matt – not that you'd understand that. I love her and...'

A sudden smarting as he slaps her face, one side then the other, over and over. Her only escape is to drop to the floor, away from his stinging palms. But not from his feet. The toe of his shoe finds a breast, and stabs into it rhythmically, repeatedly. She tries to move but is trapped by the sofa, tries to lift herself up, but her hands slip on the carpet, failing to find any purchase. She twists away from him slightly, and feels an explosion of pain as the shoe, missing its usual target, encounters bone instead. She wants to scream, to cry out in agony, but can't get sufficient breath. All she can manage are useless, shallow gasps. She lies there, silent.

Someone is sobbing. She hears her name again and again. 'Al...Oh God, Oh Christ, Al...Al...' A door slams. Then nothing.

Not daring to hope that he's gone, she doesn't move for several minutes, then starts to take stock. She experiments first with breathing. As long as she limits the intake of breath, there's almost no pain to speak of. Next she investigates arms and legs. All working, she finds, only tender and bruised. When she pulls herself up, slowly, in stages, it hurts in places she can't precisely identify, but so far as she knows, nothing broken, no permanent damage. The prospect that offers most comfort is the thought of talking to Bobbie, but that's impossible. She won't be home from the Institute – it isn't yet half past five. Instead she pours some brandy – always effective in cases of shock, though she has to sip sideways, because of the cut on her lip. She runs a bath, sinks into it gratefully, and lets the soothing waters do their work.

Wrapped in a towel in front of the mirror, she's examining her face – cheeks puffy and reddened, the cut on her lip not as bad as she'd feared – when the doorbell rings. She's not going to answer – if it's Matt, he can bloody well stay there; if it's Maggie, she'll unearth her key – when she hears a voice through the letterbox.

'Alex – Alex – are you in there? It's me. Is everything all right?'

*

All day at the Institute I'd been anxious. Only after Alex dropped me in Gordon Square, and I watched her drive off towards Hampstead, did it dawn on me how very literally we'd taken Terry's assurance that Matt would by now have left London. Part of me longed to believe it, but part of me nagged with worry. By any standards, his recent behaviour had been impulsive, extreme, unpredictable. If he turned up at Alex's flat, there was no telling what he might do.

As soon as I entered the building, I was caught up by Dr G. She'd just received a letter from the Klopstock-Gneiss Foundation (who hailed, not as I'd hoped from somewhere in Central Europe, but from an office in Swindon), requesting a detailed account of the work on which we planned to spend their money.

'And listen what they say,' said Dr G., reading from the dread communication. "A reply at your earliest convenience will ensure that projected levels of funding can be maintained.' Our earliest convenience – that is now. If we do not answer quickly, our monies will not come. You must help me, little Bobbie. Sometimes my English is not so good, but you can write strongly, with passion, to show them our great success.'

Dr G.'s command of the language always deteriorated during the holidays, when we weren't around to keep it up to scratch.

Consequently I spent the morning compiling a convincing report of our recent activities, and writing enthusiastically about our immediate plans. Dr G. was only satisfied when every statement was accompanied by statistical evidence, which meant trawling through back copies of the *Journal of Aural Studies* to find support for even the tiniest assertion. This made for a very odd document, full of bracketed instructions to consult our earlier work, and each time I wrote bossily '(See Grossmann *et al*...)', I was horribly conscious of Matt. It did occur to me that the people at Klopstock-Gneiss were hardly likely to possess a complete set of the journal so often referred to, in which case my efforts would lack all sensible point. But Dr G. brushed this problem aside.

'It matters not,' she said brightly, greatly improved in spirits now the report was almost complete. 'No-one can argue with figures. If we say that sixty-one percent of our subjects remembers a major third correctly under certain circumstances, but only twenty-four percent remembered a minor sixth, who will say it is not so? Figures suggest we are truthful – the more we can use, the more merry. And they will know our results are correct, because they have all been published.'

By the end of the morning I almost believed this myself.

At lunchtime I nipped out to ring Alex, but when I finally found a phone box in working order, there was no reply. I pictured the telephone ringing in the empty flat, and drew two consoling conclusions: Maggie was not yet home, and Alex was out. The afternoon was spent closeted with Paula analysing the tapes of our last experiment, slow and mechanical work which left plenty of time for brooding. By three o'clock I'd persuaded myself that Matt was still in London; by half past three, when we stopped for a tea break, he was holding Alex prisoner; by five o'clock, when we re-wound the tapes for the very last time, he had raped her and left her for dead; by half-past five, when I left the building, he'd abducted her off to Australia. I remembered her fear in the dovecote, and knew that I couldn't go home. At Warren Street station I made for the northbound platform and the train to Hampstead, convinced beyond doubt that something appalling had happened to Alex.

When she opened the door of the flat, I was so relieved she wasn't imprisoned or dead or abducted that I barely noticed her face. We collapsed against one another.

'He was here...he came here...he hit me, Bobbie, he hit me...My God, I thought he would kill me.' Sobs racked her body, leaving her short of breath.

'Hush,' I murmured, holding her tightly. 'It's all right. I'm here now. He's gone and I'm here. It'll all be all right.'

I helped her through to the bedroom, and while I inspected the damage, she told me exactly what happened.

'What you need most,' I said, trying to sound professional, 'is arnica. That'll deal with the bruises. Or failing that, calendula. But I don't suppose you've got either.'

'You suppose correctly.' She winced as she moved on the bed. 'I feel as though I've gone several rounds with Mohammed Ali.'

The state of her body could give that impression, but I didn't say so. Instead I asked, 'Did you manage to hurt him at all?'

'I kneed him in the goolies. Not very hard, but better than nothing.'

'Good for you. Oh, your poor, poor breast,' I said, seeing it properly for the first time. 'Is it terribly sore?'

'Not as sore as my stomach. That's where he kicked the hardest.'

'I could go to the chemist and buy some magic ointment,' I offered.

She grabbed my hand. 'And leave me alone? Don't you dare!'

'In that case there's only one thing for it. I'll have to kiss it all better.'

Alex looked down at her body. 'That may take a very long time. Before you start on the treatment, why don't we eat? There's a casserole ready. I made it for Maggie, but now I don't care if she starves. The viper – how could she? What on earth was she thinking? Pouring her heart out to Matt, of all people! If only she'd spoken to *me*.'

'And you still don't know when she's coming back? She hasn't phoned, or sent a card or anything?'

Alex sighed. 'This is Maggie we're talking about, not some thoughtful, considerate daughter. The idea of letting me know wouldn't enter her head.'

'I think,' I said carefully, 'that I'd like to have a word with her. I'll stay here tonight – I can doze on the sofa – then if she appears, I'll be ready. If she doesn't, we'll make a new plan in the morning. You've got nowhere with her so far. It's about time I had a go.'

*

Alex writes,

Dear Terry,

It's four in the morning, and I'm lying here wakeful, thinking of all you have given me: the happiest Christmas I've ever spent, the example and friendship of like-minded women, and – most precious of all – Bobbie.

It's not been a very good day. I'll spare you the details: suffice it to say that Matt reappeared and made several suggestions with which I didn't agree. He seems to think I could give up Bobbie, as one gives up chocolate or other bad habits. Whether he finally grasped that this is impossible, I do not know. As he hates being crossed, I anticipate further persuasion. But I want you and Jo to be in no doubt: nothing that Matt or anyone else might do can alter my love for Bobbie. She is firmly entwined with the thread of my being; without her, life is unthinkable, like life without music or laughter. You, I know, will understand this, as you value her highly, and are yourself in a wholly beneficent partnership. And I owe it all to your dovecote, for I think I loved her the very first moment I saw her, crossing your yard in the peaceful August sunshine.

She is now keeping watch on my sofa, an attentive and heaven-sent guardian. We await the arrival of Maggie, who's about to learn much – not all of it to her advantage.

If Bobbie knew I was writing, she would add her love to mine. As it is, I speak for us both, in joy and thankfulness.

Yours ever, Alex.

*

I heard a bump, followed by muttering and giggling. Maggie, returned from skiing, certainly wasn't alone. It was six o'clock in the morning. While prone on the sofa, I'd been carefully planning what I would say, but hadn't expected a sidekick –

195

male, by the sound of it, currently helpless with laughter. I hoped they weren't drunk or high on anything. The interview would be taxing enough, without first having to sober them up.

When I switched on the light in the hall, Maggie jumped.

'What are *you* doing here?' she asked sourly. I could see she was tired by the dark rings under her eyes. Poor soul, I thought. She's probably been travelling for hours.

'I might well ask the same,' I said, determined to seize the initiative. 'Maggie I know, but who might you be?'

The young man, tall, blonde and ungainly, had the grace to look sheepish and the manners to introduce himself properly. 'Jethro Harper-Townsend.' He was neither drunk nor stoned, I was glad to see, and shot out a hand for the shaking. 'My friends call me Jet.'

'How do you do, Jet.' I returned his very firm handshake. 'I'm Robina Sinclair, but my friends call me Bobbie. All except Maggie, who refuses to call me anything. I expect you're exhausted. Why don't you have a lie down? That's Maggie's room there,' I said, pointing helpfully. 'Maggie and I need to talk for a while, but then she'll most probably join you.'

'Hey – wait a minute!' Maggie was clearly not pleased. 'What's going on? What's happened? Where's Mum? Why isn't she here?'

I ignored her, and continued speaking to Jet. 'The bathroom's there, if you need it, and the kitchen's next door, if you feel like a coffee. But please don't make too much noise. Maggie's mother's asleep – she's recovering.'

'Right. OK. No problem.' Jet was actually whispering. I warmed to him more and more.

'No – don't go – don't leave me!' Maggie looked positively terrified at the prospect of facing me single-handed. 'You don't have to do what *she* says. I'll tell Mum you're here and . . .'

She made a move towards Alex's bedroom, but I niftily got in her way. 'Perhaps you shouldn't just yet. As I said, she's sleeping. She's been through a bad time lately. Maggie and I will be in the sitting room, Jet. Half and hour should do it.

She'll see you then, I expect.' And to my surprise I winked at
the fellow.

Maggie turned to him imploringly. 'You won't just go, will
you? Some of my stuff's in your bag.'

He shook his head. 'No sweat, Mags. I'll do what Bobbie
suggests. I need to crash out, anyway.'

'What about me?' she whined. 'I'm totally shagged. I've been
up as long as you have . . .' But Jet had already tiptoed away,
and was shutting himself in her bedroom.

'I know,' I put in soothingly. 'Travel's exhausting, isn't it?'
Docile now, Maggie let me shepherd her into the sitting room.
I shut the door but did not sit down, and started at once on
the speech I'd rehearsed.

'The thing is, Maggie, I wanted to prepare you, so it would-
n't be too great a shock. Your mother's been assaulted – quite
badly, from what I've seen.'

'Assaulted? You mean, like mugged?'

'No, no, she wasn't mugged. It happened here, in the flat.
Your father turned up – rather drunk, it seems – and knocked
her about quite a bit.'

'My Dad? My Dad came *here*?' She stared at me incredu-
lously. Obviously this hadn't been part of her plan. 'But he's
in Australia.'

'Not today, I'm afraid. He was definitely in Hampstead this
afternoon. Your mother was here all alone, and naturally let
him in. She had no idea he'd attack her.'

'And he hurt her?'

I nodded.

'How is she? You're a doctor – you must know how bad she
is.' To her credit she looked fairly shaken.

'I've done what I can to make her comfortable,' I said
evasively. 'She's severely bruised, and her face is cut, and I
think she's probably cracked a rib. Nothing that won't heal in
time, though she doesn't look pretty at present. And of course
it was all the most terrible shock. What she can't understand –
and I must say I can't either – is the cause of it all, what
prompted him to come. As far as I can gather, he'd got hold of

some very nasty tittle-tattle. We can only think that someone had deliberately poisoned his mind. But why would anyone do that, Maggie? It's quite beyond me. Can *you* think of a reason?'

It was alarming how like my housemistress I was beginning to sound. When I'd rehearsed this overnight on the sofa, Maggie conveniently broke down at this juncture, confessed her involvement (tearfully) and begged our forgiveness. The flesh and blood Maggie was less easily cowed.

'Why ask me?' she snapped. 'Why should *I* know what he's thinking? Yes, he's my Dad, but I haven't seen him for years. He left when I was like four. That's how much *he* bloody well cares.'

'I'm sorry,' I said, conscious of hitting a nerve. 'I thought you and he might still be in touch. Of course you can't possibly know what goes on in his head, or what silly gossip he's got hold of. But the thing is, Maggie, I really don't think your mother should stay here, do you? Not when he might come back and beat her up at anytime. She'd be mad to stay. Don't you agree?'

'I suppose so,' she said sullenly. 'But where could she go?'

'She could move somewhere else.'

'But she's lived here for ages. I don't think she wants to move.'

'Then it's up to us to persuade her,' I said, amazed by how easily we'd arrived at this stage in the argument. 'I'll do what I can of course, but mainly it'll be up to you. If I were you, I'd insist that she leave. She's attached to this flat because it's your home, but if you were to tell her you're ready to live on your own, she'd feel easier about moving. And you and I would both be much happier, knowing your father couldn't find her.' I paused for a moment to let this crucial point sink in, then continued disingenuously, 'Jet seems a very nice person. Did you meet on the ski slopes?'

She instantly brightened. 'Yeah – he picked me up. I mean, like literally. I'd fallen over, and he came and picked me up. From the snow,' she added, in case I had trouble picturing the scene.

'What a lovely romantic story!' I gushed. 'Does he live in London?'

'Yeah – a house in Fulham.'

'Ah, Fulham. I was reading only the other day that Fulham is tipped to become very fashionable indeed.' This was true, though why I'd retained this nugget of information, heaven only knew. 'Anyone who buys property there now can expect to make a huge return on it in ten or fifteen years time, apparently. And where does he work?'

'In investments – in the city. Not far from my office, actually.'

'I could tell that he likes you a lot,' I lied, then realised I wasn't at all certain how many ideas Maggie could absorb in one go. Better, I decided, to return to the major topic and let her love life take its course. 'So – I can rely on you then? As soon as your mother feels better, you'll do all that you can to encourage her to move somewhere safe? Somewhere your father can't find her.' I said this last part slowly, to stress her role in this drama.

'Yeah. OK. I was thinking of moving out soon, in any case. Hampstead's not really my scene any longer.'

I could at that moment have strangled the girl quite cheerfully. Instead I said briskly, 'I expect you want to see your mother now. I'll just make sure she's OK. Then how about the two of us – and Jet as well – having breakfast together? You must both be hungry.'

'I'm starving,' she said, and I might have been wrong, but I *think* she gave me a smile.

Alex, awake, was agog to hear how I'd fared.

'Mission accomplished,' I whispered triumphantly, bending to kiss an unbruised area. 'You're wonderfully black and blue this morning – quite hideous, in fact. But that's all to the good. Maggie can't help but be stricken. Be as ill as you like today – moaning and groaning, that sort of thing. Make her feel thoroughly guilty. And don't be surprised by anything she says. She swallowed it all, hook, line and sinker.'

'But what did you tell her? Oh darling, you're looking quite horribly smug. Was it really that easy?'

'I told her the truth – and no, we didn't come to fisticuffs, nor did we shout at each other. I simply appealed to her sense of responsibility. As it happens, we're about to have breakfast together. Oh, there's a chap she's brought with her – she'll tell you about him. Jet's his name. Nice chap – seems thoughtful. Should be encouraged. Ah,' I said, raising my voice, 'here she is now. I'll leave you alone together.'

In passing, I whispered to Maggie, 'Try not to be *too* upset,' and was gratified to hear her burst into tears before I'd got out of the room.

13

Risoluto

Alex, alone in the flat, hears the telephone ring. She does not rush to answer. Walking is painful enough, and if she delays, whoever it is might assume that she's out and hang up. But the summons continues. When she finally picks up the receiver, some instinct stops her from speaking. Instead, she listens. Silence. There's nothing to hear, not even a hint of heavy breathing. She waits for the sound of a definite click. Which comes, as she knew it would.

She feels spied on, beleaguered. Somebody knows she's at home. The door's double locked – Bobbie insisted – but now, unnerved, she checks to make sure. She even draws curtains and blinds, as though by complete isolation she can stave off a second attack. She's certain the silent caller is Matt, so certain that when the ringing starts again her anger boils over. She picks up the phone and shouts in a fury, 'For God's sake, leave me alone!'

'Alexandra?' Too late she recognises the oily tones of Crispian, her producer at Radio Three. 'Have I picked a bad moment?'

'Sorry, Crispian – no, no. I thought you were someone else.'

'I'm glad to hear it. Not in any trouble, I trust?' His question is light, like those questions in Latin that assume the answer is 'no'.

'Not at all.' She gathers her wits, attempts to sound calm. 'Happy New Year. Did you have a good Christmas?'

She's content to let him talk: while he's on the line, it's blocked to anyone else. She listens to a tale of a mother in Oxford, a burst pipe, some flooding.

'Dear me – and at Christmas too.' She does her best to convey sympathy for this unknown woman. 'So hard to get workmen...'

He isn't deflected for long. 'Actually, Alexandra, there are one or two things we need to discuss. No immediate rush – maybe one day next week?'

They fix on the following Friday. With luck, she thinks, and plenty of ointment, the bruises will have faded by then. It's only when she writes in her diary '3pm – Crispian' that she notices the date: Friday the thirteenth of January.

The moment she puts down the phone, she feels vulnerable once more. She decides to keep the line busy, arms herself with *Yellow Pages* and spends the rest of the day talking to estate agents who have properties for sale in West London.

*

'But you mustn't feel you have to stay in with your mother *every* evening. It simply wouldn't be fair.'

I was doing my best with Maggie. For the third time that week I'd rushed to Hampstead straight from work, only to find that tonight she'd beaten me to it, and had even offered to see to the meal. Alex – now up and limping about, but still looking gruesome – had begged me to supervise. Maggie's idea of a meal was touchingly simple: I would make toast while she heated beans. Even this pushed her skills past their limit: left to her own devices, she'd have treated the tin like an egg and put it to boil in a pan of water. Once again I was faced with the mystery of how she'd survived in Earl's Court.

'But if Dad comes back...'

'Your mother knows now not to open the door,' I said firmly, before realising she might have meant something quite different. I altered my tone. 'Or perhaps you were hoping to see him?'

She abandoned the beans and turned round to face me. 'Yeah – I'd kind of like to, in a way. He used to play with me, like when he brought me home from Nursery. He had this like metronome. He'd set it and we had to keep time with it when we talked. Like very, very, very, very quickly' – she did an imitation of demisemiquavers – 'or ve-ry-slow-ly. I was like four. It was fun.'

'I haven't seen my father for years.' I kept my voice level, and busied myself with the toast and the toaster. 'I write to him from time to time, and keep him up to date with what I'm doing, but we've not seen each other since 1967 – more than a decade ago. At my mother's funeral,' I added for reasons of poignancy. 'I don't honestly know whether I'd recognise him now, or whether I'd have anything much to say to him, if we did meet.' When the toast popped up, I added, 'People change.'

I made this assertion for Maggie's sake, but with little conviction, for I do not believe it is true. People don't change, though most of us like to think that they do. The change is in circumstances, situations, which make different demands on our repertoire. Faced with the task of amusing a four year-old, Matt might still be as much fun as ever. Since this wasn't a view I wanted to share with Maggie, I asked instead, 'How are the beans?'

'Christ!' She spun round and grabbed at the pan. 'They're all stuck at the bottom!'

'Don't throw them away!' Just in time I stopped her from dunking the whole lot in the sink. 'We can salvage a few. Why don't I scramble some eggs while you butter the toast?'

She gave me a look of appeal. 'Couldn't I do the eggs – if you showed me how?'

'Of course.' I thought of Jet in Fulham, of his manifold dietary needs. 'And tomorrow we could grill some chops, if you like – or cook steaks...'

'Not tomorrow,' she said quickly. 'There's a party. I'll probably be staying at Jet's all weekend. But I wouldn't mind doing the chops and stuff another time.'

'That's fine – whenever you like.' While scrambling the eggs, I asked casually, 'As you won't be here tomorrow evening, do you think I should drop round and stay overnight – just in case?'

Her reply showed a real sense of conscience. 'Yeah, I guess I'd feel better if someone was here.'

Perhaps she imagined I'd sleep on the sofa, or that Alex's cut lip and bruises effectively ruled out passion. If so, she was wrong on both counts.

*

There's a deluge of post on Saturday morning. Bobbie looks at the postmarks as she takes it all through to the bedroom.

'This is mostly from estate agents in Ealing,' she says, getting back into bed next to Alex. 'It's quite a haul. There should be plenty to choose from here – and as we said the other day, no other borough would suit us so well. Right on the Central Line, blissfully distant from Piers and Drusilla ...'

'And handy for the A40, to take us to Hendre. It's nicer than going by motorway, and will keep me to sensible speeds. It means we could go there at all times of the year without the hassle of first crossing London.'

Bobbie glances through the first list of property details. 'You know, we really ought to approach this logically, if we're to do it at speed. At the moment we've no idea where any of these roads are, and as for some of these flats and houses ...'

By lunchtime they've weeded out the hopeless ones, and with the aid of the *A to Z* have laid out the rest on the bedroom floor with a semblance of geographical accuracy. Two pairs of Alex's shoes are standing in for tube stations, a scarf does duty for Ealing Common. They gaze at what they've produced.

'Just here would be perfect.' Alex indicates an empty spot between the scarf and a shoe. 'A mere stroll to the station, convenient for shopping and close to the Common. But alas it has nothing for sale.'

Bobbie's more sanguine. 'Only so far as we know. Why don't we go and make sure?'

It's the first of a spate of such outings. Under cover of darkness – Alex believes she's still not fit to be seen – they cruise the borough of Ealing, making a note of its features. 'Our library,' they say, and 'Our off licence'. But never 'our house'. Not yet.

Crispian's office is spacious and bleak. A plastic poinsettia perched on a cupboard, a pristine row of reference books – complete sets of Grove and the *Dictionary of National Biography* – and, on his otherwise empty desk, a telephone and an executive toy, ball bearings on wires, designed to knock irritatingly together for hours at a stretch.

'Alexandra!' He half rises from his chair in greeting. 'You're looking very...' He fails to find an appropriate word. 'Good holiday?'

'Thank you – yes. Very good. A few days with some friends on a farm.' She likes the repeated 'f ' in that sentence, hasn't yet had a chance to use it. 'You suggested we have things to discuss?' She starts to take from her bag a notebook and pencil, then changes her mind. Too servile, too eagerly secretarial. She opts for a tissue instead.

'You remember our programme last November on funding for the arts and so forth?'

Our programme? She lets it pass. 'Indeed I do.'

'It went down very well in certain circles. Extremely well indeed.' He looks at her smugly. Alex sees he's been praised by some broadcasting bigwig, catches the whiff of career advancement. For Crispian, naturally. Not for her. 'What we need to do now is pursue it,' he continues. 'Discuss those sorts of topics at regular intervals. Make people sit up and take notice. Show what the programme can do in practical terms. Prove we've got teeth and are eager to use them.'

He seems to be quoting from some kind of manual. *Projects for Producers Pursuing Promotion* at a guess. She knows she shouldn't appear too intransigent. 'It sounds as though you want us to take up causes, to be militant. That's quite a change of direction,' she says evenly.

Crispian leans back in his chair, laces his fingers together. 'Think of it as a new breath of life. To stimulate listeners. To get them...' She waits for the next gem from the manual. 'To get them *involved*.'

'And you think this approach will win us a bigger audience?'

'I know so, Alexandra. We'd be seen to be on a mission, fighting for something important.'

'You make it sound rather aggressive.' Those producers pursuing promotion must all be men, she decides.

'That's what we need – aggression! The campaigning spirit. Let people see where our values lie, nail our colours to the mast...'

She thinks she might scream if he utters another clichè. It's time to defend her position. 'Everyone I've spoken to seems to like the programme as it is. They appreciate the way it explores its subject in depth. They like the existing breadth of its remit.' She wants to say they enjoy its kindly good nature, but knows he'll dismiss that as anodyne. 'They like the fact that it's balanced, that it's informative musically, varied and entertaining...'

He raises a palm, halting her list of the programme's merits. 'It's the people you *haven't* spoken to that we're trying to reach here, don't you see? The ones who are looking for something more...challenging.' His tone changes slightly. 'The fact is, Alexandra, we've no choice in the matter. I've agreed to do it, and do it we shall.'

'But I've already drawn up plans for the forthcoming series.' She knows it's a token objection, and Crispian knows it too.

'I'm sure if you show me the schedule, we'll manage to find a slot. Say some time in March? A report on what the November programme achieved, then, to take us forward, a look at some new issues, which we'll follow up in due course. Excellent. I'm glad we agree. I knew you would see the potential.'

Oh, Bobbie! she thinks, preparing to leave. This is all thanks to your Dr G. 'If there's nothing else, Crispian...'

'Just one more thing.' He reaches into a drawer of his desk, pulls out two packets of letters and hands them over. 'These are addressed to you.' She recognises the usual fan mail, always heaviest during the programme's winter break. 'And this' – he picks out a single sheet which he passes across the desk – 'was addressed to me. Perhaps you would read it and give me your comments.'

There's no address, no date, no signature. An anonymous letter. Typewritten.

'I feel it my duty to tell you that the esteemed presenter of *Schneider's Showcase* is a Lesbian,' she reads. 'She is currently cavorting with a girl half her age. I am sure these facts would interest her listeners.'

She reads it through twice, though it makes her feel sick. She's shaking, she realises, as she gives it back. 'How very unpleasant!'

'Exactly,' Crispian agrees. 'And untrue, I assume?'

'No,' she says carefully. 'It's essentially true. I might take exception to the word *cavorting*,' – Matt's word, she recalls – 'but perhaps that's being pedantic.'

If he's surprised, he disguises it well. 'And do you know who might have . . . ?'

'My husband, without a doubt.' She remembers Matt's threats at the flat. 'He's usually abroad, but was here over Christmas. I'm only sorry he thought it necessary to involve you.'

'Me – and who else? That's the question. There's a thinly-veiled threat of exposure here. Who else has received one of these?'

'No-one – so far as I know.'

'But can we be certain? The press, for example?'

'When did that letter arrive?'

'Delivered by hand on the fifth, apparently.'

The day Crispian rang. So that's why he called her in. He's known for a week. 'Surely you'd have heard by now if he'd sent any others. Someone would have been in touch, asking questions. Though I hardly see that it's anyone's business . . .'

'Quite, quite. But I thought it best to let you know.'

'Thank you. I'm glad that you did. And of course you've not mentioned it to anyone?'

'Alexandra!' He raises his hands in mock horror. 'Would I do such a thing?'

'Of course not. I'm sorry. I suggest we forget the whole business. It's not as if my choice of partner has any bearing at all on the programme.' She stands up, desperate now to leave not only the office, but the entire building. That Crispian, of all people, knows about her and Bobbie is ghastly enough without also suspecting he's spread it abroad. 'I'll bear in mind our earlier discussion and adjust the new schedule in line with your suggestions,' she says with polite formality. 'It should be ready early next week.'

'Thank you. Good of you to come in today.' He raises his hand in salute. 'Enjoy your weekend.'

Is it her fancy, or is there something new in his tone, something suggestive and lewd? She gives what she hopes is an enigmatic smile. 'Oh, I have every intention of doing so.' Let him make of that what he will. God knows what he thinks she gets up to.

'Bloody man!' she mutters as she walks the length of the corridor. 'Bloody, bloody man! Bloody men in general!' Outside it's already dark. She cannot now face the thought of going back to her flat, or to Maggie. Instead she summons a taxi and asks for Gordon Square.

*

When Alex turned up at the Institute, I knew all was not as it should be. Dr G., surmising nothing, was simply delighted to see her. Ever since the people at Klopstock-Gneiss agreed to fund us, she'd taken the view that Alex, alone and unaided, had rescued our threatened research. Now, beaming in welcome, she ushered her in to her office and waved me over to join them.

'We are working very hard, as you see.' Dr G. clearly felt she should give an account of our progress. 'We can learn much from the young musicians who remember long pieces for the very first time, and also we can teach. Together it bears much fruit. And thanks to the report that Bobbie has written, we have the promise of fresh monies. Alas, we are now only four, but since I am here and do not have to travel about for grants, we bring about as much as when we were six. Is that not so, little Bobbie?'

'Actually, Helga,' Alex interrupted, 'I came to ask if I might borrow Bobbie for the rest of the afternoon. I'm planning to run a follow-up programme soon, to show what's been achieved since November. If Bobbie could give me some details about your partnership with the Klopstock-Gneiss Foundation...'

'Naturally, naturally! She is the expert.' Dr G., overjoyed at the mention of a second programme, was rummaging through the mountain of papers on her desk. 'Here is the report she made of our work. Have this, and have Bobbie also, and you will know all.'

Once outside, Alex took my arm and we walked towards Warren Street station. The rush hour was just beginning, and it was while we were waiting to cross Gower Street that I heard about Crispian's plans for the programme, and about the anonymous letter.

'Of course I'm furious with Matt, though he's probably back in Australia now. The silent phone calls have stopped. I think he's shot all his bolts, and won't risk anything further. Strangely, what upsets me most is that Crispian knows about us. I've never discussed anything personal with him, partly because I don't like him very much, but also because I know he's ambitious and would do anything to further his wretched career. And now he knows this, it gives him a certain... power.'

'Yes, I see what you mean. It wouldn't be wise to cross him – not now. You'll have to go on with those tub-thumping programmes. And as for the letter, what can he do or say? It's just gossip, that's all – a nudge and a wink. As long as the listeners keep listening, he won't want to lose you. But I'm so sorry, my love – sorry this whole thing has happened. I feel I'm to blame. If it weren't for me...'

Alex squeezed my arm tightly. 'Nonsense! The tub-thumping's probably saved me; without it my broadcasting days were probably numbered. I ought to thank you for that. And if anyone's to blame for the letter, it's Maggie. That's why I plan to abandon her this weekend – make her suffer a little. I'll ring her and say I'm away until Monday on urgent business. Then, if you're willing, we'll carry out Crispian's final instructions in full – with Klopstock and Gneiss in Clapham.

*

Some time that night, Alex says, 'Tell me about it. How it will be.' And Bobbie beside her raises herself on one elbow and says, 'The music room's at the back, looking onto the garden. The Bechstein's in there – and our records of course, and my cello – and sometimes you play for me, late at night, Chopin and Schubert, as loud as you like, because no-one can hear, only us. There's a sofa as well, where we sit when we listen to records. To the Schubert Quintet, for instance...'

'With the score?' Alex asks sleepily.

Bobbie smiles. 'With the score. And on Sundays we often have friends to lunch, musical friends who bring instruments. We give them splendid meals and a great deal to drink – but never too much, because afterwards we play together. Trios, sonatas, piano quintets – it all depends who turns up...'

'Is Helga there?'

'Dr G.? Yes, she's there. In the interests of musical memory. But she also brings puddings, dishes her mother once made in the Rhineland, cheesecakes and mixtures of chocolate and cream...'

Alex adjusts her position in bed. 'I didn't think Helga could cook.'

'You're right – she can't. She's terrible at it. Her food is often inedible. So, when she's not looking, one of us – you, perhaps, or it may be me – discreetly throws it away. Of course she assumes it's been eaten, and happily brings us another concoction the following week. If we told her the truth, we'd upset her, and we couldn't do that – we love her too much.'

Alex, drowsier now, asks, 'Why do we love her?'

And Bobbie, sleepy too, says dreamily, 'We love her because she accepts us entirely. She's a psychologist. She understands people, she understands us. She can see how much we delight in each other, she knows that love has touched us both with its wing and carried us off in its flight. She's wise enough, and old enough, to recognise that love like ours is a blessing, sweeter than wine, vast, without limits, our bedrock, our treasure...'

Alex raises her head, silences Bobbie with a kiss. 'Yes,' she murmurs. 'That's how it is. And how it will always be.'

*

Alex was still with me the following evening when Terry rang with news of her own.

'Jo and I are coming up in the world, Bobbie. We've been asked to speak at this year's SPAFS Conference. We agreed to it ages ago – you know how we say yes to all and sundry – and now the programme's arrived, we find that we're on it. Not once, but twice! There are one or two whimsical items dealing with mills and barns and suchlike inferior buildings, but the Ancient Farmyard Structure that has pride of place this year is our very own dovecote! I shall spellbind the audience with a discourse entitled 'Doves in Domestic Economy', and Jo, for her sins, will expound on the architectural side of things the following day. We fully expect the *Compendium* to sell like the hottest of cakes after this – straight to the top of the best-seller list, I shouldn't wonder. I trust, dear niece, that you're duly impressed.'

Behind all the banter I sensed her enormous pride. 'Oh, I am. Exceedingly so. Double congratulations. But did you say, 'the following day'?' So far as I knew, the two of them were never away from Hendre overnight.

'Ay, there's the rub. As you rightly suspect, I'm ringing not solely to boast, but to grovel and beg for a favour. You must picture me grovelling now, in a posture of craven entreaty.'

'There's no need for that,' I laughed. 'Your request is already granted. I'll willingly come and look after the animals, if that's what you'd like. Just tell me when.'

'Bless you, my poppet. The conference is in four weeks time, all day Saturday and Sunday morning. But as it takes place in outlandish County Durham, we plan to drive up on the Friday. Could the Institute cope without you if you took a day off and came for a long weekend?'

'I'm sure it could. Maybe Alex could come as well, if she's not too busy. Her new series is starting that week.'

'Is it, indeed? That's very good news. Our Wednesday evenings have hung very heavy of late. Perhaps Alex *ought* to come with you. It's high time she learnt how to milk a goat, an art form too often neglected by those on Radio Three. Now tell me, how are you both? Have you found yourselves somewhere to live?'

'Not yet,' I said. 'But we've definitely settled on Ealing.'

'Quite right too!' was the forthright reply. 'If I'm not mistaken, it used to be known as the Queen of Boroughs, and is handy for Kensal Green Cemetery, should you wish to commune with the illustrious dead. You notice I draw a tactful veil over those tedious Ealing comedies. What news of our Christmas visitor, the diabolical Matt? We gather he made a second appearance.'

I wasn't sure how much news of Matt's recent activities I wished to impart. 'Alex can tell you about it herself,' I hedged. 'She's here, as it happens.'

'In that case, forgive my ill-timed interruption. As long as you're both well and happy, you can put the rest in a letter. My thanks, dear niece, and adieu.'

Alex was lying on my sofa looking very much at home. She studied me carefully as I put down the phone. 'You've volunteered me for something, haven't you? What terrible feat do I have to perform?'

'Oh, nothing too strenuous – only milking a herd of goats. Or should that be 'flock'?'

'Flock or herd, they'll never be milked by me!' She spoke with great determination. 'I remember only too well how painful breast-feeding can be. It would be criminal to let the poor beasts suffer my clumsy handling. But I'll happily watch while you do it.'

I explained about the conference, and Terry and Jo's commitments.

'Friday the tenth of February?' She took out her diary to check. 'It seems I'm free as a bird. Come to think of it, why don't I make that the day I call on Klopstock and Gneiss? Swindon's not much of a detour – it's virtually on the M4 – and I'd have to go there sometime. I've been reading your report, my love. Your argument's perfectly lucid, even to someone for whom the *Journal of Aural Studies* is an unknown and firmly closed book. You make a compelling case. No wonder they gave you the money; I felt like chipping in myself by the time I got to the end. Your research sounds much more focused now, more geared to a practical outcome. Or was that simply a front for the sake of your sponsors?'

'Partly,' I conceded. 'There's still a reductionist element in what we do, but I tried to keep quiet about that side of things. Klopstock-Gneiss are terribly keen on practical outcomes.'

'Aren't we all?' She smiled at me fondly. 'I'll put it in the diary, then – 'Weekend at Hendre with B.' How lovely! If in the next three weeks I ever need to be cheered, that entry will do it nicely.'

'And you did say you wanted to visit Hendre at all times of year,' I reminded her. 'Funnily enough, I've only ever been there once in February myself, for the spring half-term in my last year at school. That was a long weekend, too. On every bank, and at the bottom of all the hedges, there were carpets of snowdrops – hundreds of tiny brave flowers wherever you looked. Terry actually made me a cake with snowdrops on it, iced in white and green. For my seventeenth-and-a-half birthday. Ten years ago.'

'Two birthdays a year – what an excellent notion! A tradition like that deserves to be maintained. I'm not much good at cakes, I'm afraid – they either burn or refuse to rise – but you must let me do *something* a little special, to celebrate your twenty-seventh-and-a-half birthday.'

'In future we may want to celebrate the anniversary of our first weekend alone at Hendre,' I suggested.

'Exactly! Just leave it to me. I'll make sure it's unforgettable.'

Until we both tried to do it, I had no idea that selling a London flat could be so difficult. My Clapham estate agent, an elderly man called Parrot, was diligent in sending people to view. Their appointments were usually for seven o'clock, and perhaps they were weary by then, or in want of a meal, but none of them greeted my basement with the slightest degree of rapture. In vain I'd describe how the sun drenched the patio on summer mornings, or mention the owl in the towering black poplar: on chill January evenings, the appreciation of such features required more imagination than my prospective purchasers seemed willing to exercise.

'It's early days as yet,' Mr Parrot assured me whenever we spoke. 'And frankly not the best time of year to be selling. Be patient, Dr Sinclair. When the spring weather comes, we always experience an upturn.'

I took this to mean that basements appear slightly less gloomy when seen in a smidgen of daylight.

Alex, at second-floor level, was faring no better. Her block lacked the lift that most of her viewers expected, and once-so-desirable Hampstead was apparently now being slighted in favour of Belsize Park. The only person whose place of residence looked likely to change in the immediate future was Maggie, who more than once started a sentence with, 'When I like move in with Jet...' This, I felt sure, was thanks to my kitchen tutorials: having mastered the Scrambling of Eggs, she'd almost grasped The Grilling of Chops and was soon to embark on The Frying of Steaks.

'You spoilt her, darling,' I told Alex one evening. 'If only you'd shown her how to cook instead of doing it so effortlessly yourself, she might still be with Nick in Earl's Court.'

'I know, I know – I just never had time.' She sounded truly remorseful. 'And it honestly didn't occur to me that anyone, especially a daughter of mine, could be so utterly clueless. By the way,' she added, perking up, 'I've a plan for the catering at Hendre – for your half-birthday evening, at least. It's a secret, of course. You won't know what it is till we get there.'

It was snowing in London on the tenth of February, light, ineffectual snow that may as well have been rain. For places further north there were forecasts of heavier falls, especially in the North East of England, where two days' snow was already lying. So alarming did the weatherman sound on the radio that I rang Terry before breakfast, fully expecting to hear that she'd called off their journey. Instead I found her in very high spirits.

'Call it off? Whatever gave you that idea? We've packed the car with all we might need – a spade to deal with the deeper drifts, a thermos or two of nourishing soup, and every jumper, glove and scarf we possess. As we're travelling mainly on motorways, we intend to make it all the way – though whether anyone else will be foolish enough to run the same risks remains to be seen. There's no snow here, and none has been promised. The goats have been told they'll be fondled by alien hands for a couple of days, and have kindly agreed to coop-erate. Build yourselves enormous fires and drink our homemade wine. You've got the number of our hotel, should you need it. All being well, we'll see you on Sunday evening.'

Alex picked me up on the dot of nine. We crawled through West London, but things improved when we hit the M4, and once we left Heathrow behind us, there was remarkably little traffic.

'It's no distance at all to Swindon,' Alex blithely informed me. 'We're in plenty of time – my appointment at Klopstock-Gneiss is not till midday. Let's stop for a coffee. There's something I'm dying to show you.'

When we got out of the car at the next service station, I spotted what looked like a box of tins with their labels removed on the rear seat. Alex steered me quickly away through the drizzle.

'Don't look – not yet! It's supposed to be a surprise. All sorts of wonderful food for your half-birthday, carefully selected to form an extravagant meal. It's amazing how many luxuries find their way into tins – perhaps we ought to tell Maggie? I've even remembered to bring a tin opener, in case Terry and Jo don't possess such a thing.'

'If they do, it's probably rusty from lack of use. But surely those tins aren't all for me?'

She laughed. 'Only the ones with your name on. I thought we could share the rest.'

We took our coffees to a table by the window. Alex leant forward and held my hand. 'I never thought I'd look forward to going to Swindon, but I have been – all week. And as if the prospect of a weekend together at Hendre weren't enough, the postman brought this yesterday.' She produced a sheet of estate agent's details from her bag and handed it over with a flourish. 'I haven't said anything before now, because I know you'll feel exactly as I do. It's perfect, Bobbie – unbelievably so. I've made an appointment for us to view it on Monday evening. It's only just come onto the market; we'll have to act quickly. Read it, darling. Read it out loud.'

I looked at the sheet. '"Culverhouse Lodge",' I recited. 'Culverhouse? – but that's the Old English name for...'

'You see! You see!' Alex's eyes were shining. 'It's definitely an omen.'

'"This detached, three-storeyed house,"' I continued, '"dates from the early nineteenth century and benefits from a secluded situation adjacent to Ealing Common...."'

But I was able to read no further, for Alex interrupted. 'There's a garden all round – look! And a bow-fronted first floor sitting room – that's where the Bechstein will go. The rooms aren't enormous, I grant you, but there's a couple of decent-sized bedrooms, and all the space you and I are likely to need.' She looked at me beseechingly. 'You do like it, don't you? You want us to live there together?'

Never before had I seen her so excited. Clearly this wasn't the moment for practical details. 'I love it,' I said. 'It's perfect. Of course we'll live there.'

Alex sat back and beamed. 'That's it, then. We've found it. Our house.'

I drove the rest of the way in to Swindon. Alex had taken down detailed instructions, and we easily found the headquarters of the Klopstock-Gneiss Foundation in disappointingly modest premises at the end of a row of shops. Cars were parked solidly on both sides of the road, but none of them wore a permanent air.

'If I cruise up and down, a space is bound to appear,' I said as I let Alex out. 'How long will you be?'

'Half an hour at the most.' She winked and blew me a kiss. 'Then it's non-stop to Hendre.'

I winked in return. 'Will you give my love to Klopstock and Gneiss?'

'Not a chance! I'm keeping it all for myself.'

On my second reconnoitring cruise, a car pulled out just across the road from the Klopstock-Gneiss office. I manoeuvred into the space, and settled down to read for myself the details of Culverhouse Lodge. I'd almost got them by heart when I caught sight of Alex. I saw her look round; when she noticed the car, she waved. There was a look of such joy on her face as she started to cross the road. It's important for me to remember this: she looked totally, radiantly happy as she made her way towards me.

Coda

Adagio – arioso dolente

Alex never saw the car that killed her. I did. For weeks whenever I closed my eyes, I saw nothing else, and my impotent shouts, which she never heard, returned constantly to haunt me. I heard again the screech of the tyres, the bang as the car hit a wall, the terrible moment of silence. Much as I wish to banish those sounds, and have done my best to forget them, I find I am skilled at remembering. Memory's the process I understand best. I know how memories linger, how they lift themselves out of the everyday and take on a timeless existence. I never learnt how to forget.

There was in due course a memorial service, to which other people brought their memories of Alex. They spoke of her skills as critic and broadcaster, of her charm, the warmth of her personality and all that she had achieved. A string quartet of international renown, whose career was launched by one of her early reviews, found time to remember Alex, and flew in from Barcelona to play Schubert and Beethoven just for her.

My memories are different. I remember the way she would laugh at my jokes, the way music could move her to tears; I remember each shade of love in her look, from longing to absolute stillness. The touch of her hand, her seductive smile, her verve, her weakness, our desperate need of each other: these are the things I remember. Her voice, familiar to many, was most familiar to me. It spoke to me softly when no-one else listened, saying what no-one else said, and I hear it quite clearly still. From time to time I meet Maggie for lunch in the

City and we talk about Alex then. I costs me a great deal to do this, but I like to think Alex approves.

I've learnt not to think of her killer, the murdering boy who only knew how to hot-wire a car and didn't know how to drive it. Nor do I think of his mother, whose loss may be greater than mine. But I've yet to banish the searing guilt that racks me night after night. It accuses me unanswerably: that I ought to have parked on the other side of the road; that Alex was there at that precise moment because of a scheme I conjured with the help of Dr G.'s wine, and because of my wish to have her with me at Hendre. It can even drag me further back, with the torturing thought that she'd still be alive if, on that thundery June afternoon, I'd not changed the wheel of her car. But that would be somebody else's life. Mine – for better, for worse – was fatally caught up with Alex, and now I must live with the consequences.

For a year they have been my companions, in the basement flat which I never sold, where we spent our first night together. The happiness we shared there – the music, the laughter, the love – has not yet disappeared. Shrouded now, and only half alive, it goes around on slippered feet and whispers, but even so is strong enough to catch me unawares. I turn to Alex and she is not there; I store up things to tell her that she'll never hear; I miss her with an ache at times so piercing that I do not know how life can be endured. Words can't do justice to this dreadful sense of loss. It is a howl, an endless, inchoate scream, an unbearable sob which tears the breast and breaks the heart but will not, can not be spoken. There are no words for that. Once, on Clapham Common, I watched a crow distraught beside the body of its dead mate. Its grief was harrowing to hear – no melancholy coo, as mourning doves are said to make, but ugly, elemental pain, abrasive, plangent, harsh. That sound is in me too, and I do not know how to express it. Sometimes, just for a moment, I hear it in music, a hopeless, keening grief, sharp, open, jagged, raw. I know then that others are able to give it voice, though I cannot. Perhaps one day it may ease. Or perhaps there are some darknesses that never will be lightened, despite what I want to believe.

This weekend I am again at Hendre, because Terry and Jo have once more gone to their annual conference, this time in Sussex. Before they return I plan to do one thing. I will take from the car the box of tins that has so far never been touched. I'll remove them all, and put to one side those we'd have eaten together. But those Alex labelled as mine I will carefully open. I will lay them out here on this window seat, in sight of the dovecote, and serve them to myself, alone. I will taste them slowly, letting their flavour become a memory in my mouth. My last gift from Alex, postponed for so long, must not be hurried. And as I eat, I shall tell her that the flowers have again appeared on earth, that the time of the singing of the birds is come, but the voice of the turtle is silent. I shall say that her love is feeding me still, and fills me with every good thing.

Perhaps I shall do this tomorrow.